THE STREET WHERE SHE LIVED

Books by Mark Miano

Flesh and Stone

The Street Where She Lived

Published by Kensington Books

THE STREET WHERE SHE LIVED

Mark Miano

MARK MIANO

Kensington Books
http://www.kensingtonbooks.com

KENSINGTON BOOKS are published by

Kensington Publishing Corp.
850 Third Avenue
New York, NY 10022

Kensington and the K logo Reg. U.S. Pat. & TM Off.

Library of Congress Card Catalog Number: 97-073470
ISBN 1-57566-270-1

First Kensington Hardcover Printing: March, 1998
10   9   8   7   6   5   4   3   2   1

Printed in the United States of America

For Astrid,
who makes me so happy

ACKNOWLEDGMENTS

A sincere thank-you to my agent, Kay Kidde, and my editor, John Scognamiglio, for their input, patience, and support.

And speaking of support, many thanks to the gang at Dallas Murphy's writing round-table.

Prologue

The wonderful thing—the thing that never ceases to amaze me—is the fact that people will do anything to avoid looking me in the eye.

When I make my rounds on the street, strolling in a manner that I imagine as forceful, people try their damnedest to shake off eye contact. They look past me, above me, even straight through me, as if I'm some inanimate being, an essence, apparition, barely a presence. Even when they approach me head-on, when a glance in the face is inevitable, they allow their eyes to go soft-focus, as if they were off somewhere in a daydream or a trance.

When I was younger, it used to really bother me.

Back then, I used to interpret those lowered, inhospitable eyes as a sign of disrespect, a deliberate disregard for myself as a human being. Those dodging eyes were a signal that I didn't warrant their attention. I wasn't intelligent enough, handsome enough, witty enough, important enough. I wasn't good enough.

Especially in the eyes of women.

The women, they seem to do everything in their power to guarantee no chance encounter with my eyes. They might stare off into the distance, eyes positioned a half-inch over my shoulder, as if they're checking for the street sign down the block. Some might keep their eyes focused on the pavement, as if a hidden obstacle threatened to suddenly appear before them. Others might peer into their hands, perusing a newspaper or a magazine. The ones really adamant about not seeing me might place an object between their eyes and mine: a pair of reflective sunglasses, a raised hand, even an extreme squinting of the lids, as if it were necessary to repel the snow, rain, heat, or gloom of night.

When I was younger, such women made me very angry.

So angry, in fact, that I often did things that would demand their attention. Sometimes I would act like a crazy man, shouting all kinds of gibberish as I lurched down the sidewalk. Other times, I would exhibit a posture that can be interpreted only as menacing: fists and jaws clenched, eyes narrowed, upper lip curled with contempt. I would say things too. A whispered "bitch," a snarling "fuck," even the hissed "c" word, the most despicable word on this planet to a woman's ears. But I learned very quickly that when you act that way and say those things, people remember you. They remember your face and the way you acted. Especially the women.

Now I enjoy my anonymity.

Actually, I rely on it. To be anonymous means I have the opportunity to study the women, to inspect each one like a show judge, appraising their every feature: hair (color and sheen), clothes (quality and label), body type (fat, thin, or middling), smell (perfumed or natural). Most of all, I judge the women by their eyes. I search and search each day, looking into the faces of each woman who passes, until I spot the one particular woman who is worthy of the grand prize.

Believe it or not, today I was in the presence of two such women.

One lives on 12th Street, between Second and Third avenues. She's a spicy little number: pretty face, long black hair, big chest, and a narrow waist. When she walks down the street, she moves kind of like a fashion model, a jaunt to her step, so those tits of hers bounce up and down. I'm sure she's aware of all the men staring at her. They whistle at her and shout crude things, which I'm positive she can hear even through the headphones of her Walkman.

When I saw her, I didn't ogle those tits. I was waiting for a glimpse of her eyes.

They're a magnificent set of dark brown, wrapped in oval eyelids, like the shell of a toasted almond. When she squints, those lids wrap around her brown eyes like a pair of soft hands, as if they were being presented to me.

I know a fair amount about this woman. Her name is Irene Foster. She's twenty-seven years old, single, no children. She lives in building number 228, apartment number 6E. Her phone number is 555-0554. Her checking account at Citibank is 43110213, with a balance of $6,256. If there were any more money in there, I might start wondering how she supplements her $600-per-month scholarship money from New York University. You see, she's a graduate student in art history.

I know a lot about the other woman too. Her name is Adelle Simms. She's a thirty-six-year-old resident nurse at Cabrini Medical Center, the place where I went to get stitches after a dog bit me in the ankle last year. Adelle is married with two children, twelve-year-old Brent and nine-year-old Lizbeth. Her husband is Doug Simms, a boorish-looking certified public accountant at Walker, Thomas, and Barth. Adelle and her family live in a tiny apartment on East 8th Street.

Unlike Irene Foster, when Adelle Simms walks down the block, men never ogle. She's built like a cement igloo: five foot two in heels, and tipping the scales at one hundred and eighty pounds. When she moves she waddles, sending uneven tremors through her dimples of cellulite. But there is something about Adelle's eyes, a pair of melon-brown beauties with a dot of light in the center, an uncontainable glimmer of excitement, that intrigues me very much.

You may wonder how I know so much about Adelle and Irene. The simple reason is that I have spent time in both of their apartments, making small talk with them, cracking jokes and saying "not a problem, ma'am," whenever they said "thanks." Both of these women have stood before me and met my stare. By doing so, by making eye contact, they have sealed the contract and sealed their fate. They are among the chosen ones upon whom I will someday bestow the ultimate prize. Me.

One

On the last Saturday of an unseasonably warm May, some-where between eight-thirty and nine o'clock at night, Michael Carpo began his Black Magic ritual in the kitchen of his one-bedroom apartment on 12th Street.

Black Magic was the house blend at Java The Hut, a small-time coffee dealer just around the corner on Second Avenue in the East Village. The blend was a potent mixture of Colombian and Sumatran beans, double-roasted for added kick. Every Saturday evening Carpo ground a one-pound bag of Black Magic, refilling an old Medaglia d'Oro espresso tin that he kept in the refrigerator. The can lasted exactly six days, from Monday morning to Saturday evening, when Carpo would knock the remnants into his Rancilio coffee-maker and brew his final pot of coffee for the week.

The ritual carried almost a religious significance to Carpo, mostly because he did not drink coffee on Sundays. After feeding the addiction for six straight days, the day of abstinence was important to him; somehow it proved that he was still his own master.

Carpo poured a handful of the dark, waxy beans into a Braun grinder and pressed the on button. The beans disinte-grated in a silvery whirl as an ear-throttling screech rose from the machine. He closed his eyes and concentrated on counting slowly to twelve. One Saturday he had forgotten to count and his coffee had turned out the consistency of talcum powder instead of the desirable size of gritty sand. His Rancilio coffemaker had backed up twice that week, sending cascades of steaming brown water onto the kitchen floor.

By the count of four, the screech softened, the resistance easing on the two steel blades. In its place came another noise, a strange one, far off at first but growing steadily louder. He ignored it as he focused only on counting to twelve, but by the time he reached ten, the noise took a disturbing turn: shrill, with the hint of an echo. Carpo's eyes flew open and he forgot the twelve count, the coffee beans, and the consistency of the grind.

It sounds like a scream, he thought. *A human scream.*

His hand flew off the power button as if it had scorched him, and the screech of the grinder subsided. Carpo held perfectly still, holding his breath as he listened for the strange noise. The clock ticked off seconds on the wall over the stove. Water plinked into the sink. The refrigerator motor shifted to a higher gear.

Then he heard it again, from out on 12th Street: a woman was screaming for help, and screaming as if it weren't going to get there in time. Carpo slapped the coffee soot from his fingers and ran for the bedroom.

It was a clear, still night; both windows facing 12th Street were open, the shades halfway drawn. As Carpo drew closer to the street, the woman's voice became sharper, each scream dividing into separate, intelligible phrases: "Help me! Please, someone! Please, help!"

The window screen darkened the already dark street, reducing everything to shadows and blur. Carpo spotted a commotion across the street. A woman stood on the sidewalk, arms waving frantically, as if she were trying to flag down a rescue plane. Carpo squinted through the screen but he was unable to make out her face. Suddenly, a man in a long black trench coat burst from the shadows. He shoved the woman aside and sprinted toward Third Avenue.

What's happening, Carpo wondered. *Is it a mugging? A slashing? An attempted rape?*

His first concern went out for Candi. Often she walked home along 12th Street, when her shift had ended at Little Poland. *Could the woman be her?*

"Help me!" the woman screamed. "Please, someone!"

The telephone was in the living room, on the table beside the couch. It occurred to Carpo to use it before running downstairs; he knew he shouldn't rely on neighbors to call 911. But there wasn't time for it: to call and give his name and explain what he had seen on the street. Not if someone was in trouble. Not if it was Candi.

Please God, he thought as he unlocked the door and raced down the stairs, *please not Candi.*

Two

Carpo could see that it was not Candi as soon as he burst from his building and stepped out under the streetlights. The woman was white and shorter, with straight black hair past her shoulders and a pair of tortoise shell eyeglasses.

In the time it had taken him to reach the street, the woman had stopped screaming. She cowered on the sidewalk in front of number 228, a six-story walk-up with a dirty brick facade. The woman hugged her body and shivered violently despite the eighty-degree weather. Even her teeth chattered, and through them she whimpered "Oh, God, oh God, oh God" over and over like a mantra.

Carpo carved a wide berth around the woman before approaching. He wanted a chance to study her, to look into her eyes and possibly gauge the situation, the state of her mind. The hum of air conditioners drowned out the sound of his footsteps. When he was five yards away, he stopped and said, "Miss? Are you okay?"

She whirled around at the sound of his voice, but her eyes stayed wide and unfocused, as if she couldn't see him. Her glasses were shaped like cat's eyes. They must have been for reading, because the lenses magnified her brown eyes to the size of malted-milk balls. The eyes weren't wired or psychotic, Carpo realized, they were the eyes of someone utterly consumed with panic.

He stepped closer, hands in the air, palms forward, in a mollifying gesture. "Miss, can you hear me? I'm going to get you some help, okay? I'll be right back."

Just then, a police cruiser sliced down 12th Street from the wrong direction, roof lights spinning, siren barking a crisp *whup-whup*. The cruiser braked in the middle of the street and two officers slid out. The driver was a short, burly man with a droopy salt-and-pepper mustache. His partner was younger, with braided red hair that dangled from his police cap like the wispy tail of a rat.

Both officers stood within the doors of the cruiser, stretching their legs as they unsheathed L-shaped billy clubs from canisters in the armrests and threaded them through metal loops on their belts. They repositioned the rest of the gear at their waists: 9-millimeter, handcuffs, Mace canister, 9-millimeter again, then a quick tug at the crotch. When all was in place, they nonchalantly strolled over, hands planted on hips. They stopped even with Carpo, honoring the invisible five-yard buffer zone he had already established. The officer with the handlebar mustache nodded at Carpo without taking his eyes off the woman. "What do we got here?" he murmured.

"I don't know," Carpo said, keeping his own voice low. "She was screaming for help. I saw a guy running away from her, so I thought she was being attacked."

The officer checked Carpo's face. "Which way did he run?"

"Toward Third Avenue. That's all I could tell."

The younger officer edged toward the woman. "Hey, lady, you okay? What's the matter?"

His words were tentative, but seemed to arrest the fear in the woman's face. Her brown eyes snapped into focus and began darting between Carpo, the officers, and the spinning lights on the cruiser. Just as fast, something collapsed within her. She buried her head in her hands and began to sob.

A second police cruiser blew down 12th Street, this one headed in the correct direction, west to east. It pulled grille to grille with the first car, its wailing siren setting off a car alarm down the block. Two more cops sidled out, a man and a woman, and joined the group. After a brief huddle the officers formed a protective cluster around the woman and escorted her into the brownstone. Carpo remained on the sidewalk, wondering what the hell was happening.

Rarely did the police respond to an emergency call with two units. Under standard procedure, the dispatcher sent one car, then added a second when the responding unit radioed for backup. The demeanor of the officers also baffled him; cautious and intense, but with no real sense of urgency.

Someone behind Carpo shouted, "What the hell's happening in there?"

Carpo was surprised to find a small crowd of people behind him on the sidewalk. Five men, all young and all staring intently at him. He didn't know which one had asked the question, so he addressed the group. "That woman was screaming for help. I don't know what happened to her, but the cops took her inside."

Carpo noticed the way the men stared at him, a mixture of envy and respect. He realized that they must have heard the woman's screams too, confronted the same split-second decision of whether to run down to the street. He lowered his eyes and stepped among them, uncomfortable with their silent accolades. Deep down, he wondered how fast he would have reacted if the woman hadn't made him think of Candi.

A third police cruiser sped down the block—lights off, siren dormant—followed by a blue Dodge van with the letters T.A.R.U. painted in reflective strips on the doors. It was called the "TAR-ooh" unit, and its appearance told Carpo a lot about what was happening inside number 228. He checked down at the movie marquee, where a bank of pay phones stood on the sidewalk. He needed to call the Channel 8 assignment desk immediately.

Before he had a chance to move, the burly officer came out of the brownstone and planted himself on the lowest step. He glared into the crowd, his eyes stopping when they reached Carpo. "You the guy who was here when I arrived?"

Carpo nodded, his face growing warm as the crowd's attention turned back to him. The officer came off the steps and approached him. "Tell me what you saw again."

"The woman was standing on the sidewalk screaming like she was being attacked. By the time I got down here, she had stopped."

"No, tell me the other thing," the officer said. "You said you saw a guy, right?"

"Yes, he was over by those garbage cans. I thought at first he had done something to her, because he was running away."

"What did he look like?"

"He was a white guy. He had on a trench coat or an overcoat of some sort. It was black and long." Carpo held his hand at knee level. "Down to here."

"Where did he go?"

"He ran toward Third Avenue. I couldn't see where he went after that, but that's the general direction he was headed."

The officer rubbed his mustache, the coarse whiskers producing a sandpapery scratch. "Where did you see all this?"

Carpo pointed over his shoulder. "I live on the sixth floor of the building across the street. I ran to the window when I heard the woman's screams." He checked where his finger was aimed, noticing how high and impossibly far away his apartment looked. "I saw it from there."

Someone in the crowd said, "I saw that guy too. The dude bolted like a scared little rabbit."

Carpo recognized the man's voice; it was the same person who had asked him what was happening in the building. He was a skinny white man, somewhere in his thirties, with a prominent Adam's apple and wet blond hair.

"Where were you?" the officer asked him.

"Up there." The man pointed almost directly overhead, at the brownstone in which the police had taken the woman. "I live on the fifth floor. I heard the woman screaming too and looked out my window."

The man's apartment was half the distance from Carpo's, unobstructed by tree limbs, streetlamps or parking signs. The officer seemed to take note of that fact too. He edged closer to the man and in a soft voice, almost a whisper, said, "Tell me *exactly* what you saw."

The man pointed at Carpo. "This guy got it mostly right. It was a dude in a long black trench coat, hauling ass down the block."

"How come you waited so long to speak?" the officer asked.

The man motioned toward his wet hair. "I just got out of the shower. I 'spose I could have run down in my towel, but I called 911 instead."

The officer pulled a thin spiral-bound notepad from a leather pouch on his hip. The notepad reminded Carpo of a reporter's notebook: a narrow book with thick cardboard covers, designed specifically for writing done in the palm of one's hand. The officer flipped to a clean sheet, slid a pencil out of the spiral, and said, "Let's have your names." He looked at Carpo. "You first."

"It's Carpo. Michael Carpo."

"Spell it."

"C-a-r-p-o. Like Harpo, but with a C."

"Carpo, like Harpo with a C," the officer mumbled as he scribbled on the pad. He nodded at the other man. "And you?"

"Thomas Abilene. Tommy's fine."

"Spell it."

"T-o-m—"

"I can handle Tommy," the officer growled. "Spell Abilene."

"Shit, sorry." Tommy swallowed nervously, the nut in his throat jiggling like a Tom turkey's beard. "It's A, B as in boy, i-l-e-n-e."

"B as in boy," the officer muttered as he printed out the name. He snapped the notepad shut and slid the pencil back in the coil. "You two poets think you could ID this guy if you saw him again?"

"Definitely," Tommy said, flashing a thumbs-up for emphasis.

"And you?" the officer asked Carpo.

Carpo shrugged. "Maybe, I think. I didn't get a great look, but if I saw the trench coat, I should be able to recognize him."

"Good enough. The two of you wait by that squad car." The officer pointed at the cruiser in which he had arrived. "We're going to take a spin around the block, see if our friend in the black trench coat's still hanging around. I just got to tell my supervisor what's up."

The officer shoved the notebook in its pouch and walked into the brownstone. Carpo and Tommy headed for the assigned car.

"What the hell is going on?" Tommy asked.

"I'm not positive, but it looks like someone was murdered."

"Murdered!" Tommy stopped and looked back at his brownstone. "How do you know?"

The T.A.R.U. van had backed into an open space at the foot of the building. Two officers walked to the back and pulled out several orange cases about the size of fishing tackle boxes. They stacked the boxes on a dolly and wheeled them into the brownstone.

"See that van?" Carpo said. "Those letters stand for Technical Assistance Response Unit. It's a special police unit. They're the ones who videotape crime scenes as evidence." Carpo paused a beat, then said, "Almost every crime scene they visit is a murder."

"No shit." Tommy ran a hand through his blond mop. "I freakin' live in there."

"Do you know who that woman was on the street?"

"I've seen her a couple of times," Tommy said. "I think she lives on the sixth floor. Don't remember her name." When they reached the squad car, Tommy planted his hands on the hood and leaned over them, as if checking for his reflection in the paint. "You really think it's a murder?"

When Carpo nodded, Tommy grabbed his stomach and moaned, "Shit, I freakin' live in there."

After a few minutes the officer reappeared from the building. He rumbled down the steps and through the crowd; something about his mustache and tight-ass waddle reminded Carpo of a walrus. As he walked to the driverside, Carpo caught sight of the nameplate along the bottom of his badge: P.O. Shane Podanski.

"Hop in back," Podanski said.

Carpo opened the rear door and slid across the seat to make room for Tommy. The compartment was built like a hamster pen: wire mesh separating the rear occupants from the driver; backseat upholstered in stiff industrial plastic; handles and locks absent from the door. It smelled foul too, a permeating stench of cigarette smoke, fast food, and sweat.

Podanski started the engine, then he slid open the panel in the mesh barrier. "Sit back and enjoy the scenery," he called over the motor. "Anyone looks familiar, give me a holler."

He tossed the car in reverse, executed a sharp K-turn, and moved down the block. At Second Avenue they turned right. Carpo scooted next to the window so the fresh air would blow over his face. A half block up he could make out Little Poland's blue neon sign with its circular pledge, AUTHENTIC POLISH HOME COOKING. On the same side of the avenue, they passed Java The Hut. The sight made Carpo think of the coffee beans he had left on the counter. He wondered how much time had passed since he first heard the screams. Ten minutes? Twenty?

At 9th Street, Podanski stopped the cruiser. He stared down at St. Mark's Place, the busy skid-row thoroughfare that intersected the East Village. A man and a woman with shaved heads and multiple body piercings were locked in a passionate embrace outside a Gap store. Next to them a toothless black man strummed a busted guitar.

"Let's have a look-see," Podanski muttered. He flicked a switch on the dashboard that set the roof lights spinning and stomped on the gas.

Carpo flew against the seat, his sweaty T-shirt sticking to the plastic cover. The cruiser's red and yellow strobes played off the buildings and parked cars. At Third Avenue, Podanski flicked another switch, one that controlled the siren. He gave it quick strikes—*whup, whup, whup, whoo-up*—as they slipped into the intersection. The car knifed in and out of traffic for a block, then sliced back against the grain, onto St. Mark's. Podanski killed the lights and siren, and slowed the car to walking speed.

The sidewalks teemed with an inebriated weekend crowd. Wide-eyed tourists mingled with bikers in black leather; homeless people wheeled shopping carts filled with empty cans; pockets of young toughs huddled on the building stoops. The street-level stores displayed leather goods, silver jewelry, used vinyl, and comics. Sidewalk vendors hawked old clothing and stripped paperbacks. Carpo stared into the miasma of sound and color; nowhere among it did he spot a man in a long black trench coat.

By the time they reached First Avenue, the sidewalks had grown deserted; few working streetlights, fewer pedestrians. They passed three bodegas, a liquor store, and a fortified gas station. The liquor store had its riot gates pulled, the metal slats spray-painted with an upside-down pentacle. Carpo leaned back and allowed the desolation to wash over him; they didn't have a prayer of finding the man in the trench coat here. There were too many dark alleys and abandoned buildings. Too many places where the city could swallow up a person whole.

Podanski must have sensed the same thing, because he accelerated for the completion of the journey—up First Avenue and a left on 14th Street, another left at Third Avenue, then down two blocks and the final left on 12th Street.

The crowd outside the brownstone had ballooned to more than thirty people. Men, women, and children, all of them reeled in by the flashing lights, squelching police radios and promise of excitement. Podanski muscled the squad car through the congestion, using the siren and an exterior speaker to ward off people, and pulled next to the morgue van. Its rear doors were open, affording Carpo a glimpse of four empty metal shelves lying one atop the next.

Podanski killed the engine. "Let me get your numbers before you go. The D.A. or someone from the precinct might want to speak with you."

He flipped on the interior light and took out his notebook, then Carpo and Tommy recited their numbers. When they had finished, Carpo poked his head through the divider. "Excuse me, officer, do you know what's going on in there?"

Podanski licked his thumb and brushed it over his mustache, flattening its edges. "Tell you the truth, I don't."

"It's a murder though, isn't it?"

The officer paused before answering. "Yes, a young lady on the top floor."

Tommy pushed next to Carpo. "It must be the Sandman. That's why you guys are swarming all over here. The Sandman did it, right?"

Carpo shuddered at the mention of the name. For some reason, the possibility of the Sandman hadn't even occurred to him.

Podanski swiveled around until he was staring at Tommy. "I didn't see the victim myself," he said solemnly, "but from what I hear, it's not him."

"Are you sure?" Tommy asked.

"Far as I know," Podanski said.

"Who was that woman screaming on the street?" Carpo asked.

"She's the lucky one who found the victim. A roommate or neighbor or something." Podanski turned off the interior light. "Fellas, I've got to get back in there, but I want to thank you for coming forward. These days, it's harder to find eyewitnesses than it is criminals."

The three of them slipped out of the squad car. Officer Podanski headed into the building; Carpo and Tommy rejoined the crowd. Two men in blue jumpsuits and black combat boots had pulled a flat aluminum board from the back of the morgue van. A hush dropped over the crowd as they walked into the building, every person thinking the same thing—*the body is coming out.*

Carpo turned to Tommy. "I'm taking off."

"Now?" Tommy said. "They're about to bring out the body."

"I don't really care to see it."

Tommy frowned and shook his head, as if to say he found Carpo bizarre. "I thought everyone waited for the body."

Before Carpo could walk away, Tommy said, "Say, what's your gig anyway? You a cop or something? You seem to know a hell of a lot about what's going on."

Despite the circumstances, Carpo smiled; nobody had ever mistaken him for a police officer. "I work for Channel 8 News."

"You a reporter?"

"No, I'm a news writer. I write the stories the anchor reads on the air. Occasionally, I do some field producing."

"Is that how you know so much about crime scenes?"

"I've seen my fair share." Carpo offered Tommy his hand. "I'm sure I'll see you around the neighborhood sometime."

"Okay, dude." Tommy gave his hand a vigorous shake. "Catch you later."

Carpo headed for the telephone under the movie marquee, passing wave after wave of fresh spectators. The crowd had grown to at least fifty people. Perhaps even seventy-five. From among it, somewhere, a person shouted, "Carpo! Hey, Carp! Over here!"

Carpo scanned the crowd, unable to pinpoint the location of the person, but he did recognize the voice.

"I'm over here," Candi yelled, "right in front of you."

He spotted her before the fire exit at the movie house. She was still wearing her uniform from Little Poland: black skirt, white blouse and apron, all splattered with soup and gravy stains. In spite of the drab clothes, Candi managed to retain her unique appearance. She had a short afro knotted in two-inch strands; at least a half dozen gold bangles circled her wrists, clinking and rearranging whenever she moved her arms; her left arm displayed a tattoo of a candy cane on the biceps. Candi bent over and gave Carpo a peck on the cheek. "What's happening up there?"

"Someone was murdered in the building across the street from me."

Candi recoiled noticeably. "That's awful," she said. "What happened?"

"I'm not sure. The cops said a young woman was murdered in her apartment."

"Don't tell me, it's the Sandman again." She looked up the street and shook her head forlornly. "That guy is going absolutely nutso."

"It's not."

Briefly, Carpo recapped his evening, starting with the woman's screams and ending with his drive through the neighborhood in search of the man in a black trench coat.

"It's got to be the Sandman," Candi said when he was finished. "It's totally his type of scene."

"No, the cop said it wasn't."

"I don't care what he said, Carpo, it's got to be the Sandman. Why else would a cop have driven you around the neighborhood? You must have seen him."

"We were just looking for the man in case he was still in the area. It doesn't have anything to do with the Sandman."

Candi clucked her jaw. "You disappoint me, Carpo." She waved a hand at the activity on the street. "What do you see up there? Cops, cops and more cops. It's either the Sandman or a PBA convention."

"I already told you, it's a murder."

"And I'm telling you, this is bigger than any old murder."

"Candi, quit making trouble. The guy I was with asked straight out if the Sandman had done it. The officer told us no. Now, why would he lie?"

"Because he's a cop, he's got to lie." She dangled her slender hand in front of Carpo's face. "I'm so sure, I'll put money on it."

"It'd be like stealing candy from a baby."

She planted her hands on her hips. "Oh, really, sugar? This Candi has never lost her *candy* to any man. Come on, bet me."

"What are the stakes?"

"Dinner for two."

Carpo rolled his eyes. "I suppose that means dinner at Little Poland whether or not I end up winning."

Before he could react, she snatched his hand and shook it. "You know, Carp, you're not nearly as stupid as you act sometimes."

Three

Carpo didn't learn the outcome of their wager until eight-thirty the next morning, when two police detectives buzzed his apartment from downstairs. "Michael Carpo?" one of them said through the intercom. "Detective Weissman and Detective Spinks from the 9th Precinct. May we have a word?"

The fact that they were police detectives said little about their business; it was the precinct number that made Carpo wonder how much dinner for two at Little Poland would cost him. The 9th Precinct was located on 5th Street in the East Village: headquarters for the Sandman task force.

The Sandman murdered the woman across the street last night, Carpo thought as he buzzed the detectives into his building.

They came up the stairs slow and silent, as Carpo noticed most cops like to do. He watched them through the peephole as they approached the door. One stood in front of the door, the other off to the side, out of view. They looked younger than he would have expected for detectives, mid-thirties, and they appeared to be in good shape. Neither looked the slightest bit winded from the climb to the sixth floor; unlike the mailman when he had to deliver a package requiring a signature, who coughed and wheezed as if he had hiked to the observation deck of the Empire State Building.

The detectives were dressed in street clothes: rumpled gray suits, white shirts, and wrinkled ties. When Carpo asked to see their identification, they unzipped flat leather cases and held up their badges. Carpo noted the appropriate gold color of both shields before he unlocked his door and let them in.

The one with the badge DET. P. WEISSMAN was the taller of the two. He was a thin white man with curly brown hair. He must have shaved recently, because his face looked razor-burned and he smelled of Aqua Velva. He gripped Carpo's hand and flashed a genuinely polite smile.

Detective Spinks was also white, but looked as if he had never learned how to smile. His hair was butchered military style, high and tight, and his face was lined with a bully's scowl. His nose was crooked and flat, as if it had been busted more than once in his life. He carried a cheap photo album under his arm. Dozens of photographs poked from the laminated pages, so many that Carpo wondered if a few had sprinkled onto the stairs during their climb to the sixth floor.

Carpo cinched his robe tight to his waist. He was barefoot and, beneath the robe, naked. The intercom had roused him straight from bed. No time to shower, get dressed, or comb his hair. And no time to make coffee.

"Guys want some coffee?" Carpo asked hopefully. "I could throw a pot on."

"No thanks," Weissman said, his face still holding the ingratiating smile. "This won't take but a few minutes."

Carpo started to ask if they wanted to take a seat, but

Weissman had already lowered himself onto the couch. Spinks dropped the photo album on the coffee table, hard enough to rattle the glass, then he moved to the far wall and folded his arms across his chest. His scowl deepened as he looked over the tiny apartment with its bare walls, threadbare carpeting, and secondhand furniture.

"Michael, have a seat." Weissman patted the cushion next to him. Carpo held together the bottom of his robe and sat.

Weissman pulled a notebook with a faux leather cover from his breast pocket. He skimmed through a few pages before he said, "I want to go over the statement you gave Officer Podanski last night. You said you heard a woman screaming on the street. Tell me what happened."

"I was in the kitchen," Carpo said, "grinding some coffee beans, and I heard a strange noise. At first I thought my grinder was busted, then I realized it was a woman screaming."

"Did you run straight downstairs?"

"No, I went into the bedroom to see what was happening."

"What did you see?"

"The woman." Carpo fiddled with the lapel of the robe. "She was on the sidewalk across the street, screaming for help."

"Then you ran downstairs?"

"Yes."

Weissman gnawed his lip; the hair at his temples quivered like bunny whiskers. "Hang on," he muttered, flipping back a few pages in his notebook. "You told Officer Podanski that you spotted a man running away from the woman. Was that before or after you got downstairs?"

"I saw him from the window."

"So it was *before* you went down."

"Yes."

The easy smile resurfaced on Weissman's face. "Tell me what he was doing."

"He was running away."

"Can you elaborate? Like, was he running toward the woman or away from her? Or maybe just past her?"

Carpo tugged the robe over his knees. "What's the difference?"

"Well, if this guy was already running down the street when the woman started screaming, maybe he didn't have anything to do with her. Maybe he was out for a jog or trying to hail a taxi."

"I see your point," Carpo said. "I'm pretty sure he was running away from her. I spotted the woman first. If he had already been running, I would have seen him first." Carpo avoided Weissman's eye. "Of course, it was dark and I was looking all the way across the street. I could be mistaken."

"Describe him for me," Weissman said.

"The only thing I remember is his coat. He was wearing a long black trench coat."

Weissman stared at Carpo, waiting for the description to continue. When it didn't, the detective smiled, this time showing off a little of his teeth. "That the best you can do, Michael?"

"I'm afraid so."

Weissman edged closer to Carpo. "I want you to try something for me. I want you to close your eyes and try to picture what you saw last night. Maybe it was dark, maybe it was just a glimpse, but you still have an image in your mind. I know you do. Close your eyes and study it, see if you can bring it into focus."

Carpo blushed at the detective's earnest motivational pitch, but to his surprise, when he closed his eyes, an image of the street did pop into his head. Just a glimpse, as Weissman had described, but more than he had expected.

"Okay," Carpo said, "I see him."

"How tall is he?"

"How tall? You've got to be kidding me. It's as fuzzy as—"

"Keep your eyes shut," Weissman ordered. "Try putting the man into perspective. Is he taller than the cars? Is he as thin as the trees? How does he compare to the woman? He should be right near her."

Carpo squinted at the image. The woman was on the sidewalk, about five feet from the brownstone steps; the man was about ten feet behind and to the right of her, in the shadows of the building. He seemed shorter than her, but that could be from the distance. "I think he's about the same height as the woman," Carpo said. "Maybe a little taller."

"Then he's between five six and, let's say, five ten. See, you don't have to be exactly right, Michael, we're just trying to get a general impression. What else do you see? Is he black or white?"

"White."

"Fat, thin, or medium?"

"Tough to say, since he's got that raincoat on. Medium, I guess. No, maybe a little thin."

"Hair?"

"What about it?"

"Try color."

"Uhm, I think ... brown?" Carpo peeked through his eyelids and caught Weissman shooting a strange look at Spinks.

"You tell me, Michael," Weissman said

Carpo stared at the image. Stared and stared, until tiny white spots began flashing all over it. He opened his eyes, blinking to clear the spots. "I'm sorry, that's the best I can do."

Weissman slipped the notebook inside his jacket. "You think it's worth having you sit with one of our artists? Sometimes it helps people to work on a drawing. It makes them concentrate on the features."

"I don't think it's going to help much," Carpo said.

Spinks chipped in from across the room, "How about the album, Phil? Maybe one of those photos will jar something loose."

The album consisted of forty pages, each page covered front and back with photographs. Hundreds and hundreds of snapshots lined the pages, maybe even a thousand. Mug shots, newspaper cutouts, Polaroids, black-and-whites. Some looked like surveillance photos, the images grainy and distorted from enlargement; a few looked glossy and posed, as if taken by a professional.

The men in the photos were just as diverse: white, black, Latino, and Asian; thin, muscular, obese; from teenager on up to geriatric. Many sported jewelry, especially gold earrings. One white kid, not more than fifteen or sixteen, even flashed a silver stud through his tongue. Tattoos were also popular: naked women rendered with improbable breasts; first names crudely hacked into the skin; branded fraternity scars; gang-style teardrops. One fellow with a crazy stare had "SUSEJ" carved on his forehead, the letters inverted as if he were trying to read the name through his skull.

Over the next half hour Carpo flipped through the album. The pages smelled of mildew and plastic, like an old shower curtain. He searched each photo for something familiar. A style of hair, a way of standing, even a swatch of black trench coat. At times Weissman tried to help, pointing out various details. But as Carpo flipped through the pages, all he could think was: *What have these men done? What horrific crimes have they committed to get their faces put in a collection like this one?*

When he reached the last page, Carpo sank back against the couch. "I'm sorry," he said with exasperation, "I don't recognize any of them."

Weissman fanned to the middle of the book. He fingered a Polaroid of a young kid with stringy black hair and a pot smoker's squint. "Does he look familiar?"

The kid was white and, if he was wearing a long black trench coat, might have looked similar to the man Carpo had seen. Of course, under those circumstances, two hundred other men in the photo album might have looked similar as well.

Carpo's stomach tightened; suddenly, he couldn't be certain of anything he had seen. "I'm real sorry, Detective Weissman, I'm not sure."

Spinks came across the room and dropped an envelope on the table. "Have a look at those," he said.

Inside, Carpo found six photographs. As soon as he saw the first one, his hands began to shake. It was a photograph of Rose-Marie Crostini, a thirty-three-year-old paralegal who had been found strangled in her apartment on East 10th Street. That was back in December 1996, before the police even had an inkling that a serial killer was on the loose in the East Village.

Carpo knew the names, ages, and a brief history for each of the photos in the envelope. He had stared at enough file tape, field-produced enough press conferences, and hammered out enough news copy to know bios on each woman. He also knew how they had died. Strangulation, of course, but a lot of other stuff too. Things like torture, mutilation, and cannibalism. Things that Channel 8 and other stations had decided not to report for fear of upsetting the public. Things Carpo did his best to forget as he flipped through the snapshots.

The third photo was of Adelle Simms, a thirty-six-year-old resident nurse at Cabrini Medical Center. She had died last June in her apartment on East 8th Street while her husband was away on a business trip. It was after her murder that the police first started to notice the common detail among the spate of butcherings in the East Village. At about the same time the local papers began dropping hints: *"Killer Known As 'The Sandman' Strikes Again"* or *"Sandman Notches a Third."*

Carpo found the Sandman tag revolting. It derived from the mythical creature who sprinkles sand in the eyes of children to put them to sleep. The name partly referred to the killer's skill at slipping unnoticed into the apartments of his victims. He floated past doormen and nosy neighbors, evaded locked doors, bolted windows, even the suspicion of solitary women.

But the real reason for the nickname, the one that so repulsed Carpo, was the killer's obsession with eyes. Once the Sandman had finished off his victim, he used a sharp, needlelike implement, most likely an icepick, to pluck out their eyes.

Carpo felt a bead of sweat run down his back as he handed the packet of photos to Spinks. "I've seen those before," he said hoarsely, "I know what they mean."

"Take a look at this one." Weissman pulled a glossy eight-by-ten from his breast pocket and placed it on the table.

The photo showed an attractive white woman, mid-twenties, with long blond hair and a dimpled, all-American smile. Her eyes were large and molasses brown, with a mischievous twinkle in the center. She was wearing a navy blue uniform that had a set of gold wings sewn onto the jacket pocket.

Carpo had never seen the woman before, and the fact that Weissman was showing her photo to him meant that he would never have the chance of seeing her again. Alive, that is.

"Sorry," Carpo managed in a ragged whisper. He put the photo facedown on the table and got to his feet.

"Where you going, Michael?" Weissman asked.

"I'm making coffee. You guys want some or not?"

It was like torture watching the detectives ladle milk and sugar into their mugs until his special coffee blend looked as diluted as the brew from a Greek diner. It might even have offended him if they had done it after taking a sip, but they had gone for the additives immediately. Carpo figured it was habit for them. Drink enough shitty cups of coffee in your life and you automatically reach for something to mask the flavor.

"Coffee's good," Weissman said after he finally got around to sipping some.

Carpo took a gulp from his mug; the scalding liquid numbed his tongue. "So I saw him, didn't I?"

"Who?" Weissman asked.

"The Sandman."

The detectives shared another one of their silent cop stares. Weissman shrugged. "It's possible."

"Another guy saw him too," Carpo said. "He lives in the building where it happened."

"Thomas Abilene," Weissman said. "We talked to him before coming here."

"I think he has a better view of the street than me," Carpo said. "He's closer and lives on a lower floor."

Weissman nodded. "He thought one of the photos looked familiar. The one I made you check twice."

Carpo recalled the white kid with the bloodshot eyes. "Didn't ring a bell with me. But again, my view's not as good."

From across the room, Spinks slurped his coffee with the suction of an emptying bathtub drain. Weissman cleared his throat and said, "So what do you do, Michael?"

"I work for Channel 8 News."

"You a reporter?"

"No. I'm a writer."

"Channel 8?" Spinks asked. "Isn't that Major Sisco's operation?"

"Yes, it is."

Spinks chuckled heartily. "Sure don't envy you, buddy. That Major is one hard-ass SOB. And that's strictly off the record."

Weissman joined in with his own chuckle.

Major Sisco was executive producer of Channel 8 News, known throughout the industry for his legendary fiery temper. Carpo let the detectives enjoy their joke for a minute, then he said, "So I'm right about the Sandman, then. He killed the woman across the street."

Weissman's smile vanished from his face. He looked into his coffee. "Yeah, we think so."

"Who was she?"

"Twenty-six-year-old woman by the name of Cheryl Street. A flight attendant with TWA."

"What time did it happen?"

"We think around three or four. We know the victim was on a flight that got into LaGuardia about noon. She took a yellow cab to her apartment, the meter indicates she arrived at the building at two-fifteen."

"That woman screaming on the street last night," Carpo said, "was she the one who found her?"

"Mmm-hmm."

"What's her story?"

"Out all day running errands, came back a little before nine. As she unlocks her door, she notices the neighbor's door is open. She pokes her head inside and . . ." Weissman shrugged, as if to say, You fill in the rest.

"Anybody in the building hear anything?"

"Not a peep."

Carpo looked between the detectives. "You guys have any leads at all?"

"We're here, aren't we?" Spinks said.

"Then you really think I saw him. I mean, it's more than a possibility."

"At this point, Michael," Weissman said, "anything is possible."

Carpo drank more of his coffee as he mused over the concept that he may have seen the Sandman. If only he had known at the time, he might have paid more attention. But it had happened so fast. The woman was screaming and that had commanded all of his attention.

More signals were flying between Spinks and Weissman—knowing glances, then a slow, stiff nod from Spinks. Carpo ignored them as he finished his coffee. When they finally stopped, it was Weissman who did the talking. He leaned toward carpo, elbows propped on his knees, coffee mug extended like a panhandler's tin cup. "Michael, here's a little word to the wise: You might want to watch your back for a couple of days."

"What do you mean?"

"I'm saying, it wouldn't be a bad idea if you kept your wits about you."

"Wits about me?" Carpo frowned at the detective's suggestion. "Do you mean I should watch out for the Sandman? He only goes after women."

Weissman shot another glance toward Spinks. "You're right, there's probably nothing to worry about. All the same, I'd stay on my guard."

The warning seemed unnecessary to Carpo, but he said, "Okay, I'll watch out."

"I also want you to do me a favor." Weissman's tone made it clear that Carpo didn't have a say in the matter. "I want you to keep an eye out for this character in the black trench coat. Even though you didn't get a great look at him, you might recognize him again. If he is the Sandman, we have reason to believe he'll return to the crime scene."

"I'll keep my eyes open," Carpo promised.

Weissman produced a stack of business cards held together by a rubber band. He pulled a card free and dropped it on the coffee table. "Call me if you remember anything else. Anything at all. The pager number on there is good twenty-four hours a day." He pushed himself to his feet, smoothing out his slacks. "Who knows, maybe you'll bump into this guy on the street and save us all a lot of hard work. Now, wouldn't that be a nice way to crack this case?"

Four

Six cups of coffee remained in the Rancilio after the detectives left, and Carpo stayed on the couch, in his bare feet and threadbare robe, and drank them, one after the next, until the carafe was empty and his pulse was firing as rapid as a Mac 9.

Carpo held his hand up and watched his fingers quiver, thinking: *Must be from all the excitement.*

He carried his mug into the kitchen and set it in the sink, next to the mugs used by Weissman and Spinks. Then he walked into the bedroom and threw open the windows, letting the cool breeze off the East River sweep into the humid apartment. Across the street, a police cruiser was idling outside number 228, sandwiched between a U.S. Post Office van and a live truck from Channel 2 News. The truck's central mast was raised high above 12th Street, higher than the buildings, its microwave dish aiming for the repeater atop the Empire State Building. The truck was feeding video back to the station, its big generator rumbling with the force of ten air conditioners. The sound drowned out all other sounds along the block.

From his perch Carpo could imagine the b-roll they were probably transmitting back to the newsroom: the lone police officer sitting in his cruiser; crime-scene tape fluttering in the breeze; a bouquet of flowers that someone had left on the front steps. The images would be strung together in an edit room and used to cover a voice-over or a short reporter package, perhaps for the local cut-in during the morning talk shows.

And that's when it hit him: *The other stations must know about the Sandman.*

Carpo went straight to the phone in the living room and dialed the Channel 8 assignment desk. After a dozen or so rings, the desk assistant, David Brandt, answered with the harried shout "News!"

"Dave, it's Michael Carpo."

"What's up, Carp?"

"I'm just making sure you know about the Sandman." In the background Carpo could hear telephones ringing and the scanners barking their coded language. "By the sound of things on your end, you already do."

"We're on it."

Dave's tone implied he was in a rush to get off the phone, but Carpo asked, "Have you talked to Sisco yet?"

"Ten minutes ago."

"Is he headed in?"

"He's on the way. Listen, Carp, there's like ten people on hold."

"Is Sisco calling in extra people?"

Just as Dave said "I don't think so," a beeper went off. "Shit, that's Jerry. The knucklehead probably needs directions down to 12th Street. Carp, I've got to go. I'll see you tomorrow."

Carpo set the phone back in its rest, a hot spot forming

in the middle of his chest. He lightly punched the spot, thinking: *Must be from all the coffee.*

He went to the medicine chest, shook out six antacid tablets, one for each cup of coffee he had drunk. He crunched on them as he walked into the bedroom. Down on the street, Channel 2 was setting up for a live shot. An engineer was unrolling a length of cable to the steps of number 228, where a metal tripod supported a Betacam video camera. Off to the side, a male reporter was brushing powder on his forehead, nose, and cheeks.

Carpo checked toward Third Avenue, expecting at any second to see the Channel 8 live truck pull onto the block. He swallowed another antacid tablet, the fragments feeling like shards of glass as they passed through his throat.

This is my story, he thought, *Cheryl Street was my neighbor. She was murdered on my block, right across the street from my building.*

I might have even seen her killer.

He turned his back on the street, suddenly fearful of spotting the Channel 8 live truck. He didn't want to stand there all morning and watch the reporter, Jerry Russo—the knucklehead of the newsroom—interview people from the neighborhood and shoot the stand-up for his package.

I can't stay on the sidelines, Carpo thought. *I'm a part of this story.*

Without looking out, he lowered the blinds and began to quickly dress for work.

WIBN-TV, Channel 8, is located in the Chrysler Building, the needle-nosed, art deco skyscraper located in the heart of midtown Manhattan. The newsroom sits on the forty-fifth floor and occupies the entire southern half of the building, a wide, uninterrupted space with low ceilings, bright fluorescent lights, and a picturesque view of lower Manhattan.

Often when Carpo entered the newsroom, he got the impression he was stepping into a giant beehive. The room was arranged like honeycomb: a pentagonal formation of desks, cubicles, and screening racks. Every flat surface was littered with the detritus of journalists: newspapers, press releases, show scripts, phone directories, fast-food menus, and abandoned cups of coffee.

Since it was the weekend and still early, a little after noon, the newsroom was quiet. But Carpo could already sense the buzz of activity at the assignment desk.

David Brandt was hunched behind a row of scanners, deciphering intermittent police bulletins. When under pressure, Dave had a habit of gnawing on the back of his hand. Right now he was attacking the knuckles of his left hand, clenching each one between his teeth as if he would pry them loose. A college intern sat on either side of Dave. One was looking up names in a Cole's—or Reverse—Directory; the other was jockeying the ringing telephones. At the far end of the desk, perched like a queen bee monitoring her drones, sat Major Sisco.

Even seated, it wasn't hard to imagine how Ardell Scott Sisco had gotten the nickname Major. Six feet four inches tall, Sisco owned the wooden pose of a soldier: stiff back, angular jaw, and a pair of eyes that could shoot a deadly glare clear across the newsroom. His stare was surpassed only by his voice: an impossibly deep rumble, which had the effect of snapping people to attention.

While the military tag fit, Carpo preferred to think of Sisco's nickname in a different light.

The major was executive producer of Channel 8 News, the city's top-rated local news show for five years running. At thirty-eight years of age, he was the youngest E.P. in the city by a decade. He was also the only African American in the market to hold a management position in a television newsroom.

Quite simply: Major, as in Major Accomplishment.

From across the newsroom, Sisco greeted Carpo with a resounding "Carpo!" pronouncing the name in two distinct syllables. "Don't even think of leaving today. We've got a major story breaking."

"That's why I'm here."

"You heard about the Sandman?"

Carpo dumped his knapsack on the floor. "Tough not to, seeing as how I live on the block where it happened."

Sisco gave a little jolt. "That's right, you're down on 12th Street. Any chance you know something we don't?"

"Probably," Carpo said. "Two detectives dropped by my apartment this morning to question me."

Sisco snapped his fingers at Dave Brandt. "Kill those scanners," he said, then motioned for Carpo to sit. "What did they tell you? Was it the Sandman? We can't get an official confirmation yet."

Carpo nodded grimly. "It's him."

"Who was the victim?"

"A young woman who lived across the street from me, building number 228. She lived on the top floor."

"She have a name yet?"

"Cheryl Street."

Sisco emitted a low whistle. "Un-fucking-real, isn't it, the way he keeps getting into apartments? What else do you know about this woman?"

"The detectives had a snapshot of her. She was a white woman, looked to be in her early twenties, quite attractive. The cops told me she worked as a flight attendant for TWA."

Sisco snapped his fingers at the desk assistant again. "Dave, on the double, call LaGuardia Airport and see if we can get permission to shoot in the TWA terminal." Sisco turned back to Carpo. "Were the cops casing your block?"

"I don't think so."

"How'd they end up at your place?"

"I was at home around eight last night, when a woman started screaming for help."

Sisco's face knotted with confusion. "Was it the victim?"

"No, a different woman. I never caught her name. She apparently had just discovered the body."

"What does that have to do with you?"

"When I heard her screams, I ran to my window to see what was happening. She was on the steps of the building across the street, the building where the murder happened."

"And?"

"And I saw another person. A man."

"Who was he?"

"I don't know, Sisco. At first I thought he was attacking the woman; now it seems he was just running away." Carpo leaned closer to the major and lowered his voice. "The cops seem to think I might have seen a suspect."

"Holy, holy, holy shit!" Sisco leapt to his feet and pointed at Dave. "Get Jerry on the horn, right now. Tell him to finish shooting the crime scene and hightail it back here."

"What for, Sisco?" Dave asked. "He's still got to interview the neighbors."

"Not anymore, he doesn't," Sisco said. "He's going to interview Carpo."

Carpo got to his feet, slow and deliberate. "Now, wait one minute, Sisco, who said anything about me doing an interview with Jerry?"

"If I heard correctly, I did."

"But I don't want to be interviewed."

"The hell you don't," Sisco said. "You're a player, Carp, the cops think you saw the Sandman."

"They're not sure who it was. And besides, I got a crappy look at the guy. It wasn't even good enough to send me to a sketch artist. I don't have anything interesting to say for an interview."

"Tell me what he looked like."

"I don't know," Carpo said. "It was dark and all the way across the street."

"Dammit, Carpo, describe him. Tell me exactly what you told the cops."

"He was a white guy wearing a black trench coat. That's all I could make out."

"Good enough for me," Sisco said. He looked at Dave. "Radio Jerry."

Carpo blinked with disbelief. He had wanted to work on the Sandman story, not become the center of attention in it. He stepped between Sisco and the assignment desk. "No, Sisco, please don't do that. I really don't want to go on camera."

"Nonsense," Sisco said. "What you just described is fine.

Talk about the woman screaming, then describe the guy in the trench coat."

"But I'm not comfortable with it."

Dave had the radio in front of his mouth. "Jerry's on the line, Sisco. What should I tell him?"

"To get up here."

Carpo grabbed the Major's arm. "Wait, there was another guy who saw him too. His name's Tommy Abilene. He lives in the building where it happened and got a much better look at the guy. Have Jerry interview him. He's probably home right now."

"How do you know he got a better look?"

"We rode around in a cop car together, looking for the suspect. His description to the cops was much better than mine."

Sisco's eyebrows cemented into a single angry furrow. "You rode in a cop car last night looking for the Sandman and waited until now to tell us?"

Carpo released Sisco's arm and backed away. "Sisco, I didn't know what was happening last night. The cops didn't know it was the Sandman. We were just looking for some guy who had run from a crime scene."

"Wouldn't common sense tell you to call it in?"

"I did call it in as soon as I got out of the squad car. You can ask Anita, she was on the desk last night. And I called again this morning, right after the detectives left my apartment."

"It's true, Sisco," Dave said, the radio still positioned in front of his mouth. "I took Carpo's call about ten-thirty this morning."

Sisco whirled on the desk assistant. "What do you need,

an engraved invitation? Tell Jerry to get his ass up here. Now!" Sisco glared at Dave until the radio was put to use, then he turned and shoved an index finger into Carpo's chest. "Not another word out of you, Carpo, not one peep. You're doing the interview."

Before he could say something he would later regret, Carpo snatched up his knapsack and stormed away from the assignment desk, crossing the newsroom to his cubicle. He had a mind to keep going, to walk out the door and back to his apartment, where he should have been spending his Sunday in the first place.

It isn't fair, he thought. *Reporters can't force people to be interviewed, how can the executive producer?*

His cubicle was located by the window. The desk-top held a computer, a caller-ID-equipped telephone, and a stack of city reference books. On the cork-board walls he had tacked a five-borough street map, a police precinct map, and a sheet listing the formula for locating avenue addresses. He had also pinned a few of the wackier headlines from the local rags. One of them jumped out as he took a seat: *"Need a Hand, Man?"*

The headline came from the *New York Post* a year and a half earlier. It referred to the futile state of the police investigation after the Sandman had killed his fourth victim, Rachel Thomas. Carpo wondered what tomorrow's headlines would bring. Surely, something to do with the woman's last name. *Killing Street? Street Sweep? The Sandman's Street?*

His thoughts were interrupted by the sound of Sisco clearing his throat behind him. "Carpo," the executive producer said, "word with you, please?"

Carpo swiveled in his chair and stubbornly crossed his

arms. He wasn't going to argue with Sisco, but he certainly wasn't going to be a patsy either.

"I'm sorry if you don't agree with the interview," Sisco said. "It's just, we've been working so long and so damn hard on this story, it'd be a shame to overlook a new angle. What do you say, Carp? Will you do the interview for me?"

"A minute ago you said I didn't have any choice."

Sisco exhaled with an exasperated *phoosh*. "Of course you have a choice. I can't force somebody to do a TV interview."

An idea came to Carpo, one so inviting that he feared his face had already given it away. He waited a few seconds, just in case Sisco had noticed it, then he calmly asked, "How would you feel about cutting a deal?"

Sisco closed his left eye, cocking his head to the side. "What's the trade-off?"

"I'll do the interview with Jerry if you let me work on a little project."

"I'm listening."

"I want to do a special report on the Sandman."

Sisco studied Carpo, eye still closed, before he shook his head. "I'll let you do a special report, but not on the Sandman."

"Why not?"

"I've already got too much dedicated to it. Tonight alone there'll be three reporters covering the murder. I can't expend any more resources."

"But my project is different from theirs."

Sisco pulled a chair over from the next cubicle and sat down. "Let's hear it."

"I want to do a profile on Cheryl Street," Carpo said, "a

two- or three-parter. Something that'll go in depth on her life, find out who she was, what she was really like."

"Give me the breakdown. Let's say it's a three-parter."

"I haven't had a chance to work out the specifics, but I'd probably divide it into the major stages of her life. Part one could be her upbringing. We could find out where she grew up, speak to her parents and neighbors. Part two: her teenage years. Interview her friends, boyfriends. Maybe we could trace how she ended up in New York City. Then, part three: life in the city. We could look into her job, friends, day-to-day existence."

Sisco stayed quiet for a while, lips pursed, then he shook his head. "Sorry, Carp, I'm not interested."

"Why not?"

"It's too Mickey-Mouse. It won't fly with our audience."

Carpo's face drew tighter than a drum. *Why didn't I just walk out of the newsroom,* he wondered, *save myself the humiliation?* "Fine," he muttered, "so it wasn't the most original idea."

A raspy chuckle bubbled from Sisco's throat. "You giving up that easy? Shit, Carpo, I thought you had some moxie in you."

"I said I haven't had time to think it through. It came to me only this morning, when the cops showed me her photo. All I could think was Who was she? Who was Cheryl Street? It doesn't seem fair that we'll never be able to find out."

"Life's not fair."

"Come on, Sisco, of course life's not fair. Otherwise there wouldn't be lunatics running around the East Village, strangling women." Carpo squirmed to the edge of his chair, hands gripping the armrests. "But let me tell you something, the cops are going to nail this guy. Somewhere, somehow, he's going to mess up. And you know as well as me, we'll be spending weeks looking into the Sandman's background. We'll interview his parents, his friends, probably even his damn kindergarten teacher. We'll dissect his whole life until people know every cracked-up thing that happened in his childhood that would make him want to run around the East Village, poking out women's eyes with an ice pick. I'm sick of it, Sisco, absolutely fed up with it. It's disgusting, and still we do it every time."

Sisco didn't even blink as he fired back, "Then change things."

"What do you think I'm trying to do?"

"You're not going to change anything with that simpleton idea for a series. Come up with something better."

Carpo clenched his jaw so tight, it felt close to shattering. "I told you," he muttered, "I haven't had time to think it through."

Sisco leaned back and put his hands over his eyes, as if he had fallen into a deep trance. "You've got to get Cheryl to the city sooner," he whispered. "That's all people are going to care about. Start with part one: a look at Cheryl Street's entire formative years, birth onward, concluding with her move to the East Village. Part two: the day-to-day stuff. Job, friends, hangouts, hobbies. Make her three-dimensional, make her real for people. Then let's go current for part three, really ground the series in some fact. Talk to the cops about the crime and have them discuss their theories. It might even be cool if you got those detectives from this morning to help out. Maybe they'd be willing to give you the inside track on their investigation."

Carpo's pulse quickened. "When can I start?"

Sisco opened his eyes. The corners of his mouth curled into a smile. "Hold off there, Slick, there's some ground rules."

"Figured as much."

Sisco ignored the comment. "I can't afford to spare a reporter or a camera crew right now, not with three stories a night already covering the Sandman. You'll have to pre-interview your contacts, then set up one day to shoot the interviews."

"One day!"

"That's what I heard myself say. You can do your interviews in the studio. It'll save you travel time."

"But, Sisco, it's still not enough time. I'd have to stack them like cordwood. Not to mention that I need to shoot b-roll."

Sisco held up his hand. "See how it goes. Most of your b-roll is going to come from the other reports we've done. If things get too hectic, maybe I can squeeze in a second day."

"Okay, Sisco." Carpo stood and extended his hand. "I promise I won't disappoint you."

Sisco stared at the hand without taking it. "I'm not done yet," he said. "I want all three parts of the series, shot, written, and edited, by June first."

"June first! That's the first night of Sweeps. It's ten days away."

"Thanks, Carpo, but I own a calendar. What good is a three-parter if I can't use it during Sweeps? And before you get a sour puss on that mug, I said I'd help as much as possible. If things get too hectic, I'll make special arrangements."

"How about a few days off to do research?"

Sisco shook his head. "Can't spare you. There's too much going on for me to start taking warm bodies off the schedule."

Carpo didn't fight the final edict. The newsroom was on a perpetually tight budget and an even tighter staffing. If so much as one person missed their shift, it placed a major strain on the operation. He was lucky Sisco had even agreed to the series. "When can I start?"

"You've got ten days until it's due. I'd get cracking yesterday."

Carpo felt the hot spot form in his chest again. He'd never heard of anyone completing a three-part series in such a short time. Especially while they were still keeping to the regular schedule.

Sisco pushed himself out of the chair. "And one more thing."

"There's more?"

"Bet your ass there is, and listen up good, because it's the most important one." Sisco waved his finger in front of Carpo's face. "I don't want to hear one thing about screwups or ethical quandaries on this story, okay? And I certainly don't want to read about you in the papers."

"You're the one who wants to put me on TV."

"You know what I'm saying, Carpo. Lord knows, it's always something with you. Just do your job and steer clear of trouble."

Carpo didn't say anything; he did know what Sisco was

talking about. Twice in his five years at WIBN he had nearly been fired for problems he had created while covering stories. The last time had even resulted in a two-week suspension. He doubted if Sisco would be understanding if something happened again.

Sisco started for the assignment desk. Before he got five steps, he stopped and said, "And one more thing, Carp."

Carpo's shoulders slumped under the mounting burden. *Now what?*

When Sisco turned around, there was a mischievous grin on his face. "You might want to powder your nose a bit before Jerry interviews you. I wouldn't want you to look bad on TV tonight."

Five

"When was the last time you had a date?" Candi asked.

"What do you mean?" Carpo asked guardedly.

"Just what it sounds like. A date. Something you never seem to go on."

It was late Sunday night. Candi was picking through the remnants of her victory feast at Little Poland: cabbage soup, potato pancakes, mushroom gravy, corn on the cob, and string beans. She was still wearing her apron, stained with many of the same dishes she had just consumed.

Candi wiped her mouth with a napkin. "You going to answer me or not?"

Carpo answered by shoving his plate aside. Candi rummaged through her purse for a pack of cigarettes. She fished one out, lit it. "Last time I saw you with a woman was two years ago," she said as she squinted through the smoke. "What was her name? You know, that skinny little brown-haired waif-of-a-thing. Not much to look at."

Despite his best efforts, Carpo couldn't help smiling at the description. "Karen Blackwell?"

"Yeah, that's her. Karen." She blew a cloud of smoke over his head. "What ever came of her?"

"Candi, I don't want to talk about it."

"So be it," she said, shrugging. "But I'm guessing she was the last one."

"The last what?"

"The last girl you . . . dated."

Carpo crumpled his paper napkin and tossed it on the table. "I said I don't want to talk about it."

The owner of Little Poland, Devon Jacek, limped to the booth with a pot of coffee. He was a short, stoop-shouldered man with a mountain of snowy hair. "How was dinner?" he asked in a thick Polish accent as he refilled Carpo's mug.

"It was delicious, Devon," Carpo said. "Thank you."

"And yours, Can-dee?" Devon asked.

"Great as usual, honey," Candi said. "I'm stuffed to the gills." She stacked her plate on Carpo's and handed them to Devon, who carried them back to the kitchen.

Carpo sipped his coffee, a mass-produced Colombian blend. It was a bit watery, but passable as far as diner coffee went. He reached across the table and shook a cigarette from Candi's pack. She produced a book of matches, struck fire, and held it to the end of the cigarette.

"Two whole years," she mused softly.

"Candi, would you give it a rest?"

She gave it a rest for about thirty seconds as she fiddled with the cover on the matchbook. Finally, she tossed the matchbook on the table. "Come on, Carpo, nice guy like you. Good-looking. Got yourself on TV tonight. You should be beating them off with a stick."

"Candi, you're ruining dinner."

"Maybe it's your clothes."

Carpo gagged on a mouthful of smoke. "What's wrong with my clothes?"

"I don't know. They're boring."

He fought the urge to check what he was wearing. "What's boring about them?"

"You wear the same outfit every day. Wrinkled khakis, wrinkled shirt, and those god-awful, clodhopper hiking boots. You look like the Swiss Family preppie."

"I like my hiking boots."

"You live in Manhattan, Carpo, not Maine." She wiggled closer. "I'm telling you this only because I care about you. I think there's something wrong with the fact that you haven't dated anyone since this Karen Blackwood chick."

"Blackwell."

Candi ignored the correction. "I want you to tell me the truth. Is she the last woman you've been with?"

"What do you mean by that?"

"You know darn well what I mean."

Carpo crushed out his cigarette. "If I tell you, will you leave me alone?"

"Okay."

"Promise?"

"Cross my heart."

"Fine," Carpo said. "She's the last one."

Candi slapped the table, an impish grin spreading across her face. "Holy cow, Carp, it's been two years since you got some? No wonder you're such a grouch all the time."

"I don't know why I trusted you," Carpo grumbled. He caught Devon's attention and signaled for the check.

"What are you doing?" Candi said.

"Getting the check."

"But I'm not done yet."

"You are now." When Devon was still fifteen steps away, Carpo said, "We'll take the check now, Devon."

"Hold on a sec," Candi said louder. "I won the bet. I want dessert."

"I thought you said you were stuffed," Carpo said.

"Well, I found a little room." Candi turned to Devon and said, "I'll take a chocolate egg cream and a slice of that strawberry cheesecake we just got in from Lindy's. Some whipped cream too, honey."

"And more coffee, please," Carpo called after Devon.

Candi folded her napkin into a neat square and set it on the table. "I didn't mean to hurt your feelings," she said sincerely. "It's no big deal that you're not dating, you're just in a funk. It's called a broken heart, Carpo, it happens to the best of us."

Carpo sighed heavily. "It's more than that. I don't have the patience for it anymore. I'm too busy with work, and when I'm free, I'm too tired to bother. I can't deal with the whole bar scene any more."

"But a bar isn't the place to meet a woman anyway. Least, not the type for a relationship." Candi tapped Carpo's arm to get him to look up. "I'll bet you didn't meet Karen Deadwood in a bar."

"No," Carpo admitted, "I certainly didn't."

Devon arrived with a double portion of cheesecake and placed it between them. He also set down forks, fresh napkins, then he returned to the kitchen for Candi's egg cream and the coffeepot. Candi slid a piece of cake with a giant strawberry into her mouth. "Mmm, f'real good," she said, pushing the plate toward Carpo. "Fry frum."

Devon returned with their beverages. As he filled

Carpo's mug, he said, "We see you on TV tonight, Michael. Second story on ten o'clock news. You are a big star."

"I'm no star, Devon," Carpo said. "I just happened to be around when that woman was screaming in the street."

Devon gave a solemn shake of his head, the coffee sloshing in the carafe. "It is terrible, this thing. The poor, poor girl. Nobody deserve a death like that."

"Did you know her?" Carpo asked.

"No, no, I never see her before. But I feel bad. Very, very bad." Devon shuffled back to the kitchen, still shaking his head.

"Come on, Carp." Candi slid a fork across the table. "Try a bite."

The cake was moist and creamy on the inside, with plump red strawberries and clouds of thick whipped cream. Carpo sampled a bite. It tasted like heaven, especially when he washed it down with a gulp of coffee. As he went for a second forkful, he said, "What about you?"

"Don't worry, I'll have more."

"No, I mean the woman. Did you recognize her?"

"The Sandman victim?"

"Yes."

"No, I've never seen her." Candi set her fork down. " 'Course, that doesn't mean she didn't come in here. Most people in the neighborhood do at one time or another." She lit another cigarette; the spent match perfumed the air with burnt sulfur.

"Are you . . . freaked out by it?" Carpo asked.

" 'Course I am, aren't you?" She stared at him for a moment, then blew a cloud of smoke toward the ceiling. "Actually, you probably aren't."

"What do you mean? I'm terrified."

"No you're not," she said. "Not the way a woman is." She flicked ash into the ashtray and went right back for another hit. "You ever notice how it's always women? These wackos never seem to prey on solitary men in their apartments. Christ, I've got so many locks on my door, I could keep out King Kong if I had to."

"You really that scared?"

"Mmm, scared to death. When I get home at night, the first thing I do is check my apartment. I look in the closets, behind the sofa, under the bed. I even pull aside the shower curtain, just to make sure he doesn't grab me while I'm brushing my teeth."

Carpo smiled at the image. "And what would you do if he was there?"

Candi put the cigarette in her mouth and squinted through the smoke. She cocked her head in a tough way. "I'd kick the ever-living shit out of him."

Carpo couldn't help laughing; Candi was tall, but she wasn't a pound over one-twenty. "What if he's big?" he asked.

"Don't matter if he's a giant." She reached into her purse and took out a small metal canister about the size of a lipstick dispenser. "Handle that with care," she said as she put it on the table. "I bought it from the guy who runs the bodega on my street."

"What is it?"

"Pepper Mace."

"That stuff's illegal."

"No more illegal than murder. The guy says it'll blind a person twenty minutes. By the time those twenty minutes

are up, Mr. Sandman will wish he'd kicked sand in someone
else's face."

Carpo smiled again, but this time he didn't laugh. Candi's
eyes had a different glint to them, a bright spark that burned
in the center like white hot embers. He had a hunch she
wasn't bluffing.

He took another bite of cake, followed by a swig of coffee,
then he said, "How do you think he does it?"

"What?"

"Get into their apartments."

She dropped the Mace in her purse. "Seems simple
enough to me: He knows them."

"But the cops have already checked out that theory.
There's no pattern to the women he kills. The only thing
that links them is the fact that each one was home alone at
the time of the murder."

"True," she said, "but you're leaving something out."

"What?"

"The place where they live." Candi stamped out her cigarette as if she were pressing it into the Sandman's eye
sockets. "All of his victims lived in the East Village."

It was well past midnight by the time Carpo settled the
bill at the register. The chairs were upside down at the
tables so the busboy could mop the floor. The odor of pine-
scented disinfectant slowly erased the aroma of home-
cooked food.

The tab came to fourteen dollars and change—Devon
had thrown in the strawberry cheesecake and Candi's egg
cream gratis. He also had not uttered a word of complaint
when they lingered in the booth talking for a half hour after

closing. To show his gratitude, Carpo pinned a ten under the ashtray on the way out of the diner.

He walked Candi to the bus stop on 14th Street and waited until she had boarded an M15, then he started for home. The neighborhood had grown quiet in the three hours since he had arrived downtown. Most of the bars were empty, and every shop along the block had its riot gates pulled. Traffic had petered out as well, just a few vacant cabs and an occasional delivery truck. Far off in the distance, somewhere past St. Mark's Place, an ambulance siren wailed in its plaintive way.

The sense of desolation in the neighborhood seemed unusual to Carpo until he remembered that it was Sunday night, the next day a workday, and most people were already in bed. Most people, that was, except for the small band of kids lingering on the steps of a brownstone halfway down the block. They drank cans of beer out of paper bags and the breeze carried a hint of reefer. Carpo wondered why the curfew governing work nights didn't also apply to school nights. He avoided them by crossing the street.

It wasn't until he was halfway across the avenue, glancing over his shoulder for any oncoming traffic, that he noticed the police cruiser tailing him down the block.

The car was twenty yards back, headlights off, tires hugging the shadows of the parked cars. The engine was barely audible as it rolled along, matching his pace. Outlined in the windshield were the heads of two officers.

Carpo pretended not to see the car as he continued down the opposite sidewalk. He maintained a normal pace, his body language casual. At least that was the way he hoped it appeared; for some reason, he felt as though he had forgotten how to walk. He knotted his hands into fists and trudged along, the subtle grumble of the car unsettling the air behind him.

When he reached 12th Street, the squad car roared to life. The roof lights flashed on and the motor flipped into high gear. Carpo froze, half expecting the officers to jump out and arrest him on the spot. But the cruiser sped past him, turned onto 11th Street, and disappeared.

Carpo wiped his clammy palms on his blue jeans and kept walking, silently fuming over the incident. *What are the cops hoping to accomplish? Do they plan on catching the Sandman by tailing every solitary male pedestrian in the East Village?*

The idea seemed ludicrous to Carpo, especially since it was common knowledge that the Sandman didn't stalk his victims on the street. He worked from the inside, outwitting the array of locks and bolts. He sneaked past doormen and next-door neighbors without raising suspicion. And then he got past his victims, who were already living in fear of him. In essence, he persuaded them to unlock their doors and invite him inside to murder them.

No, Carpo thought as he started up the steps to his building, *tailing people down the street isn't going to change a thing. In fact with that plan the police are never going to capture the Sandman.*

The phone started ringing as Carpo slid the key into his door. He hurried inside and answered it before the answering machine could. It was Candi, calling to say that she made it home and that her apartment had checked out safely.

She also extended a hearty "Thanks, Carp" for the lengthy victory dinner.

After hanging up, Carpo puttered around his apartment, straightening it for the start of the work week. He washed the pile of coffee mugs in the sink and set them on the counter to dry. He also folded a pile of laundry that he had washed Saturday morning, before all the craziness had begun. A little before one A.M. he grabbed a Coke from the fridge and turned on the television.

Like the other local independents, Channel 8 rebroadcasted its ten o'clock news show at one in the morning. Carpo found the practice odd, since the news no longer lived up to its billing, but he guessed it was cheaper than buying a rerun of a sitcom or an old western to fill the time slot. Some nights, especially big news nights, the rebroadcast actually won the hour in the ratings.

With the latest Sandman killing, Carpo figured more than a few television sets were turned to the repeat. And Channel 8 had obliged them by stacking the entire first section with coverage of Cheryl Street's murder. Most of it was standard local news fare: heavy on shots of the crime scene and file tape of the previous vicitms; light on official police comment and overall substance. His interview with Jerry Russo hit second in the show.

The interview ran just a minute and a half in length, though it felt much longer to Carpo. They had taped the spot in the community affairs studio, down on the 43rd floor of the Chrysler Building. The room was painted bright blue, with Channel 8's latest ad slogan stenciled on the walls—
CHANNEL 8 NEWS. THE WAY NEWS OUGHTA BE.

When his face appeared on camera, Carpo cringed. He

had worn a solid black T-shirt during the interview and that, coupled with his charcoal-black hair, had sucked all of the color from his face. At times it was hard to tell if he even had a nose or a mouth. He wished he had obeyed Sisco's makeup tips.

Carpo stayed tuned for the entire first section and ended up learning one pertinent fact about the latest Sandman victim. In the stand-up of the third package, the reporter, Mary Snow, revealed that the police had been unable to locate Cheryl Street's next of kin. As a result, her body lay unclaimed in the morgue at the chief medical examiner's office.

Imagining the body at the morgue, stretched out on a cold metal gurney sent a shiver up Carpo's spine. Dead and unclaimed: to Carpo it seemed the most horrific tandem in the world.

Six

The most obvious sign of the murder—the crime scene tape—was absent from the exterior of number 228 the next morning. In its place, a small memorial had sprouted on the front steps of the building: three bouquets of flowers arranged in a pile. Carpo made sure he didn't step on them as he entered the brownstone to begin research for his series on Cheryl Street.

The intercom in the tiny entrance listed twelve apartments, two on each of the six floors. Carpo took a moment to jot down the name of each resident in his notebook. He noticed that someone had placed a piece of black tape over the first name on the list. He peeled it back to reveal: C. STREET-6W.

Carpo winced at the sight of the apartment number. 6W was the west apartment on the sixth floor, the same number as his own. He replaced the tape and pressed the buzzer for the adjoining apartment: I. FOSTER-6E. After a short wait the intercom squelched, "Gawool izit?"

"Ah, yes?" Carpo said. "Hello?"

"Ishrumadee ayre?"

The speaker on the intercom was covered by a dented metal plate punctured with nail holes. Carpo placed his mouth near it and slowly enunciated his words. "My name is Michael Carpo. I work for Channel 8 News. Can I talk to you for a moment?"

"Ahsoldjew ahleevee ahloan!"

Carpo stared at the speaker, unable to decipher the scrabbled words leaking from it. "I'm sorry, but I think your intercom's busted," he said. "I can't understand a thing you're saying."

There was no reply, but a slight crackle of feedback indicated I. Foster was still listening.

"If it's not too much trouble," he continued, "I'd like to speak to you about Cheryl Street. I promise it won't take long."

The silence lasted several seconds more, then the interior door began to vibrate. Carpo grabbed the handle before it stopped and pushed his way into the building.

As the names on the intercom suggested, number 228 had the same layout as his own building, only flip-flopped: E, or east apartments, on the left half; W, or west apartments, on the right.

He stood in the hallway, waiting for his eyes to adjust. Drab gray wallpaper covered the walls, its ancient floral design faded to transparency. The carpet was stained with old muddy footprints, and the plastic skids on the stairs were chipped to the wood. Even the lighting seemed dingy, leeching from a glass fixture caked with years of grime and bug parts.

Far overhead, a door slammed, then a woman shouted, "I told you guys to leave me alone. Get out, or I'll call the police."

Carpo walked to the stairs and peered up the narrow

chute that ran between the landings. At the top, he could make out a woman leaning over the railing.

"Are you deaf or something?" she asked smartly. "I said, get out."

"But I'm not the same people," Carpo said. "I've never been here before."

"Didn't you say you were from Channel 5?"

"No, Channel 8."

She dismissed him with a swipe of her hand. "Eight, five, whatever. I'm sick of you people buzzing my apartment. Now go away."

Carpo nodded but didn't move. "I understand how you feel. Some of these reporters can be really pushy. If I could just have a few minutes of your time, I'd like to ask you—"

"Get out."

"But let me explain what—"

"I said, get out!"

Carpo put his hand on the railing, as if to show that he didn't intend to budge; inside, he felt his will evaporating. What would Major Sisco say in this instance, he wondered. Sisco always seemed able to coax people to speak to him. He called it perfect pitch. What pitch would he use now to get the woman to talk?

Carpo would have liked to ponder that question, perhaps even try a few lines on her, but the woman slapped the railing and said, "Have it your way, I'm calling the cops."

All Carpo could manage was a weak "But why?"

"Why? Why?" the woman sputtered. "Because I've told you four times to leave and you're still standing there. That's why."

"No, I mean, why won't you talk to me?"

"Because you people are sick. You won't stop at anything. None of you seem to understand that I don't want to be on TV or on the radio. I don't even want my name in the papers. All I want is to be left alone."

"Look though," Carpo said, motioning around the hallway, "I'm all by myself. Even if I wanted to, I'd have no way of taping you."

The woman let go of the railing and stepped back from the chute, out of sight. "Answer's still the same," she called out, "no interview."

The sound of footsteps moved across the building. *I'm losing her*, Carpo thought. *She's going back to her apartment.*

He cupped his hands over his mouth and shouted up the chute. "For what it's worth, I live across the street. I was home the other night when that woman started screaming and I ran down to her. I don't know who she was, or what she saw, but I care . . . about her and about this story. Not because I work for a TV station, but because it happened in my neighborhood."

He stopped talking when he no longer heard her footsteps. It had been the wrong approach. He had been pleading with the woman and that almost never worked, especially when talking to a stranger.

"Did you say you ran down to the street?"

Carpo looked up the chute, startled to find the woman standing at the railing again. He suppressed the urge to smile, realizing he had used the perfect pitch after all. "Yes," he said quietly, "I ran down to her."

The woman nodded, her long black hair falling over her

shoulders in a waterlike cascade. "Stay where you are," she commanded. "I'm coming down."

Her descent was marked by the volume of her footsteps: light squeaks growing into sharp taps, then flattening into hollow thuds. When she turned the final landing and came into full view, Carpo remembered what it was that he had found so striking about her the other night: her eyes. They were large and dark brown, a shade lighter than espresso; they held his stare like a pair of magnets.

The woman eased down the last steps tentatively, toes extended, as if she were testing the floorboards for weakness. She was wearing a pair of blue jeans and a faded NYU T-shirt. Two steps above him, she halted, negating his slight height advantage. Her hair was black and so shiny that it looked as if she had brushed it with boot polish. She folded her arms and appraised him with one sweep of her eyes, from his hiking boots to his face, so sharp and quick, Carpo felt disemboweled.

"You don't look like a reporter," she said.

"Maybe that's why I'm not one." He handed her his press pass, a laminated, picture ID issued annually by the police department. The card granted Carpo access to fire and crime scenes anywhere in the five boroughs. It also granted proof of his employment. "I'm from Channel 8 News. I'm a news writer."

She glanced at the pass, then handed it back. "What are you doing here, then?"

"Occasionally, I get sent out as a field producer. Right now I'm working on a special report." Carpo returned the

ID to his pocket and extended his hand. "My name's Michael Carpo."

She accepted it reluctantly. "Irene. Irene Foster."

"Do you . . . remember me?"

She stared at his face, studied each part of it, as if searching for something in it. She shook her head. "For some reason, I don't. I was trying to make out your face from up there, but even here I can't remember you. I guess I blocked it out."

"Do you remember being on the street?"

"All I remember is the police arriving. The siren must have jolted me out of it. Everything else is very fuzzy." She frowned and looked down at her hands. "I don't even remember running to the street."

"You must have been in shock."

"Maybe," she said. She lifted her head and offered what could pass as a smile; mouth only, and no real sparkle to the eyes. "Anyway, I guess I owe you a thank-you. The police told me what you did. I don't remember it, but I'm sure I appreciated it at the time."

"It wasn't a big deal."

She exhaled slowly, her shoulders relaxing. "So tell me about your special report."

"I'm doing a profile on Cheryl Street. I'm trying to give people a sense of what she was like in real life. Do you think you could help me?"

She shrugged. "I could try."

Carpo took out his notebook and a pen. He held them up and asked, "Mind if I take notes?" She nodded her assent, so he uncapped the pen. "Let me start by asking, did you know Cheryl?"

"Yes."

Carpo waited for her to continue, but the woman's mouth stayed firmly shut. "Could you elaborate?" he asked.

"We were next-door neighbors. And friends."

Carpo tapped his pen on the pad. *How can I get this woman to loosen up?* He decided the best way was to fire a quick sequence of questions. He started by asking, "How old was Cheryl?"

"Twenty-six."

"What did she do?"

"She was a flight attendant for TWA."

"For how long?"

"I'm not sure. Four, maybe five years."

"Did she like it?"

"Yes, she loved it."

Carpo waited a moment, then said, "Do you know why, Irene?"

The woman shrugged and said, "She was great with people and she wanted to see the world. Flying was her dream job, a perfect fit."

"Did she get regular work?"

"She'd go short stretches without any routes, a week or so—called them her dry spells. But then the phone would ring and she'd be off to Miami, Chicago, the West Coast. Once in a while she'd even get an overseas route."

"Where did she fly in from Saturday?"

"Los Angeles. Cheryl was supposed to stay through the weekend and fly back today. Friday night I got a message on my answering machine saying a slot had opened on an earlier flight. Some luck, huh?"

Carpo grimaced in agreement. "Did Cheryl have a boy-friend?"

"Yes."

"Know his name?"

Irene raised her eyebrows conspiratorially. "Will it get back to me?"

"Never seen you before."

She smiled, this time a real one. "His name's Steve. Steve Plotkin."

"Where does he live?"

"Somewhere in New Jersey. I'm not sure where."

"What does he do?"

"He works on Wall Street, some kind of bigwig invest-ment banking type. I never understood exactly what he does besides make a lot of money."

"Do you know which investment house?"

"I'm not sure." She stared up at the ceiling, one eye closed, as she pondered the question. "I think he's at the one with the bull as its logo."

"Merrill Lynch?"

"I think so. Chery used to have a T-shirt with that logo on it. I'm pretty sure Steve gave it to her."

"Were they serious?"

"Steve sure was."

"And Cheryl?"

"I think she liked him."

Carpo stopped writing. "That doesn't sound very con-vincing."

"Cheryl was a little strange about him. He was like a drug to her. She complained about him nonstop, always say-ing that his heart wasn't in the relationship, that they didn't have a future together, but then the telephone would ring or he'd buzz downstairs and off she'd go, running to be with him. I never could understand it."

"I can understand it," Carpo said. "Lots of people exist in relationships like that."

"Maybe so, but I used to wonder how serious she was about him. Anyway, it doesn't matter much anymore, does it?"

"Has Steve been notified of her death?"

"I assume so. You'd have to be living on another planet not to hear about it."

"Was Cheryl dating anyone else?"

Irene avoided Carpo's eyes. "I think she may have been."

"Anyone serious?"

"I don't know. It wasn't something we ever talked about, but I know she went on dates with other men. I got the impression that she might have been seeing some of them."

"Where would she meet them?"

"Work, I guess. That's how she met Steve."

"On an airplane?"

Irene frowned at Carpo's tone. "Keep your hat on, pal, it's not a capital offense. Cheryl was a pretty girl and she came into contact with lots of eligible men. It's only natural that she'd find some of them attractive."

"I didn't say it was a capital offense."

"Not directly."

Carpo shook his head, needled by the comment. "Nor indirectly."

Irene seemed needled as well. She cast an overt glance at her wristwatch, then another one up the stairwell. "Is this going to take much longer?"

"Just two more questions." Before the woman could back out, Carpo said, "I take it that you're the person who found Cheryl's body."

The woman's eyes widened and locked onto his, as if she were shocked that he could ask such a question. Carpo held his breath and waited.

Will she answer me?

She continued to stare, mouth open a pinch, the space taken up by her perfect white teeth. For twenty or thirty seconds she didn't blink. Then all at once she closed her eyes and said, "Yes, I was the one who found her. I found her while I was coming home. Her door was open. I noticed it while I was unlocking my door."

"Did you go inside?"

She nodded but didn't elaborate.

Should I push further? Should I ask what she found in there? What she saw that made her bolt down six flights of stairs, screaming into the street?

Instead, Carpo said, "Let's move on to something else."

The woman exhaled with relief. "Sounds good."

"Last topic, I promise. I heard in a news report that the cops are having trouble locating Cheryl's family. Do you know where they're from?"

"Pennsylvania. I think from Lancaster, though it might have been another town."

"Cheryl grew up there?"

Irene nodded. "She used to tell people she was born and raised in Dutch country." Irene smiled at the memory. "She would get a big kick if someone thought she meant the Netherlands."

"Was Cheryl close to her parents?"

"No, I'd say just the opposite. She never liked to talk about them. I got the sense it was a taboo subject with her."

"Do you know how she ended up in New York?"

"She got transferred here out of flight school."

"Did she like it?"

"The city? I think she loved it. She always used to rail against small town life. I think she couldn't wait to escape."

Carpo closed his notebook. "What about you? Where are you from?"

"Clinton, Ohio."

"Are you a grad student?"

The woman pretended to wipe her brow. "Is it stamped on my forehead or something?"

"No, it's your sweatshirt that gives it away. What are you studying?"

"Art history." The woman caught Carpo making a face at her answer. She pointedly asked, "Something wrong with art history?"

"No, I just used to date someone with the same major. It brings back bad memories."

"Then I guess it's a good thing we're not dating," she snapped. She glanced at her watch. "I also guess this means we're done talking about Cheryl."

Carpo managed a brief nod before the woman turned and stomped up the stairs.

After her footsteps had receded within her apartment, the gloom pressed in on Carpo. He felt as if he were suffocating: the shoddy wallpaper, the dreary light, the deafening quiet. Unfortunately, that was the way he needed things: quiet and empty of people.

He started up the stairs two at a time, feet placed wide to minimize the creaks. He moved as fast as possible, ears tuned for the sounds of people. Each time he passed an apartment, he crouched beneath the peephole, in case some-one happened to be looking into the hallway. At 3E the noise of a television dribbled under the door. The program sounded like a game show: bells, wild clapping and excited squeals from contestants. On the way past 5E, a small dog started barking. Carpo stayed motionless until it stopped.

As he rounded the corner for the fifth and final flight, Irene's apartment, 6E, came into view. He slithered forth on all fours, hands gripping the stairs above, until he reached the landing. He grasped the banister and eased himself upright, one inch at a time, until he could see 6W.

Three strips of yellow crime scene tape sealed the door shut: top crack, doorknob, and bottom jamb. Two longer strips formed a narrow **X** over the entire frame. Printed on the tape, again and again, was the phrase *CRIME SCENE: DO NOT ENTER.*

The sight of the taped-up door spooked Carpo: a giant, neon X-marks-the-spot where a murder happened. He couldn't imagine how it made Irene feel, having to pass it every time she entered or left her apartment.

Carpo noticed two decals on the door. One was a sticker for Amnesty International, a candle entwined in barbed wire. It was affixed to the lower left side of the door. The sticker looked old, and since he knew Cheryl had lived in the building no more than two years, he figured that it probably had not come from her. The other sticker looked newer and was displayed more prominently, dead in the center of the door and an inch below the peephole, where no visitor could miss seeing it. In blue block letters it read: *PROTECTED BY ADT SECURITY SYSTEMS.*

Spooky, Carpo thought as he made a silent retreat down the stairs. *Spooky as hell.*

This building was not some yuppified, Upper East Side, doorman-patrolled compound. It was a six-story tenement located on the fringes of one of Manhattan's tougher neighborhoods. And by the look of things, Cheryl Street had known that. Two solid locks on the door, probably a dead bolt on the inside, and that burglar alarm. There wasn't a chance in the world someone could have forced their way into the apartment without raising attention.

No, Carpo realized, what had happened to Cheryl was exactly what had happened to the others. Cheryl must have gone to the door, undone the locks one by one, and then invited the Sandman into her apartment.

Candi is right. Cheryl Street must have known her killer.

Seven

It took the better part of Monday afternoon to track down Cheryl Street's boyfriend. Carpo had expected an easier time of it, possessing Steve Plotkin's name and place of employment. Most of the problem he blamed on Wall Street, the world of button-down collars and buttoned-up lips, especially when it came to revealing the members of its secretive, closed fraternity.

Carpo did the work from his cubicle in the Channel 8 newsroom. Phones were ringing nonstop all around him, so it didn't look unusual for him to have a mouthpiece wedged under his chin. The phone at his desk also afforded him unlimited use of directory assistance; at seventy-five cents a pop, he would have been forced to flip through the white pages if he had made the calls from home.

On his first call to 411, Carpo learned that Merrill Lynch had five branch offices scattered throughout the tri-state area. He started with the firm's headquarters, located in the World Financial Center in Lower Manhattan. The switchboard operator informed him that eight employees worldwide were listed under the name Steve or Stephen Plotkin. Three he eliminated on the spot: employees stationed in Paris, Tokyo, and Hong Kong. Cheryl may have been a flight attendant and her boyfriend may have been rich, but distance alone precluded the weekly visits described by Irene.

When Carpo asked for a list of the five local Plotkins, the operator claimed that company rules prohibited him from giving more than one number per inquiry. Carpo figured the man was dodging the chore of reciting the listings, but each time he called back, the same rule applied. He printed the names and their corresponding numbers in his notebook, then he started calling them.

By a process of elimination, he ruled out four of the five names—Plotkins working in Westchester, Connecticut, and two in New Jersey. Each of the Steve or Stephen Plotkins who answered the phone professed no relationship with a Cheryl Street. It wasn't by accident or from bad luck that Carpo happened to call the wrong Plotkin each time; he was using the phone calls to test his pitch. By the time he dialed the final number, his pitch felt crisp, confident and—he hoped—perfect.

"Mr. Plotkin, this is Michael Carpo calling from Channel 8 News. Did I catch you at a bad time?"

The man on the line didn't say anything for a moment, then muttered, "No."

"I'm sorry to call you under these circumstances," Carpo said, "but I was wondering if I could talk to you about Cheryl Street."

The pause lasted longer this time, a full five seconds, before the man said, "What was your name again?"

"Michael Carpo."

"Yes, Michael, listen, you *have* caught me at a bad time. Can I call you back another time?"

Carpo circled the man's name, adding asterisks beside the number. "Sure," he said, "but why don't you let me explain why I'm calling first."

"You said it was about Cheryl."

"That's right, I'm working on a profile of her, a short bio. I'm trying to get in touch with the people who knew her best: family, friends, the people closest to her."

The man cleared his throat. "I'm afraid I won't be of much help."

"That's not true, Mr. Plotkin, you'd be a tremendous help. From what I understand, you were one of the closest people in the world to Cheryl. You could help give a sense of her, the real Cheryl, what she was really like."

"Michael, how did you get my name?"

Carpo remembered his promise to Irene. "I've been doing some interviews with people who knew Cheryl. Your name came up in a few of the conversations."

"And what did they say about me?"

"Just that you and Cheryl were dating." Carpo switched the phone to his fresh ear. "Would it be possible for us to meet, Mr. Plotkin? It doesn't have to be a formal interview. No cameras or tape recorders. We could talk over lunch or coffee."

"I don't think that's a good idea right now. I'm not . . . up to it."

"I understand, Mr. Plotkin. But can I leave my phone number with you? If you change your mind, maybe you could give me a ring."

Carpo recited his home and work numbers, then they disconnected. He leaned back in his chair and exhaled all the tense air that had been collecting in his chest. He felt tired and weak, as if the conversation had taken a severe physical toll on him.

Knocking on doors and cold-calling strangers were the parts of his job that he hated most. Especially when the story was murder.

For the rest of the evening Carpo played catch-up with his regular writing. The news editor had assigned him seven stories, an average weekday load, but *The Ten O'Clock News* had already started by the time he finished the last one. It was a late-breaking murder story unrelated to the Sandman killing. Police had arrested a seventy-two-year-old woman for rewiring a toaster so it would electrocute her husband. When paramedics responded to the emergency call, they found the woman still at the breakfast table, calmly munching a piece of toast, her husband facedown beside her.

To Carpo, the story exemplified his biggest gripe with local news. If the woman had shot, poisoned, or even bludgeoned her husband, the murder wouldn't have raised an eyebrow in the newsroom. But zap him while he pulls the lever on his English muffins, and the story rockets straight to the first section.

After work Carpo rode the bus down to 12th Street, where the late picture had just finished clearing out. Crowds of people lingered under the bright marquee, amid the smell of popcorn and melted butter. Carpo had planned to grab a piroshki at Little Poland, then head straight off to bed, but the sight of all those people made him yearn for something different. He reversed course and headed south, down half a block, to Orson's.

Orson's was a pint-sized bar on Second Avenue, wedged between an all-night newsstand and an all-you-can-eat sushi restaurant. It was dark and cozy inside, with cobalt-blue lights that cast a velvet glow over the room. People ate dinner at small tables surrounding the bar and Billie Holiday crooned over the sound system. Above the rest rooms, a model train chased itself around a circular track, the tiny light on the locomotive slicing into the rising cigarette smoke like a lighthouse beacon through fog.

Carpo selected a stool at the end of the bar, where the blast from the air conditioner was most direct. To his left, a pair of women sipped from champagne flutes and chain-smoked cigarettes. To his right, an empty stool separated him from a woman writing postcards with a bottle of Heineken perched before her.

The bartender approached Carpo. "Can I get you something?"

Carpo pointed at the woman's beer. "I'll take one of those."

The bartender produced a bottle from under the counter, snapped off the cap, and set it before Carpo. "I'll run a tab," he said as he slid over a bowl of peanuts. "Give a holler when you're ready for another."

Carpo took a sip of beer, then he pulled out his notebook and set it on the bar. As he did so, he glanced at the woman on his right, the one writing postcards. Something about her intrigued him; he wasn't certain what. Taken in parts, the woman's face seemed skewered: narrow eyes, crooked nose, a mole on the left cheek, another mole higher up on the right. Taken all together, the woman was mesmerizing, even striking, much like a Medigliani cubist painting.

Carpo didn't realize he was staring at the woman until she looked up and caught his eye. Before he could look away, she smiled and said, "Hi."

"Hi," he said, the word coming out like a gasp.

He took a pull from his beer then flipped through his notebook until he found the notes from his interviews with Irene Foster and Steve Plotkin. His body tingled as he skimmed over the words, none of them making sense. When he tilted the bottle back for another gulp, he noticed that the woman was still looking at him, a curious smile splashed on her face. He turned to her, but she bent her head down and resumed writing her postcards.

What's going on? Am I reading too much into a smile, or is this woman interested in me?

He held the bottle in front of his face and squinted at the label as if he were trying to memorize the list of ingredients. His palms felt sweaty despite their contact with the chilled bottle.

I should try talking to her before she leaves. But how should I approach her? Should I slide over to the empty stool? Stand up? Stay right where I am?

The thought of engaging the woman in conversation sent a nervous current through his body, from his stomach out through his arms and legs. He couldn't remember the last time he had felt this way—a tightly coiled ball of agitation. Not since Karen, that was for sure.

He drained his beer in three gulps and signaled the bartender for a replacement. *Should I check to see if she's staring at me? And if she is, what should I say?*

Hi, my name's Michael Carpo?

Hi, are you from the neighborhood?

Hi, do you come here often?

The bartender placed the fresh beer on the bar. Carpo took several gulps, hoping to deaden his nerves. He glanced at the woman from the corner of his eye. This time she wasn't looking. She was writing on a postcard, front teeth gripping her lower lip as she concentrated on the task. A strand of hair had escaped her ear. It dangled back and forth across her forehead, mimicking the quick movements of her hand.

Carpo bit his own lip and closed his eyes. He inhaled deeply, as if experiencing something very painful, and he thought, *I could make you so happy.*

Sweat stung his forehead and upper lip; he picked up a cocktail napkin and dabbed it across his face. An insane urge came over him to reach across to the woman and brush the strand of hair off her face. He longed to do it, to initiate some sort of contact. Suddenly, more than anything else, he wanted to hold her in his arms, very close, and whisper that he loved her.

Love her? Carpo's eyes popped open. *How can I say I love her when I don't even know her?*

He peeked again and the feeling remained. *Yes, I love you,* he thought. *I love you because you said hello to me and smiled at me twice, and you've made me realize just how terribly lonely I am.*

He had almost forgotten the loneliness; it had been with him so long that he had stopped noticing it. He knew it was there, deep inside him, behind a wall of diversions that he had created just so he could forget.

He stared openly at the woman and thought, *if you gave me the chance, I could make you so happy.*

It was time.

Carpo set the bottle down. His hands were shaking, his knees pumping like pistons. *Take a deep breath, scoot one stool over and introduce yourself. No coy moves or tired lines. Just move next to her and say Hi, my name's Michael. Would you mind if I joined you?*

As he started to slide into the empty stool, the door opened, letting in the humid air from the street. The woman's head came up and the smile resurfaced. She looked right at Carpo and said, "I thought you'd never make it over here."

"I'm a real slow mover," Carpo said before he realized that her statement was not directed at him. She wasn't looking at him, she was looking past him, at a man who had just entered the bar.

"Hi, Amy," the man said as he staked claim to the empty stool between them. "Sorry I'm late. I thought you said this place was on Third Avenue."

Carpo lowered himself to the stool, watching as the man wrapped his arms around the woman and pulled her close. The ache was perceptible again, scorching his chest, reminding him why he had built that wall of diversions in the first place.

Yet he looked at the woman and still he thought, *I could make you so happy.*

Eight

On his way home from Orson's, Carpo ducked into the all-night newsstand next door. He stood at the magazine rack, flipping through the various publications until a pair of trucks built like armored cars rolled up to the curb. The drivers tossed bound stacks of *Daily News* and *New York Posts* onto the sidewalk. Carpo waited for the clerk to slash the plastic bindings, then he snagged a newspaper from the center of each bundle. The papers were still warm and smelled of wet ink—literally, hot off the presses.

The cover of the *Post* had a bold three-inch headline that read: *CLUE-LESS*. It featured a picture of the police commissioner, Roy Chesire, presiding over the Sandman briefing earlier that afternoon. In the photo Chesire was scratching his head, his flabby cheeks balled into an expression of anguish. Beneath him, in smaller lettering, the caption read: *Top Cop Stumped by Sandman*.

The *Daily News* aimed for the sentimental with its headline: *THE STREET WHERE SHE LIVED*. The cover featured two photographs: the makeshift memorial that had sprouted on the steps of number 228 and a snapshot of Cheryl Street. Carpo immediately recognized Cheryl's picture; it was the same one Detective Weissman and Detective Spinks had flashed Sunday morning. Carpo paid for the papers, then he walked around the corner for a firsthand look at the memorial.

The memorial had more than doubled in size since the *Daily News* photo had been taken, transforming the bottom of the staircase into something that resembled a makeshift altar. More than a dozen flower bouquets rested on the steps, wedged among flickering votives, a pair of rosary beads, and a wicker basket heaped with dollar bills and spare change. On the railing, someone had taped a recruiting poster for the National Organization for Women. Taped beside it were two flyers: one listed the confidential police hot line, 577-TIPS; the other announced a ten-thousand-dollar reward for information leading to the arrest of the Sandman.

Seeded among the items was an assortment of messages, prayers, and testimonials; they were scribbled on paper scraps, pieces of cardboard, fast-food menus, and the backs of business cards. Most of the messages expressed sorrow or outrage over the murder. One message, written in a shaky, childlike script, spoke directly to Cheryl, as if at any moment she might stroll out of the building to look at her own memorial. It said: "Keep your head up, gal! And don't forget, we luv ya!"

Carpo studied the collection of objects for several minutes, something about it making him seethe inside. These people didn't love Cheryl Street. The were probably the same people who had gathered three days earlier to gawk at Cheryl's body as it was rolled out of the building; tourists, out soaking up the local color.

Carpo tucked the newspapers under his arm, thrust his

hands in his pockets, and crossed 12th Street. A few spaces down from his building, a late-model sedan was double-parked with its engine idling. As Carpo passed, the window on the driver's side lowered with a faint electrical whir, and a familiar voice said, " 'Evening, Michael."

"Hi, Detective Weissman," Carpo said. He walked to the car and leaned his head into the window. Weissman was in the driver's seat; Spinks on his right. "What are you guys doing, staking out the memorial?"

"No," Weissman said, "we were waiting for you."

Carpo motioned toward his building. "Want to come up?"

"Naw, this shouldn't take but a minute or two," Weissman said. "Why don't you hop in the back?"

Carpo opened the rear door and climbed inside. The interior smelled showroom fresh: plastic, rubber, and virgin upholstery. The air-conditioning was cranking at high speed; the icy blast evaporated the sweat on Carpo's body. Compared to the backseat of Officer Podanski's cruiser, this car felt like a padded, climate-controlled cocoon, Carpo thought. One that still had knobs for the windows and locks on the doors.

Weissman twisted his body around until he was facing Carpo. "So how are things, Michael?"

"Pretty good."

"Been busy at the TV station?"

"Yes. Very busy."

"I saw that interview you did last night. Wasn't quite what I had in mind when I said you should keep a low profile."

"Sorry about that," Carpo said, avoiding Weissman's eyes. "I kind of got roped into it."

"Believe it or not, it actually triggered a few leads," Weissman said. "People calling to say they saw the same guy."

"Anything come of it?"

"Not yet, but we're still checking. By the way, is there anything else you remember about the guy?"

"Nothing," Carpo said. "It's almost like I've blocked the whole thing out. Sometimes I can't even picture the trench coat he was wearing."

"Don't give up on him," Weissman said. "Sometimes an event will trigger the memory—a face in the street, a picture in a magazine. Usually it'll happen when you're least expecting it."

"If something comes to me, I promise I'll give you a call."

"You do that." Weissman rubbed his chin, then flexed his jaw as if it were sore. "So, things are going well at Channel 8?"

"Yup, everything's fine."

"Working on anything to do with the case?"

"The past two nights we've done little else. Sunday night we devoted the entire first section to the murder. And tonight we had three packages leading the ten o'clock show."

"No, Michael, I meant, are *you* working on anything?"

"Oh," Carpo said, "yes, I am."

Weissman glanced at Spinks, who continued to look straight ahead. "Care to share it with us?" Weissman asked.

"I'm putting together a series for the upcoming sweeps. It's a profile on Cheryl, probably two or three parts. I'm interviewing the people who were closest to her. Friends, neighbors, anyone who can give a sense of what she was like."

Weissman turned forward in the seat. He grasped the rearview mirror and angled it so he could still see Carpo's face. "You know, Michael," he said, "we could really use your help."

"What kind of help?"

"Getting out some . . . information."

"What kind of information?"

The detectives exchanged a brief glance. "You know how we were having trouble finding Cheryl's family?" Weissman said. "Well, we've located them."

"You did?"

"Actually, they found us. They contacted us this morning. They're not from the area, so it took a few days for the bad news to reach them."

"And you want me to report that?"

"No, not that," Weissman said. "Mr. and Mrs. Street are planning to hold a small funeral when they arrive in town, probably on Thursday. We were wondering if Channel 8 would consider producing a pool feed of the service."

"I'm sure we'd be interested," Carpo said. "It's one of the biggest stories of the year."

"Hear me out before you say yes," Weissman said. "There's a few stipulations involved."

"Such as?"

"First off, your station would be there as a passive observer. The parents want nothing to do with the media, so no interviews."

Carpo nodded. "Channel 8 would probably agree to that."

"You've also got to make sure this story stays under wraps until after the funeral."

"You mean we can't report that there's going to be a funeral?"

"No."

Carpo pushed the hair off his face. "Can I ask why?"

"Like I said, we're trying to keep this low-profile. If the local press catches wind of it, they'll be crawling all over the cemetery come Thursday."

"Couldn't we just say it's closed to the public?" Carpo asked.

"What the hell are you having trouble with?" Spinks asked sharply; the first words he had spoken that evening. "Like Phil said, the stipulation is no prior reports on the funeral. Period."

Carpo glared at the back of Spinks's head, irked by the detective's brusque tone. "In that case," Carpo said, "you guys can find another station to cover it."

"No, no, wait, Michael," Weissman said. "We want you to do it."

"There's six other TV stations in this city that would cover it in a heartbeat," Carpo said. "Ask one of them."

"But I want you," Weissman said.

"What's the point?" Carpo asked. "No interviews, limited shooting, no pre-reporting. Why do you guys even want a pool feed? Keep it closed to the public and everybody will be happy."

Weissman shot a hard glance at Spinks. "That's not the way we want to handle it," he said, rubbing the stubble on his chin. "It's important this story gets done in the right way. We need to work with someone we can trust. Someone like you."

Carpo stared out the window at Cheryl Street's memorial. He was honored by Weissman's statement, but he couldn't fathom why the detectives were so adamant about not mentioning the funeral before it happened.

What would Major Sisco do, he wondered. What would he say if the cops approached him with a deal like this one?

Weissman shifted on the seat again until his body was turned all the way around. "So what do you say, Mikey? Will you help us?"

Carpo sucked in his breath. "All right, I'll do it," he said, then, taking a cue from Major Sisco, added, "but I've got a few stipulations of my own."

Spinks bellowed, "What the hell is—"

Weissman cut off his partner with a curt "Shut up, Joey." He nodded at Carpo. "Go ahead, let's hear them."

"First, Channel 8 gets exclusive on the first broadcast of the video. We'll share it only after it airs Thursday night."

"Done," Weissman said.

"Second, if I can't have interviews with the parents, then I want interviews with the two of you for my profile on Cheryl. And none of this 'sources say' baloney either. I want you guys on camera, faces showing."

"We could probably accommodate," Weissman said, "just as long as it doesn't jeopardize our investigation."

"Next, I've got to clear all this with my boss. Major Sisco's got to know why we can't report it before Thursday, otherwise he'll never let me sign out a crew."

Weissman's mouth relaxed, his lips curling into a smile. "We can accept that. The funeral isn't for two more days. Talk it over with him and give me a call tomorrow. Here, take my card."

"I've got one in my wallet already."

"Great, and listen, Mike, I want you to know how much I appreciate this." Weissman nudged his partner. "How much we *both* appreciate it."

Carpo didn't move. "I'm not finished with my conditions."

Weissman's smile hardened like plaster on his face. "Oh?"

"This is an agreement between us," Carpo said, "quid pro quo. I'm shooting the funeral for you the way you want it. Now you've got to kick something back."

"We're letting you air the video first," Spinks said.

"I want something else. Something nobody else knows about. I'm sure you guys have a lot of theories about the Sandman, throw me a little bone. It's only fair if you expect me to do this story this way."

Weissman tapped his fingers on the steering wheel. "You could report that we found the parents. How about that?"

"It's not enough."

The detectives were silent for a few seconds, then Weissman looked at Spinks and said, "Can we tell him about the eyes?"

"You insane?" Spinks cried. "That's nowhere near ready for public consumption."

"What if he promises not to report it?" Weissman said. Spinks gave a perturbed shrug, then turned and looked out the window.

Carpo's interest picked up. "What're you guys talking about?"

Weissman turned back to him. "This is a good one, Michael, but it's just between the three of us. Got that? Nobody, but nobody can hear about it."

"I can't report it?" Carpo asked.

"No way," Weissman said. "I'm just telling you so you know how serious we are about the funeral coverage. Deal?"

"Sure, why not."

"Okay, here we go." The easy smile returned to Weissman's face. "And grab your seat, kid, 'cause this is going to knock your socks off."

"I'm ready."

"You know how the Sandman got his nickname, don't you?"

"From the fairy tale," Carpo said. "The imaginary creature that sprinkles sand in people's eyes to make them fall asleep."

"There's a little more to it."

Weissman stared at Carpo, the tension building between them. Carpo noticed the bleary redness in the detective's eyes, the wrinkles on his forehead, the five o'clock shadow leaning toward one A.M. stubble. His heart started knocking against his chest as he wondered what Weissman was about to tell him.

"It's not just any eyes he collects," the detective said, the smile fading from his face. "The Sandman only kills women with brown eyes."

Nine

Tuesday morning, Cheryl Street's memorial looked like the trampled mess found in Times Square the day after New Year's. The flower arrangements had wilted in the eighty-degree heat and were scattered across the sidewalk. The candles had melted into puddles of congealed gray wax. The morning dew had soaked the posters until they were as transparent as onion skin. Nothing had escaped unscathed, not even the collection basket. During the night, someone had pocketed the spare change and dollar bills, then stomped the wicker basket to shreds.

Carpo stepped through the refuse as he made his way into the foyer of number 228. After consulting the names on the intercom, he began to buzz the apartments, starting with the fifth floor and working his way down. There was no response in 5W, 5E, 4W or 4E, but his luck changed with 3E, listed to a V. Mendez; it was the apartment where he had heard the television blaring Monday morning.

Carpo launched his usual spiel through the broken inter-com, reciting his name, place of work, and reason for ringing. Within a minute he had persuaded V. Mendez to let him into the building.

The television was playing much softer when Carpo

reached the second floor. He knocked, and a moment later footsteps padded to the door. There was the sound of labored breathing as someone inspected him through the peephole. Finally, a man's phlegmy voice said, "Who are you?"

"Michael Carpo."

"Yeah, but which TV station?"

"Channel 8." Carpo took his Press ID from his pocket and held it to the peephole. "Would it be possible to talk for a minute?"

"What about?"

The lovely weather, Carpo felt like snapping. Instead, he said, "I'd like to speak to you about Cheryl Street."

A lock clicked and the door swung open. Behind it stood a short, pudgy man in a cherry-red robe. The robe carried the Marlboro cigarette logo on the front pocket; Carpo recognized it as one of the Adventure Miles promotions. Something along the lines of: Smoke five thousand packs of cigarettes, win a free robe.

The man had a Marlboro going now, perched daintily between his thumb and forefinger. Smoke curled past his flushed cheeks and watery blue eyes. He leaned into the hallway, past Carpo, and checked all around. "Where's the camera?"

"I'm not a reporter, Mr. Mendez, I'm a news writer. I'm working on a special project for Channel 8. If our interview checks out, I might come back in a few days to speak to you on camera."

The man shrugged, his chin pancaking into three distinct layers. "What do you want to know?"

"I'm trying to gather information on Cheryl Street. I'm wondering if you knew her?"

"Yeah, I knew her. I used to see her almost every day."

"Great," Carpo said. "What can you tell me about her?"

"Let's see," Mendez said, scratching his nose, "I think I read in the *Post* she was a stewardess or something."

Carpo smiled politely. "I read that too, Mr. Mendez. I'm more interested in the things that didn't get into the papers."

The man took a draw on his cigarette. "Okay, so maybe I didn't know her well," he admitted, "but I still know some stuff about her."

"Such as?"

The man's voice dipped to a whisper. "Like, for starts, I know the girl got around."

"As in, she traveled?"

"No, I'm talking *got around*." The man checked the hall-way to make sure no one was watching, then he pumped his fist crudely up and down. "She used to have lots of visitors up there. Male visitors. A few of them spent the night. I doubt if they was chatting about the mayoral race." The man broke into a raspy chuckle; cigarette smoke leaked from his nose and mouth as if his head were on fire.

Carpo held his breath until the smoke stopped coming. "How do you know this?" he asked.

"I used to watch her when she walked past my apart-ment." Mendez shoved a finger toward the peephole. "You can learn a lot about a person just by observing them."

"A close friend of Cheryl's told me she had a serious boyfriend. Are you sure that wasn't the guy you were seeing?"

"No, no, I know him, a real prick of a guy. It was other men."

"What was wrong with her boyfriend?"

Mendez studied the end of his cigarette as he prepared his answer. "He's a rich guy, you know? A typical yupster. The kind who thinks they're superior to everyone."

"Why do you say that?"

"He talked like a big shot, always blabbering on about how he was going to move her out of this dump, set her up someplace respectable. He treated her like crap too."

"How so?"

"He was bossy with her, always complaining about her clothes or the way she wore her hair. Nothing was good enough for him." Mendez leaned closer. "The dude had a real quick trigger too."

"You mean they got into fights?"

"Mmm-hmm, nasty ones. One night they got into it so bad, the cops showed up." Mendez puffed some more on his cigarette, his elbow perched on his belly. "You ask me, the cops oughta take a look at that fellow. He's no saint."

"What are you saying? You think Cheryl's boyfriend killed her?"

The man's eyes narrowed; like two slits in a cream puff. "I got to thinking the other day," he said, "how do we even know the Sandman did her? I mean, how hard would it be to make it look like the Sandman did it? For chrissakes, the whole city knows how he works."

And that's why Spinks and Weissman are keeping their brown eyes theory out of the papers, Carpo thought. *It reduces the chance of copycat crimes, not to mention the number of crackpot claims.*

"When you say Cheryl brought home lots of men, how many are we talking about?" Carpo asked.

"It's not like I kept a tally."

"No, but you make it sound like it was frequent."

Mendez crushed out the cigarette on the sole of his slipper and dropped it into his pocket. "Once or twice a week or so."

"Were they different guys each time? Or were there times she brought home the same one?"

"The boyfriend was the only one I saw more than once."

"Did you get a look at any of the others?"

"A few of them."

"Anything you remember about them?"

"They all looked the same to me." Mendez winked in a knowing way. "I get the feeling Cheryl liked a man with a big . . . wallet."

Carpo held his breath as the man broke into another prolonged chuckle. When he finished, Carpo asked, "What's your first name, Mr. Mendez?"

"Victor."

"What do you do, Victor?"

"I'm a graphics designer. You know, like computers and shit."

"Where do you work?"

"I'm a freelancer."

Carpo thought about taking down Victor's phone number but decided it wasn't worth the effort. By the man's own admission, the only knowledge he had of Cheryl came from what he had seen through his peephole. He was nothing more than a Peeping Tom.

The thought sent a jolt through Carpo. "Victor, by any chance were you home Saturday?"

"Yeah, the whole day."

"Did you see anybody suspicious in the building? Anything out of the ordinary?"

"The cops asked the same thing," Victor said. "The answer's no. I didn't see or hear nothing."

"What about Cheryl? Did you see her when she got home?"

"I didn't see her, I heard her."

"What do you mean?"

Victor motioned toward the stairs. "I heard her coming up the steps."

"How do you know it was her?"

"There's only four people who live higher than me. After a while, you get to know what they sound like climbing stairs."

"Was Cheryl alone?"

"Far as I could tell."

"What time was it?"

"Sometime in the early afternoon. Maybe one or two."

"Did you hear anybody else on the stairs?"

"That I ain't sure about. I was watching TV and I dozed off for part of the afternoon. I didn't hear anything out of the ordinary until that woman started screaming her brains out."

"Do me a favor, Victor." Carpo pulled a business card from his wallet and handed it to the man. "Call me if you think of anything else about Cheryl."

"Sure thing." Victor dropped the card into the same pocket he had deposited the cigarette butt. "Oh, and say, when's the reporter coming by to interview me?"

"I'm still not sure who we're going to interview."

Victor stepped back inside his apartment, wiping his

palms down the front of his robe. "Give me a little warning next time. I'll be sure to put on nicer clothes."

Instead of walking all the way to the foyer to ring the intercom, Carpo knocked on the door of each apartment that he passed. There was no answer at 3W or 2E. At 2W an elderly woman came to the door but refused to open it or answer any questions. Carpo couldn't blame the woman, G. Santorini; under the circumstances, he wouldn't have opened the door either.

There was only one apartment on the first floor. Instead of an apartment number, it had a plastic tab affixed to the door that read G. BENTO-SUPT. Carpo knocked on the door, waited a few seconds, then knocked again.

"Coming, coming, coming," someone shouted from inside.

A man in a tank top opened the door. He had oily black hair pulled into a ponytail and a two-day stubble on his sallow cheeks. "You here to see 6W?" he asked Carpo.

"No. My name is—"

The man cut him off. "Even though it's listed in the paper, I can't show it for another week. It's having some . . . ah . . . work done on it." The man put his hand over his mouth before he continued speaking, as if he feared a lip-reader was watching. "But if you're really interested," he whispered, "I can show you 5W instead. Layout's the same, and the guy who lives there won't be back until late. You'd be smart to check it out, 6W's gonna go fast."

"That's okay, Mr. Bento, I'm not here to see apartments. I want to ask you about the woman who used to live in 6W."

The fingernail on Bento's pinkie was long and filed to a

point: a portable toothpick. He used it to dig at something wedged between his teeth. "Where you from, guy?"

Carpo had his press ID ready. "I work for Channel 8 News. My name's Michael Carpo."

"You wanna interview me?"

"Not on camera. At least, not yet. I'm trying to get some information on Cheryl Street."

Bento examined something on the end of his fingernail. He rolled it around his fingertips and flicked it onto the floor. "I don't talk to nobody unless they pay for my time."

"I'm sorry, Mr. Bento, but I'm not allowed to do that."

The super smiled in a sly way, head cocked to the side, one eye shut, as if to show that he knew Carpo was trying to cheat him out of his fair due. "Seems to me everyone pays for interviews these days."

"Some shows do," Carpo admitted, "but not regular news shows. It's not considered ethical."

Bento chuckled coolly. "Then maybe you oughta tell some of your pals that. Yesterday I got a ten spot off a reporter just for talking to him."

"You're kidding me."

Bento made a sign of the cross. "God's honest truth," he said. "It was the guy on Channel 5. Ed something-or-other."

"Ed Thomas?" Carpo asked. "Is that who?"

"Yeah, that's the guy."

Carpo made a sour face; he had worked with Ed Thomas for four years at Channel 8, and the memory still left a bitter taste with him.

"I'm sorry, Mr. Bento," Carpo said, "but I don't pay for my interviews."

Bento pressed a strand of hair against his head. It stuck

to his oily scalp like a glue trap. "Then, Mr. Capra, I don't think I can be much help," he said, flashing a crooked grin. "I got my wallet and my own well-being to be addressed first."

Carpo thought about handing the man one of his business cards but decided against it. Bento would probably charge him to take it.

As he turned to go, Bento said, "And don't forget about 6W. Like I said, it's a real nice pad."

When he left Cheryl's building, Carpo noticed the mailman's saddlebag cart parked outside his building. He decided to drop by and see if the mail was distributed yet.

As he climbed the front steps, he could see the mailman through one of the windowpanes, stuffing pieces of mail into the mailboxes. It was the regular mailman: a short white man dressed all in blue—shirt, slacks, and a plain baseball cap.

Carpo stepped into the foyer, unlocked the second door, and pushed into the hallway. As he did so, the man started like a skittish colt, shouting, "Ooh!"

The man glared at Carpo, then the expression cleared, replaced by an embarrassed grin. "Gosh," he said, patting his chest, "you scared the daylights outta me."

"Sorry," Carpo said. "I was just wondering if the mail was ready."

"Just about." The man squinted at Carpo. "You're the guy in 6W, right? Michael Carpo?"

Now it was Carpo's turn to look surprised. "Wow," he said, "good memory."

"You do this long enough, and eventually you remember

stuff like that." The man extracted the few pieces of mail from Carpo's box and passed it to him. "There you go."

Carpo stuffed the bundle into his knapsack. The mailman had a silver nameplate on his chest that read DARRYL FOOTE. Carpo noticed that he was still breathing heavily. "You sure you're okay, Darryl?"

"Yeah, I'm fine." The man pushed the cap to the back of his head and scratched his forehead. "I was standing here, sorting the mail, thinking about that psycho who's killing all these women. I was wondering how the hell he sneaks into so many buildings without anyone seeing him. Sure enough, you come along and sneak right up on me. I didn't even hear it when you unlocked the door."

The man's statement reminded Carpo of what Candi had said Sunday night when she had claimed that men weren't as frightened by the Sandman as women were. *Maybe she's wrong*, Carpo thought. *Maybe the Sandman has the entire city spooked, male and female. Spooked to the point where people don't feel safe even in broad daylight.*

Carpo patted the man's shoulder. "Don't worry, Darryl," he said. "You can rest assured, I'm not the Sandman."

Carpo took an M101 bus up Third Avenue to 42nd Street, then he walked east an avenue and a half, to the Lantern Diner.

The Lantern was a mediocre greasy spoon that attracted a sizable lunchtime crowd, mainly due to the lack of cheap eateries in the midtown area. The diner had a strange way of closing down every few months from grease fires, city-code violations, or unpaid back taxes. Despite the air of scandal, Carpo liked the place. It was close to Channel 8, the waiters were friendly, and the coffee decent.

He grabbed an open stool at the lunch counter and ordered a cheeseburger, side of fries, and a Coke. As he waited for the food, he pulled out his notebook and began reviewing the notes from his interviews.

So far he had talked with four of the ten residents in number 228: Irene Foster, Victor Mendez, George Bento, and G. Santorini—the woman who had refused to open her door. Since Cheryl was one of the ten tenants, that left six people with whom he still needed to speak; this after two full mornings spent knocking on doors. With little more than a week until his series was due to air, Carpo wasn't even close to shooting interviews.

When the food arrived, Carpo closed his notebook and slid it back into his knapsack. As he did so, his hand brushed against the bundle of mail. He took out the pile and began flipping through the items.

Altogether, there were five pieces of mail. A plain white envelope with the return address Simon Judd Realty went back in his knapsack unopened; It was the May rent check for nine hundred dollars. The next three pieces of mail were discarded on the counter: an offer from the local gym; a fund-raising letter from his alma mater, Georgetown University; and a discount coupon for an airport limousine service. The final item was a postcard.

The front of the postcard had a photograph of the Chrysler Building taken in the midst of a thunderstorm. Somehow, the photo had been snapped at the exact moment that a bolt of lightning had struck one of the building's art deco gargoyles. It was such an incredible shot, with the gargoyle's eyes glowing red, that Carpo wondered if it was the product of trick photography. On the back of the card, written in scrawled block letters, was the following message:

> MINE EYES ARE MADE THE FOOLS O'
> TH' OTHER SENSES,
> OR ELSE WORTH ALL THE REST

> WHAT YOU SAW FROM YOUR WINDOW
> WAS NOTHING BUT THE VIEW OF A
> SENSELESS FOOL

Carpo read the card, then reread it. His immediate reaction was that someone had mailed it after seeing his interview on Channel 8 Sunday night. That would explain the photograph of the Chrysler Building and the passage about the view from his window. The news report had supplied his name and street address. A quick check in any city directory would have completed the address.

But it wasn't until his third reading of the card that he realized the note lacked a postmark and address for him. The card had been hand-delivered.

Did someone from my building put the card in my mailbox?

He wondered if the interview had offended one of his neighbors. Perhaps they felt he had sensationalized the murder by describing what he had seen from his window. Or maybe they were angry that he had brought more ill attention to the block.

More than anything else, Carpo wanted to toss the post-card on the pile of discarded mail; chalk it up to a nut case or an irate neighbor, and forget about it. Instead, he slipped the note back inside his knapsack, flagged down the waiter, and ordered a fresh cup of coffee.

Ten

The morning meeting, as the employees called the first meeting of the day, was under way when Carpo reached the Channel 8 newsroom. The entire staff was present, twenty people total, in a tight U-shaped formation around the assignment desk. At the top of this horseshoe stood Major Sisco, a sharp yellow pencil in one hand, the Metro Rundown in the other.

The rundown was the list of the day's top ten local stories—called "issues" by the major. The issues were stacked according to their relative newsworthiness: major stories at the top, starting with "issue one"; lesser stories following accordingly. Sisco typed the rundown a half hour before the meeting, and he tinkered with its lineup throughout the afternoon and evening. Depending on how each story developed, some issues would drop down the list, others would be dropped altogether.

Carpo grabbed a copy of the rundown from his desk and joined the meeting, avoiding Sisco's frosty glare. "Issue seven," Sisco called out, "the Boss is breaking balls in the Bronx again.

"Steinbrenner has reopened negotiations with the Meadow-lands about transplanting the Yankees to the Garden

State. Karl Desotto is the reporter. So far, he got 'sots' from a team rep, an official at the mayor's office, and the head of the Meadowlands Sports Authority."

Sisco turned to his desk assistants with a remark on the logistics of covering the story. "If nothing breaks by tonight with the Sandman case," he said, "I may turn this into a live shot. We can post Karl outside the stadium for some fan reaction." Sisco clutched his chest, feigning a sudden outbreak of heartburn. "God forbid if the Bombers move to *Joisey*. I may have to start rooting for the Mets."

Sisco resumed strolling through the group, his thin frame weaving in and out of the rows of desks like a knitting needle. "Issue eight: The mayor's dusting off Operation Clean Sweep.

"In case you folks forget, Clean Sweep is the mayor's get-tough-on-drugs policy he introduced during the 1994 campaign. Now that it's election season again, he's bringing it back to life.

"Caitlin James is the reporter. She's got bites with some police brass, a lawyer with the New York Civil Liberties Union and few man-on-the-street interviews. Caitlin may also get Milt Trendell, the Harlem activist who filed a harassment suit against the city over random police shakedowns."

As Sisco continued on to the next story, Carpo glanced over the issues he had missed. He was surprised to see that the Sandman investigation had dropped out of the top spot, supplanted by a shooting spree at a Jackson Heights A&P. A former employee had opened fire in the supermarket, killing three workers and a customer before turning the gun on himself. Carpo figured that fresh blood and a high body count were the only things that could bump the Sandman from issue one.

When the meeting broke up, Carpo waited with the other news writers for the editor to hand out their assignments. He was given the lead to the Sandman and the Yankees relocation stories, plus two other voice-overs—a three-alarm fire in a Bensonhurst diner and a Park Slope Girl Scout troop that had racked up record cookie sales. Four stories was a light load, but two of the spots were potential live shots. That would likely mean a hectic night; taking in live feeds and inserts from the reporters, then banging out leads and story tags for the anchors.

Carpo pulled a coffee mug from a desk drawer and filled it with some deadly-looking brew in the employee lounge. He carried the mug to the assignment desk, where Sisco was on the two-way with Sylvia Phipps, the reporter on the Sandman story. Carpo settled into a chair and began flipping through a newspaper. By the sound of the conversation, the desk was having trouble pinning down a lead for Sylvia.

"Don't look so busy," Sisco growled once he was off the radio. "The way you're sitting there, you look as if you've got everything figured out."

"Maybe I do," Carpo said, a trace of cockiness to his voice. "I've learned some stuff that might clear up your problems with Sylvia."

"Oh?" Sisco slipped into the chair next to him. "Then I presume things are coming along on the series?"

"No, just the opposite," Carpo said, "I'm up against a complete brick wall. I don't even know if it's worth continuing."

"What's up?"

"Mainly, I can't find anyone worth interviewing. I've talked to nearly half the people now in Cheryl Street's building, and, so far, only one of them has anything worthwhile to say."

"Who is it?"

"Her name's Irene Foster. She's the one who discovered the body on Saturday night, the one who was screaming in the street. Irene was Cheryl's next-door neighbor. They lived on the sixth floor."

"Were they tight?"

"According to Irene, they were. But I'm finding out that Cheryl wasn't close to many other people. She wasn't on good terms with her family, and her job kept her out of the city a lot. Even her relationship with her boyfriend sounds suspect."

"Have you talked to him?"

"Yesterday," Carpo said. "His name's Steve Plotkin. He's some sort of investment banker at Merrill Lynch. Not the most helpful guy either, I might add. He wanted nothing to do with me when I called him."

"So call him again."

"I plan to, just as soon as I get back to my desk."

Sisco pulled the yellow pencil from his shirt pocket and began drumming the eraser on the table. "So what do you think? Should I pull the plug on your series?"

"Give me until the end of the week, just to see if I can scrape anything else up. So far, I've concentrated only on Cheryl's building. I might learn something by snooping around the neighborhood. I also want to talk to some people who worked with her at TWA."

Sisco rolled the pencil between his palms, producing muffled clicks whenever it ran over his wedding band. "I thought you said you had something for Sylvia."

"I do," Carpo said, "but can we discuss it in private?"

The pencil stopped in Sisco's hand. "All right," Sisco said

as he rose to his feet and pointed toward his office. "Step in there."

Sisco's office, in the corner of the newsroom, was constructed of three solid-glass walls overlooking the newsroom. As they walked inside, Carpo noticed all eyes in the newsroom following him. A closed-door meeting with the Mayor was grist for the newsroom rumor mill; they probably figured he was about to get in trouble.

Sisco moved behind his large desk and took a seat. "I'm all ears, Carp."

Carpo chose one of the chairs that faced the desk. "I received another visit from those two detectives," he said. "They were waiting for me when I got home last night."

"Learn anything interesting?"

"Plenty." Carpo paused a beat, then said, "They've found Cheryl Street's parents."

Sisco sat up in his chair. "When?"

"Sometime yesterday. Apparently the parents are from out of state and it took this long for them to learn their daughter had been murdered. They're headed here as we speak."

"When are they due in?"

"Today. In fact, they may already be here."

Sisco slapped the desk. He got up and stuck his head out the door. "Yo, Dave," he said to the desk assistant, "get Sylvia on the horn. Tell her to drop everything and find a land line."

"Sure, Sisc," Dave said, "but why a land line? Can't she use the radio?"

"This is too big to put over the airwaves," Sisco explained. He left the door and returned to Carpo, choosing the chair opposite him. "Did the cops tell you where the parents are from?"

"They didn't say."

Sisco's eyes narrowed with suspicion. "They didn't say, Carpo, or you neglected to ask?"

Carpo felt his face heat up. "I didn't ask."

"What about their names?"

"I assume it's Street, just like their daughter."

"Thanks for the insight," Sisco said, "but I'm talking about their *first* names."

"Oh, I'm sorry." Carpo said, his cheeks starting to feel like a pair of boiler plates. "I'll call Detective Weissman just as soon as we're done and find out the answer to both."

"You do that." Sisco planted his hands on the armrests and began to lift himself.

"Hang on, Sisco, there's more." Carpo waited until Sisco had returned to a sitting position, then he said, "The parents are holding a funeral for Cheryl the day after tomorrow."

"What the hell's the rush?"

"I don't know."

"Where's it being held?"

"I don't know." After he answered, Carpo held his breath, awaiting the inevitable follow-up question.

"Did you ask?"

"I will when I call Detective Weissman about the other stuff."

Sisco shook his head impatiently. "You've got to think of these things ahead of time, Carpo. You won't always get a second chance."

"Sorry," Carpo said, "I got so excited about the tip, I didn't think to ask for the specifics."

"Have the cops told any other stations about this?"

"This is what I wanted to talk to you about," Carpo said.

"The funeral is strictly off limits to the press. The detectives are asking us to keep it quiet until after it's over."

"How come?"

"They say the parents are paranoid about the media. They don't want anything to do with us while they're here."

Sisco's eyes narrowed. "So why'd the cops tell you at all?"

"Because they want us to cover it as the pool camera."

Carpo briefly outlined his conversation with Weissman and Spinks, telling everything except the part about the brown-eye theory. When he was finished, Sisco leaned back in the chair. "Call me suspicious, but why are the cops being so chummy with you?"

"I don't think it's me they care about, I think they're worried about pissing off the parents. I guess they had to promise that only one TV station would be covering the funeral."

"But why let us cover it at all? Why not close the thing to the media altogether? That way, they could guarantee no one will bother the parents."

"I think they know it's impossible to totally shut out the media. This way, the TV stations and newspapers will get their pictures without anyone bothering the parents."

The explanation seemed to satisy Sisco. He reached over and patted Carpo on the back. "Any rate, Carp, nice work. You've found us at least two exclusives on the Sandman for this week. We'll report on the parents tonight, then we'll scoop the entire city Thursday night with news of the funeral."

Back at his desk, Carpo fished Detective Weissman's card out of his wallet and dialed his desk number at the 9th Precinct. A recording of Weissman's voice came on the line and instructed him to leave a message or, if it was an emergency, to try a beeper number. Carpo chose the latter. Five minutes later the phone started ringing on his desk.

"Channel 8 News. Carpo here."

"Yeah, Michael, it's Detective Weissman." The detective sounded like he was talking from a cell phone. "You beep me a minute ago?"

"Yes, thanks for calling back so fast. I wanted to tell you, I got clearance to shoot the funeral."

"Great, great," Weissman said. "Maybe the old major isn't such a hardass after all."

"He wanted me to ask one more time if you'll change your mind about promoting the funeral. Tonight we'll be doing a report on the discovery of the parents. It seems like a logical spot to mention Thursday's service."

"I'm going to have to insist that you don't do that. Please, Michael, it's real important that we keep this under wraps."

The stipulation nagged at Carpo, so he said, "Can I ask why?"

"Like I told you last night, if word of this funeral gets out, every reporter in the tri-state area is going to be calling me for information. Not to mention, the parents are totally against it. I had to push them just to let you there."

"Okay," Carpo said. "By the way, what are their first names?"

"Myron and Alice."

"And what time will the service be held on Thursday?"

"Four o'clock sharp."

"That's where?"

"St. John's Cemetery," Weissman said. "It's in Middle Village, Queens. You need directions?"

"No, I can figure it out." Carpo glanced at the map pinned to his cubicle. Middle Village was far into Queens, several miles past LaGuardia Airport. "Is there any special place we should meet?"

"Just park in the main lot. There won't be many people, so it shouldn't be hard to spot each other. And make sure it's four on the button. We can't be sitting around, waiting for you to show up."

"I'll be there," Carpo promised. "I've got one other question for tonight's broadcast. Where are Cheryl's parents from?"

"Virginia," Weissman said. "Roanoke, Virginia."

"Have they arrived in town yet?"

"They're due any time now. In fact, I really should get going."

Carpo thanked the detective for the information and hung up the phone. He pulled out his notebook, scribbled the details on the funeral, then he flipped through the pages until he found Steve Plotkin's number. He took a sip of coffee and dialed it.

After a half dozen rings, a woman answered the line. "Steve Plotkin's office."

"May I speak to Steve, please?" Carpo asked.

"I'm sorry, he's on another line. Would you care to hold?"

"Yes, please."

"May I ask who's calling?"

Carpo thought about identifying himself, then decided against it. "Just tell him it's a personal call."

The woman put Carpo on hold. He listened to a recorded message that implored him to open a brokerage account with the bank. The sales pitch sounded intriguing—*"Earn returns of up to twenty percent on your hard-earned money*"—until the voice mentioned a required minimum balance of ten thousand dollars. Carpo already had trouble maintaining the minimum on his regular Citibank account, and that was just fifteen hundred dollars.

Suddenly, the line clicked and Plotkin said, "This is Steve. Can I help you?"

"Hi, Steve, it's Michael Carpo calling from Channel 8 News."

"A personal call, huh?" Plotkin said, his voice hardening noticeably. "What do you want?"

"I'm sorry, have I caught you at a bad time? If I have, I can call back later."

"Anytime is a bad time. I thought I made that clear the other day. I have nothing to say to you."

"I understand," Carpo said, "but I just wanted to tell you that there's going to be a funeral for Cheryl on Thursday. I'm not supposed to tell anybody about it, but I figure you deserve a heads-up."

The line was silent for a few seconds. When Plotkin spoke, some of the punch had left his voice. "Where are they holding it?"

"St. John's Cemetery in Middle Village, Queens. Four o'clock sharp. The funeral is closed to the media. It'll be Cheryl's parents, a few close friends, and that's it."

"So they finally found her mom and dad?"

"Yes, the parents contacted the police yesterday."

"Are you guys going to be there?"

"I'll be there with one camera to shoot some b-roll," Carpo said, "but that's it. No other stations are attending."

Plotkin cleared his throat. "I guess I should say thanks for the tip."

"No problem, Steve." Carpo paused a moment, half expecting the man to hang up. When he didn't, Carpo decided to make one more pitch. "Listen, I know my calls are making you uptight, but I want you to know if you need someone to talk to, I'm here."

"No offense," Plotkin said with an uneasy chuckle, "but you're about the last person I'd talk to."

"So be it. I'm just putting the offer on the table."

"Well, you can pick it right back up. I wouldn't trust someone from the media as far as I could throw them."

"And well you shouldn't," Carpo said, "because most of us really are just out for the story. I'm not saying I'm better than anyone else, but you sound like something's troubling you. I'd be willing to talk to you off the record, no camera, no bullshit. I want you to know that you're not alone."

It took Carpo a few seconds to realize that he was the one all alone; Plotkin had hung up on him. He sighed heavily and slammed the phone back into its cradle, thinking to himself, *Somehow, some way, I'm going to reach Steve Plotkin.*

Eleven

Wednesday morning Carpo crossed 12th Street to complete his interviews with the residents of Cheryl Street's building. It was earlier than the other visits, a little after eight, so the sun hadn't had a chance to bake the neighborhood. The air felt moist and cool, and the street smelled fresh.

Carpo got a response from the first apartment he buzzed: T. Abilene in 5W—the man who had toured the neighborhood with him on the night of the murder. After explaining his way past the intercom, he headed up the stairs. The hallway seemed darker than the previous times, the noises different. Televisions and radios played in most of the apartments. Water pulsed through pipes in the walls, a muffled gush, as people took their morning showers.

By the look of things, Tommy Abilene had just finished his shower. He was waiting on the fourth flight of stairs, his hair slicked off his forehead, just as Carpo remembered from Saturday night. "What's up, dude?" Tommy called down, the lump in his throat bouncing like a pink Spaldeen.

"Not much, Tommy. How are you?"

"I'm cool, man." They exchanged a brief handshake, then Tommy said, "Tell me your name again? I forget."

"Michael Carpo."

Tommy snapped his fingers. "That's right, Carpo, like Harpo, but with a C. How could I forget? What can I do for you, Carpo?"

"I was hoping we could talk about the woman who lived above you, Cheryl Street."

"Sure, sure, we can talk." Tommy pointed to his apartment. "Want to come in?"

The apartment was a small studio, a perfectly shaped square, with two windows overlooking 12th Street. A queen-sized mattress was on the floor by the far wall, beside a television set with a wire hanger serving as antennae. Dirty clothes were scattered on the floor and over the two chairs at the breakfast table. A half-eaten bowl of cereal sat on the table next to an open box of Cheerios. Tommy pushed the clothes off the chairs and offered Carpo a seat.

"This won't take long," Carpo said.

"No sweat, I've got plenty of time. I don't have to be at work until ten-thirty."

Carpo took out his notebook. "What do you do, Tommy?"

"I'm a paver with Costanza Construction."

"I don't think I've heard of them," Carpo said. "Where are they located?"

"Pine Street, in Brooklyn. Most of my projects are in Manhattan, so thankfully, I only have to go out there only on paydays."

"What site are you working now?"

"Columbus Avenue, Upper West Side." Tommy flicked a Cheerio off the table. "Every time we lay down the surface, the city finds another problem and we got to rip the whole street up again. Rate we're going, we'll be up there through the millenium."

"Yeah, we did a story on that a few weeks back," Carpo said. He made a writing motion with his pen on the notebook. "Listen, Tommy, I'm working on a special project at Channel 8: a profile of Cheryl Street. I was wondering if I could ask you a few questions about her."

Tommy's face turned serious. "Sure, Carpo, I'll answer as best I can."

"I can't remember if we talked about this Saturday night or not, but did you know Cheryl?"

"Not very well. We used to say hi when we passed in the hallway or down by the mailboxes, but that's it. I didn't even know her first name until I read it in the papers."

"Did she keep to herself?"

"She did with me."

"Tell me about Saturday," Carpo said. "Were you here during the day?"

"Yeah, most of it. I slept late, made some chow, cleaned the apartment. Then I went to Dan Lynch's to catch the Mets game. Didn't get back here until right before all the excitement."

"How long were you here before that woman started screaming?"

"Maybe an hour. Maybe longer."

"Did you hear anything unusual during that time?"

"I didn't hear a peep," Tommy said. His face balled into a quizzical look. "It's a shame I didn't come home earlier. If I'd been here, I might have seen or heard something."

"Did those two detectives show you that book of mug shots?"

"Yeah, how'd you know?"

"They came to my place afterward." Carpo set his pen

down. "I didn't think any of them looked like the guy on the street. What about you?"

"One guy looked familiar, but it's hard to say when you're staring at so many pictures. Everyone starts looking the same after a while."

"Tommy, a lot of people in the building have been telling me about Cheryl's boyfriend. Have you ever seen him around?"

"I passed him a few times in the hallway."

"What's your impression of him?"

Tommy flicked aside another Cheerio. "He seemed like an okay guy. In public, that is. In private, I get the sense he wasn't too cool."

"How so?"

"The dude had a temper. A bad one."

"How do you know?"

Tommy pointed at the ceiling. "The walls in this place are paper thin, man. They must have forgot to put down insulation when they framed it out."

"So you heard arguments?"

Tommy nodded. "They used to fight all the time. I could never hear what they were saying, but sometimes I'd hear them wrestling around, throwing things."

"Wrestling?" Carpo asked, barely able to control his shock. "These fights were physical?"

"I wasn't there to see it, but sometimes it sounded like shit was flying all over the place. Tough to tell what was doing the flying—the furniture or the people."

"Either way, it was violent."

Tommy tilted his head to the side. "Like I said, Carpo, the dude has a temper."

Carpo flipped to a fresh sheet of paper. "One person I talked to claims he saw Cheryl with a lot of men. He made it sound like she was promiscuous. Any truth to that?"

"I'll bet that blimp, Victor, told you that." Tommy shoved his cereal bowl aside in disgust. "The guy thinks any woman who says hello is trying to hop him. Carpo, it ain't true."

"About Victor or Cheryl?"

"Neither one. Victor couldn't get laid if he was paying for it, and I never saw Cheryl with anybody but Steve."

Carpo looked up from his notes. "So you do know him, then?"

"Who, Victor? Yeah, he's always looking out his damn peephole when I'm walking past. I guess he's hoping I'm one of the women who lives above him."

"No, I mean Cheryl's boyfriend. You just said, Steve. That's his name, Steve Plotkin."

"Did I say Steve?" Tommy chuckled. "I didn't even hear myself say it. I must have heard Cheryl use it in the hallway or something, because I've never met the guy in my life."

"Is there anything else you can tell me about Cheryl? Maybe you heard her say other things in the hallway."

"I wish there was more I could tell you," Tommy said. "She seemed like an awfully nice girl, always smiling, and super friendly. I used to be able to hear her getting dressed in the morning. Footsteps going back and forth across the ceiling, back and forth, back and forth. Man, it used to drive me crazy."

Tommy put his thumb on a Cheerio ring and ground it into dust. "Funny thing is, right now I'd do just about anything to hear those footsteps again."

* * *

Violetta Ignacio lived across the hall from Tommy Abilene, in 5E, the apartment with the snippy dog.

She talked to Carpo with the chain fastened on the door. At her feet the little dog yapped insanely at Carpo, its tiny body whirling in agitated circles. Finally, the woman clapped her hands and shouted, "Suki! Enough!"

The dog yelped once, as if it had been slapped, then it slumped to the floor, a prolonged growl rumbling in its throat.

"I'm sorry," Carpo said. "I don't think your dog likes me much."

"It's not you," Violetta said. "Suki always barks at strangers."

"She's a real good watchdog. The other day she made a racket when I walked past your apartment."

Violetta dismissed the ball of white fur with a wave of her hand. "Suki is, how do you say, all bark and no bite. Once she gets used to your smell, she won't make a peep."

"She must have made a commotion Saturday night with that woman screaming and all of the police walking past."

The woman knelt and patted the dog's side. "No, my little girl was quiet that night, very quiet. I think she sensed it." The dog rolled onto its back and spread its stubby legs so the woman could scratch its belly. It began groaning ecstatically as the woman cooed, "Yes, you knew, my little one. Mama knows you did."

"You think she could tell someone had died?"

Violetta looked up at Carpo, her face serious. "I believe she could, yes. Animals are very . . . perceptive of such things. That is the correct word, no?"

Carpo nodded to show that it was.

"Yes, yes," the woman whispered. "Mama's little girl is perceptive."

Beyond the introduction to her clairvoyant pet, Carpo learned little from Violetta Ignacio about Cheryl Street. Just as every other tenant in number 228 had mentioned, Violetta said that she used to pass Cheryl from time to time in the hallway or down by the mailboxes. She also said she used to run into Steve Plotkin infrequently, and mentioned Suki's contempt for the boyfriend, a supreme distaste that stemmed back to an incident last January when the dog had bitten him on the ankle.

So much for all bark and no bite, Carpo thought.

Carrie Bellows lived one floor below, in apartment 4E. She was an elderly black woman with thinning hair and milky gray eyes. She wore a faded calico dress with sweat stains under her arms. Bellows told Carpo that she had moved into the building three months ago, after losing the lease on an old apartment. In that short time she had never met or run into Cheryl Street or Steve Plotkin. She told Carpo that the murder had upset her so badly, she was already seeking a new residence. Adding to Carrie Bellows's displeasure with the building, Carpo learned, was the incessant scraping of Suki's claws on the ceiling above.

Carpo's final interview was with Ludwig Monroe, in apartment 2E. Ludwig was a West Indian man in his late fifties, with square gold-rimmed glasses and teeth that were stacked as even as piano keys.

Ludwig told Carpo that he was the oldest tenant in the

building, going on sixteen years that September. And he said, over those years, he had never come across two people so compatible and so obviously in love as Cheryl Street and Steve Plotkin had been.

Before leaving the building, Carpo reviewed the names on the intercom one last time. So far, he had talked with seven of the ten residents in the building. The only people he had missed were in apartments 4W and 3W—D. Lee and R. Doyle. During his three visits to the building, neither tenant had answered the door or responded to the intercom. Carpo figured they were either on vacation or hiding from him.

Among those he had interviewed, Carpo noted the wide range of opinion on Cheryl Street. Some (Irene Foster, Tommy Abilene, and Ludwig Monroe) had described her as friendly, smart, and optimistic. Others (Victor Mendez) had insinuated that she was a stuck-up flirt. The range of opinion on Steve Plotkin was even greater. Irene and Ludwig had described him as being very much in love with Cheryl. But Tommy had remarked on their frequent violent arguments, and Victor had even insinuated that he might be responsible for the murder.

Carpo was fairly sure that none of the people he had interviewed was lying. He knew from his work at Channel 8 that people often interpreted the same event differently. Still, the central question remained: With six days until he was due to begin editing his piece, whom should he interview?

Take your pick, he thought.

Irene Foster, definitely. Of all the people in the building, she was the closest to Cheryl, perhaps the only one who had gotten beyond a simple hello while passing in the hallway. He was also leaning toward Ludwig Monroe and Tommy Abilene, and perhaps Violetta Ignacio. Carpo was skeptical of Victor Mendez's motivations, and that was enough to scratch his name off the list. He also crossed off George Bento's name, since the super had demanded money for an interview.

Other than that, he thought, *take your pick.*

When Carpo stopped by his building, he discovered another strange postcard in his mailbox. Like the other card, this one had no address or postmark written on it. The front of the card showed the exterior of Java The Hut, the coffee store on Second Avenue that Carpo frequented every Saturday afternoon. Carpo remembered that the store had a stack of the cards on the counter that people could take for free.

At a glance, the handwriting appeared to be from the same person who had written the first card. It also carried, Carpo believed, more than a subtle hint of threat.

> THE VIEW FROM A WINDOW
> IS THE SIGHT UNTO ANOTHER LIFE.
> BUT THE SIGHT FROM YOUR WINDOW,
> IS THE VIEW OF ANOTHER DEATH.

Carpo stood by the mailboxes, postcard in hand, and stared at 12th Street, trying to make sense of the letter and the many questions it raised. *Who sent it? How are they getting it in my mailbox? And am I in danger?* He shoved the card in his knapsack and ran out to the street. The sidewalks were empty save for a few women pushing strollers and a man smoking a cigar. Standing near the steps of his building was Mrs. Garbanzo, the old woman who lived in the apartment beneath him.

"Hi, Mrs. Garbanzo," Carpo said. "How are you?"

"Hi, Michael," the woman said, her prunish face breaking into a smile. "Thanks for taking my garbage down the other day. I certainly appreciate it."

Often, Mrs. Garbanzo left her garbage bag in the hallway, next to her door. Whenever Carpo saw it on his way out, he made a habit of carrying it to the garbage pails.

"No problem, Mrs. Garbanzo," Carpo said, "I don't mind at all. Listen, though, I was wondering if you've been standing here long?"

Mrs. Garbanzo checked the watch on her wrist. "For about twenty minutes. My girlfriends are supposed to meet me for a lunch date. They're late as usual."

"Have you seen any strange people go into the building?" Carpo asked. "I mean, anyone you don't recognize as living here."

Mrs. Garbanzo thought for a moment. "There were a few people I didn't recognize," she said, "but that doesn't mean they don't belong here. I can't remember all the faces from our building like I used to."

"What about the postman? Did you see him?"

"He just headed up the street. Is something wrong, Michael?"

"No, there's nothing wrong. I'm just trying to find out where one of my letters came from." Carpo smiled to reassure the woman that everything was okay. "I'll talk to you later, Mrs. Garbanzo."

Carpo jogged up 12th Street until he came across the mailman's saddlebag cart. It was parked outside building number 212, a large apartment complex near Third Avenue. Carpo walked inside the lobby, where he found the mailman stuffing letters into a row of bronze boxes.

"Hi, there," Carpo said. "Can I ask you a question?"

The mailman looked at Carpo with a puzzled expression, then he tapped his forehead. "Sure, I remember you," he said, "you're the fella from the building up the street. Matt or something, right?"

"It's Michael," Carpo said. "Michael Carpo."

The mailman stepped forward and shook his hand. "That's right, Michael Carpo. Sometimes I have trouble placing people when I don't see them in their buildings. Must have something to do with not observing them in their natural setting. Anyway, what was it you wanted to ask?"

"I have a question about one of the letters I found in my mailbox today." Carpo pulled the postcard out of his knapsack. "Do you remember delivering this?"

"Let's see." The mailman took the card and checked both sides. "No there's no way I delivered it. The card doesn't have an address or a postmark."

"That's what I thought," Carpo said. "Someone must have hand-delivered it, right?"

"More than likely. If there's no address, they wouldn't even sort it at the post office."

"Thanks," Carpo said as he stuck the card back in his knapsack, "I just wanted to check with you to be sure."

He turned to leave the building, when the mailman said, "Maybe it's just a coincidence, but I think that girl who got murdered was getting postcards like that one."

Carpo stopped dead in his tracks. "Which girl? Cheryl Street?"

"Yeah, her. She left a note in her mailbox last week asking if I was delivering postcards that didn't have her address on it." The mailman shrugged. "I completely forgot about it until you showed me that one."

"Did you see her postcards?"

"I never got the chance to. She left the note on, I think, Wednesday or Thursday, and she was killed Saturday." The mailman shrugged, hands turned up. "The postcards must be from someone in the neighborhood. I can't imagine any other way you'd both be receiving them."

Twelve

"It doesn't surprise me, not one bit," Candi said later that night. "I've seen men and the way they act. I've seen it firsthand. Nothing they do surprises me."

It was the end of Candi's shift at Little Poland, and she had joined Carpo in his booth. She looked pale and tired, with dark circles under her eyes. A cup of herb tea sat before her, next to an ashtray cradling a cigarette. Smoke and steam meshed into one as they lifted past her face.

"You think it's normal for a man to kill a woman and then lance out her eyes with an ice pick?" Carpo asked. "I'm sorry, Candi, but I don't know many men who feel the urge to do that."

Candi picked up the cigarette and inhaled. She held the smoke inside for a moment, then blew it above her head, the smoke expanding in a cartoonish thought cloud. "You seem to forget my other career, Carpo," she said in a gravelly voice, "when I had to wait on men in an alley or the backseat of their car. I've had them ask me to play their mother or their sister. I've even had some ask me to be their daughter. Listen to me when I say I'm *not* surprised by what the Sandman does."

Carpo fidgeted with the handle of his coffee cup. "I believe you. I just don't agree that *all* men are animals."

"Show me one."

"One what?"

"One who isn't."

"Why, that's ridiculous," Carpo said indignantly. "What about me? I don't get into stuff like that."

Candi studied his face closely, as if really seeing him for the first time. "You seem nice enough," she said finally, "but I don't know what you're really like. I mean, what it is you crave deep down inside."

"Candi, that isn't fair. You're lumping all men into one bracket. I'm a man so I must be an animal? I'm surprised at you."

"Calm down, Carpo, it's got nothing to do with you. I know you're not an animal." She stamped out her cigarette in the ashtray. "Shit, I'll never forget all the things you've done for me. I totally owe you. But it doesn't change the way I feel. Plain and simple, I don't trust men."

Carpo sipped his coffee, silently brooding. Even though it went against his principles, he knew Candi had a point. She most certainly had seen and experienced things he could never imagine. Terrible things.

"Let's change the subject," Candi said. "You're starting to get all moody on me, and I hate when you do that. What's happening on the dating front? Any new prospects?"

"Any prospects!" Carpo exclaimed. "Didn't you just get through telling me that all men are animals and that you could never really trust one, not even me?"

Candi grinned maliciously. "Did I say that?"

In spite of himself, Carpo smiled too. He grabbed the

pack of cigarettes and shook one out. "No news on the dating front," he said after the cigarette was lit. "I'm still single. I still haven't met any women. And there still aren't any prospects on the horizon."

"Problem with you, Carp, is you work too hard. Every time I see you, you're either coming from or going to the TV station. Even when you're here, you've always got your notebook out, scribbling notes for some special project. I should call you damn robo-Carpo."

"I just don't have the time or patience for it. Last night I went to a bar and practically made an ass of myself trying to speak to a woman."

"Didn't I tell you a bar isn't the place to meet women?"

"Where else can I meet them?"

Candi ladled two spoons of sugar into her tea and stirred it. "You've got to go places where you'll find people with the same interests."

"The only place I can think of is Channel 8," Carpo said, "and everyone there is either dating or married."

"I'm not talking about people at work. Don't you have any hobbies outside of Channel 8?"

"I like to read."

Candi rolled her eyes. "Real interactive, Carp. And knowing you, you probably read books about Dan Rather and Peter Jennings. I'm talking about a real hobby. Like lifting weights or gardening."

"Who ever heard of gardening in the city?"

"I'm just throwing out suggestions. Like a foreign language, for instance. You could take one of those beginner classes at the New School. I'll bet there's dozens of eligible women there, waiting to meet a guy just like you. You could study French or Italian, learn if they really are Romance languages."

Carpo grimaced at Candi's wordplay. "I'd love to study a foreign language, but there's not enough time for it."

"That's another problem, you need to make time. A woman wants a man who's strong, someone who won't take no for an answer. You've got to pursue her."

"Candi, I'm not about to pester a woman for a date."

"I'm not saying you have to stalk them. Smile and try to be yourself." Candi reached over and ruffled Carpo's hair. "You've got a lot going for you, Carp', it's time you started acting like it."

Just then the front door to Little Poland opened. Candi looked at the person who had entered, squinting her eyes to make them out. She leaned closer to Carpo and whispered, "Take this one, for instance. Here's a pretty young lady who looks like she's got half a brain in her head. Check her out."

Carpo continued facing forward. "I'm not looking."

"Why not?"

"Because it's silly."

"She's all alone, Carp. Ask her to sit here."

"No way."

"How come?"

"Because, I said, it's silly." Carpo gripped the edge of the table as if he feared Candi would drag him over to the woman. "It's too . . . desperate."

Candi lowered her eyes. "Here she comes," she whispered without moving her lips. "Ask her."

"No."

"What's the worst thing she can say?"

"How about Get lost, you animal."

Carpo heard the woman approaching, her shoes clicking on the linoleum floor. He felt an incredible urge to peek at her, to see what it was about her that had so intrigued Candi. But the idea of inviting a stranger to sit with him seemed ridiculous. He wouldn't even know how to ask her.

Candi didn't have the same problem.

"Excuse me, miss?" Candi said in an innocent, little-girl delivery, "my name is Cassandra Wilson. I work here at Little Poland and I'd like to introduce you to a dear friend of mine, a really sweet man. His name is Michael Carpo."

Carpo kept his head immobile; his neck was so rigid, he felt a kink develop. Even if he had been facing the woman, he wouldn't have seen her. His eyes were squeezed shut.

"Oh my God!" the woman exclaimed. "Michael, is that you? I was just thinking of you."

Carpo's first glimpse was of Candi's enormous smile. He turned to the woman: It was Irene Foster, Cheryl Street's next-door neighbor. "Irene, what a surprise. How are you?"

"I'm doing okay." Irene shook his hand and then Candi's. "Would it be okay if I joined you guys? I'm all alone tonight."

"Yes, yes, of course," Candi said. "Carpo ... I mean, Michael ... doesn't mind at all. In fact, I was just about to bring him more coffee." Candi scooted out of the booth and guided Irene into her spot. "Take my seat, honey, I'll bring a menu straight over." Candi made a beeline for the kitchen and disappeared through the swinging doors.

"She's awfully nice," Irene said.

Carpo managed a weak smile. "Yes, very."

"Do you know her from here?"

"No, I knew her before. She used to work in the neighborhood." Carpo chuckled uneasily, not wanting to delve too deep into Candi's past. "I don't think I've ever seen you here before."

"I've been in a couple of times, usually just to get take-out." Irene glanced around the diner. "Maybe I should start coming more. It's got a nice feel to it, the way everybody knows each other, sort of like a family."

Candi returned to the table. She topped Carpo's mug with the coffee and handed a menu to Irene.

"Would you like to join us?" Irene asked.

Before Candi could accept, Carpo said, "Don't you need to start closing out the register? You know how Devon gets when you're late."

"Yes, you're right, Michael, I almost forgot." Candi kicked him under the table as she smiled broadly at Irene. "He's so sweet, really he is. Just wait until you get to know him better. I know he looks all stiff and grumpy, but inside he's got a heart the size of Manhattan."

"Candi," Carpo said under his breath.

"I'm going, I'm going." Candi backed away from the table. "You kids take your time, there's no rush. I'll come back and take your order whenever you're ready."

Irene opened her menu. After a minute she peeked over the top. "What do you recommend?"

"I had the piroshki tonight, which are a specialty here, but everything on the menu is excellent."

"I think I'm in the mood for soup. Borscht, that sounds good." Irene closed the menu and set it aside. "How's it going with your special project? Find any good interviews?"

"So far you're the only one who interests me." Carpo blushed when he realized how his statement could be interpreted. "What I mean is, you're the only one who's been helpful."

Irene didn't seem to notice the gaffe. "What about Steve Plotkin? Any luck finding him?"

"I found him, but he's reluctant to talk. Actually, it's worse than that. He wants nothing to do with me."

"He's probably still upset about Cheryl."

"Maybe you're right." Carpo took a sip of coffee. "I should tell you they're holding a funeral service for Cheryl tomorrow."

"Who is?"

"Her parents."

Irene's body tensed noticeably. "The police found Cheryl's parents?"

"Didn't you watch the news last night? It was all over the place."

"I haven't turned on the TV since Sunday. What happened?"

"The parents contacted the police yesterday. It took a couple of days for the news about Cheryl to reach them."

Irene rubbed her hands back and forth as if they were cold. "I'm happy to hear that," she said. "I can't tell you how it's been bothering me, thinking about Cheryl at the morgue these past four days. Where's the funeral going to be?"

"St. John's Cemetery, in Queens. The police haven't released the information because they're afraid of creating a big media crush at the service."

"Who'll be there?"

"I think just family and close friends. Why don't you go? I'm sure no one will mind."

"I don't know if it's appropriate," Irene said. "I've never met Cheryl's parents before."

"It doesn't matter, Irene, you were her friend." Carpo waited a moment, then added, "You know, it might be good for you to go, help put some closure to this. Worse comes to worst, if things don't feel right, you can leave."

Irene didn't answer. She stared across the diner, lost in her thoughts.

Carpo took a sip of coffee. "Irene, did Cheryl ever say anything to you about receiving strange letters or post-cards?"

"Not that I remember."

"Nothing about letters that were hand-delivered, or had no return address?"

"Not at all," Irene said. "Why do you ask?"

"It's just something I was wondering. Nothing important."

Candi returned to the table. "Ready to order, honey?" she asked Irene.

"I'll have the borscht and a diet Coke," Irene said.

"Is that all?" Candi said. "Let me bring you a side order of something. A piroshki or some dumplings."

"I'm not too hungry," Irene said. She looked at Carpo. "Unless you would help me with a piroshki?"

Carpo started to say no, but Candi cut him off. "Of course he'll help you. I'll bring the soup first. You two keep chatting."

Once Candi was out of earshot, Irene said, "Gosh, she's so nice. I can tell she likes you a lot."

"What she really likes is to tease me."

Irene took a sip from a glass of ice water on the table.

"Thanks for telling me about the funeral. I never would have found out in time."

"No problem."

"I guess it's an advantage having a friend in the media. You must learn a lot of things before anyone else."

Carpo chuckled quietly. "Not as much as we'd like people to believe."

"What do you mean?"

"Most of the time, we just rehash the facts. It's sort of like tossing salad. Give it a few spins and it sounds like a fresh lead."

"If the cops are trying to keep the media away from the funeral, how did you find out about it?"

"The day after the murder, two detectives showed up at my door. They asked me some questions about the guy I saw on the street."

"Was it those two detectives? Weissman and Spinks?"

"Yeah," Carpo said. "Did they stop by your place too?"

"Sunday afternoon." Irene wrinkled her nose at the thought. "They made me look through this humongous book of photographs with some of the most frightening men I've ever seen."

"I looked through the same album. I didn't think any of those men looked familiar."

"No, me neither." Irene rubbed her eyes. "I still don't remember much at all about that night."

"Did Weissman show you the other photographs? The ones in the envelope?"

"You mean the other victims?" Irene asked. When Carpo nodded, she said, "Yes, they did."

"Since we're on the subject of photographs," Carpo said,

"would you have any photos of Cheryl I could borrow? It might be helpful if I have something to flash at people when I ask them questions."

"What about the one the detectives had?"

Carpo shook his head. "I don't want to use that one. It's been plastered all over the media."

"Is that a bad thing?"

"It can influence a person's answers. They look at the photo and remember it was in the paper, then they remember all the stories they read about the case. Before you know it, you're hearing all the rumors stated as if they were fact."

"I'll lend you a photo if you want."

"Great." Carpo started to go for his coffee, then stopped. "Did Cheryl look like that photograph anyway? It seemed a little too perfect, as if someone had retouched it."

"You're right, it didn't look like her. Cheryl was a pretty girl, but she never wore that much makeup. She also wore her hair differently."

"How so?"

"She had long, straight hair which she wore down to here." Irene held her hands at shoulder length. "The photo you saw was a TWA head shot, so she had it up in a bun. That's the way she had to wear it when flying."

"What about her eyes?" Carpo asked, remembering what Detective Weissman had told him about the brown-eye theory. "The detectives mentioned that she had brown eyes. Were they very noticeable?"

"Yes, they were beautiful, the kind of eyes that are difficult to look away from." Irene's brow knitted into a frown. "But that's a real strange thing for the detectives to say."

Carpo picked up his coffee cup again. "It came up while they were showing me the head shot."

"No, it's not strange that they mentioned it," Irene said, "it's strange about the color."

Carpo kept the cup in front of his mouth. He could smell the aroma of the coffee, but still he didn't drink. "What do you mean?" he asked. "What's so strange about the color?"

"Cheryl didn't have brown eyes," Irene said. "Her eyes were blue."

Thirteen

Carpo set the coffee cup down without drinking from it. "Say that again."

"Cheryl's eyes were blue."

"Are you sure?"

Irene nodded solemnly. "One hundred percent positive, I can picture them right now." She held his stare, her own brown eyes wide and unblinking. "Why does it matter?"

Carpo looked into his mug. According to Detective Weissman's theory on the Sandman, Cheryl's eyes had to be brown. It was the only common link between the victims.

"I asked why it matters."

"It's just strange." Carpo mumbled, his mind racing for an explanation, "Very strange."

"Michael, tell me what's going on."

Although the detectives had insisted that he not tell anybody about their brown-eye theory, Carpo felt the circumstances warranted an exemption. He decided he trusted Irene enough to tell her.

He leaned closer to her and said, "I found out a huge angle in the Sandman case last night, bigger than finding her parents and even the funeral."

"What is it?"

It hasn't been made public yet, so you've got to swear you won't tell anyone."

"Of course, I won't," Irene said. "I swear to God."

Carpo lowered his voice in case anybody could hear them. "The police think they've figured out the major link between the six murders. They say each of the victims had brown eyes."

Irene hugged her arms to her body. "God, that's so creepy," she said, shivering noticeably. "The Sandman steals the eyes from only brown-eyed women?"

"No, he steals all their eyes. He preys only on women with brown eyes."

Now it was Irene's turn to be silent. She stared across the diner, off into the distance, arms still wrapped around her body.

"Irene," Carpo whispered, "how can we find out what color her eyes were? If they weren't brown, there must be a record of that somewhere. Like a driver's license."

Irene shook her head. "Cheryl didn't drive."

"How did she get around?"

"She lived in New York. Public transportation."

"What did she do when she got carded at bars?"

"She used her work ID from TWA."

"Would that have her eye color on it?"

"I don't know."

"What about an eye doctor? Wouldn't they have a record of it?"

"Maybe, but I don't think Cheryl went to an eye doctor. She once told me she had perfect vision. Twenty-twenty or something."

Carpo fiddled with the salt and pepper shakers, clinking

their metal tops together. "There must be some way we can find out."

"I can't think of one."

"If we got inside her apartment, there must be something that would show it. A photograph, passport, or some other official document."

"Yeah, but how do we get in there?"

"You wouldn't happen to have a spare set of keys hanging around, would you?"

"No," Irene said her eyes snapping back into focus, "but even if I did, it wouldn't work. The police sealed up her door with crime-scene tape. They'd know in a second if someone had gone inside."

"Not to mention the burglar alarm," Carpo said. "If it's armed, we'd end up setting it off."

"Cheryl didn't have a burglar alarm."

"But there's a sticker on her door that says she had one."

"That thing? It's a fake. They sell them at Peddler's Hardware. It's supposed to deter criminals. A lot of good it did Cheryl."

Carpo waited a few seconds, then said, "Come on, Irene, think. There's got to be some way we can find out her eye color."

"I can't think of anything, Michael, besides breaking down the door." She stared at Carpo, her lower lip trembling. "What do you think this means anyway?"

"I don't know. It could mean the cops are wrong about their theory. Maybe the Sandman doesn't prey just on women with brown eyes." Carpo shrugged. "It could mean some other things too."

"Like what? You think the Sandman didn't do it?"

"I'm not saying he did it or didn't. I just think it's something worth looking into."

Irene shook her head back and forth very quickly. The movement caused her hair to fan across her shoulders, creating a faint rustling noise. "No, no, no," she said, her voice cracking, "it was him. Believe me, I was the one who found her. I saw what he . . . did to her. It has to be the Sandman, it just has to be. Only an animal could have done something like that."

After they had finished eating, Carpo escorted Irene back to 12th Street. Thick clouds coated the night sky, as black and heavy as wood smoke. The street itself was quiet, the silence interrupted by the echo of their footsteps and an occasional passing car. Carpo was thankful for Irene's company. It was so dark and quiet along the block, he might have felt spooked walking home by himself.

When they reached number 228, they stopped at the front steps. "Will you go to the funeral tomorrow?" Carpo asked.

"Yes, I think so."

"Do you need a ride?"

"How are you going?"

"I'll be in the Channel 8 News truck. It's just me and a cameraman, so there's plenty of room."

"No, that's okay, I can just as easily take the subway. I'm sure there's a stop nearby."

"I don't know about that," Carpo said. "It's all the way out in Middle Village, way past LaGuardia. Even if there is a stop, it would be an awfully long trip."

"I'll find my way," Irene said. "It's nice of you to offer,

but I'd feel like I was getting in the way. You have work to do."

She climbed the steps and stopped at the door. "Thanks for this evening, Michael. It was nice running into you, even if you did shock the hell out of me." She rustled through her purse for keys and unlocked the door.

Is this as far as it goes, Carpo wondered. *Bye, see you later?*

She had unlocked the door and taken a step inside the foyer before Carpo reacted. "Hang on a sec." His throat felt dry, voice hoarse. "I was wondering if maybe you'd like to get together sometime. Dinner or drinks. I don't know what your schedule is like, mine's pretty hectic, but maybe we could find a night when we're both free."

The yellow light over the door cast a warm glow to her face. Her hair fluttered in the light breeze and she smiled at him. "You're so polite."

"Pardon me?"

"I said, you're so polite. The way you speak, it's so, I don't know, considerate."

Carpo could feel the color rise in his cheeks. "I'm sorry," he said again, "I guess I'm too—"

"I'd love to."

"Pardon me?"

"I said, I'd love to. Have dinner, that is."

"Great."

She stepped into the foyer and waved good-bye. Before the door could shut, he called out, "So when are you free?"

She stuck her head around the side of the door. "Anytime. Whatever's good for you."

"Not tomorrow. I might have to stay late at the station.

How about Friday or Saturday night? Which one's better for you?"

"Let's shoot for Friday." The door started to close.

"What time?" Carpo said.

Irene poked her head back into the light. Carpo was relieved to see that she was still smiling. "How about eight?"

"Sounds great."

"I'm looking forward to it." Irene gave a little wave and said, "Sweet dreams, Michael."

Carpo waved back, but the door had shut and she was gone. He stood there for a moment, as if she might reappear. When she didn't, he crossed to the other side of 12th Street. It wasn't until he had reached the foyer of his building that he realized he was smiling.

Her words had been so simple—*I'm looking forward to it*—but they carried an inherent promise, one that made him want to burst out laughing. For the first time in a long time, Carpo realized that he, too, had something to look forward to.

"Sweet dreams," he whispered. "Very sweet dreams."

Fourteen

The alarm clock jarred Carpo from sleep at nine the next morning. With his eyes still closed, he slapped the snooze button, then he flipped onto his stomach and faded back to sleep. Raindrops rapped on the windowpanes like tiny hammers. Farther off, the sky rumbled ominously.

After a few more swipes on the snooze bar, Carpo mustered the energy to get up and put on a pot of coffee. It was so dark in the kitchen, he had to turn on the lights to see what he was doing. He shaved and showered while the coffee brewed, then he wrapped a towel around his waist, poured himself a mug, and carried it into the bedroom. He sat on the edge of the bed—chin cupped in hand, hand rested on knee—and stared blankly out the window.

Like a dull hangover, the rain fell steadily on 12th Street with no sign of abating. It darkened the bark on the trees and pooled in tiny beads on the hoods of parked cars. It turned the sidewalks gray and the asphalt glistening black. Across the street it created a shimmering waterfall down the windows of Cheryl Street's apartment.

The sight of the windows captured Carpo's attention. He had lived in his apartment going on five years; during that time he had stared across the street countless times.

Strangely, he couldn't recall a single time when he had taken note of the apartment directly across from him. Cheryl Street had lived thirty feet away, and yet she might as well have existed in a parallel universe.

He pulled Detective Weissman's business card from his wallet and called him from the living room. For once, Weissman was at his desk—not at all an illogical place to be, Carpo thought, considering the weather.

Carpo identified himself and asked, "Are we still on for this afternoon?"

"Of course we are, Michael," the detective said. "What would make you think otherwise?"

"Have you looked out a window recently?"

"Not a pretty sight, is it?"

"Doesn't it affect our plans?"

Weissman chuckled a little too long. "We're going to a funeral, Michael, not a baseball game."

"I'm just checking," Carpo said defensively. "Besides, it's not even the reason I called."

"What's up?"

"Last night I ran into the woman who lived next door to Cheryl Street. Her name's Irene Foster. She's the one who found the body."

"Foster, Foster, Foster," Weissman mumbled. "Okay, I remember her. Irene Foster, the nice-looking brunette, right?"

"Yes, that's her," Carpo said coolly.

"What about her?"

"We were talking about Cheryl and she told me something amazing. She said Cheryl didn't have brown eyes. Her eyes were blue."

"You told her about our theory?" Weissman asked, his tone rising with accusation. "I made a point of telling you not to, Michael. That information isn't public for a reason."

"I know, I wasn't intending to tell her, but we were talking about Cheryl and she mentioned that Cheryl had blue eyes. Don't worry, she won't tell anybody. I made her promise to keep it secret."

"Let's hope she does a better job than you," Weissman grumbled. "That little tidbit is the only way we can be sure the Sandman committed a crime."

"That's just my point, Detective Weissman, the color of Cheryl's eyes doesn't match your theory."

Weissman was silent for several seconds. "Hang on a sec while I pull the file."

When Weissman returned, he didn't speak. Carpo could hear him rooting through papers, muttering an occasional unintelligible word. Other noises filled the background: telephone rings, muted voices, and the clatter of an electric typewriter. The sounds reminded Carpo of the way a newsroom sounds: a sustained bustle of energy and urgency that seemed to illustrate the importance of the work being done there.

Finally, Weissman cleared his throat. "Okay, I've got the coroner's report in front of me. It lists Cheryl Street as having brown eyes."

"How would the coroner know?"

"It's standard on the form."

"It must be wrong," Carpo said. "Irene was adamant about this. She said Cheryl had blue eyes."

Without breaking stride, Weissman said, "Also in the file are two color photographs of the victim. One is a picture we took from her apartment, the other is her employee ID from TWA. In both her eyes look brown."

"I'm telling you, Irene wouldn't make this up. She knew Cheryl better than anyone in the city. Don't you think it's worth checking out?"

"It is an interesting point," Weissman conceded. "I'll look into it once we're off the phone."

"What are you going to do?"

"I'll put a call into the coroner's office. I'll have an M.E. reinspect the body."

"How many days will this delay the funeral?"

"What are you talking about?"

Carpo frowned. "Won't this take a while to sort out?"

"It'll take a half hour, max. All the M.E. has to do is check the eyes, then we'll toss the body in a casket and get it over to St. John's. The service will go off at four, you'll shoot your video and get it on the air tonight, just like we've been planning all week."

Carpo's frown deepened; something about Weissman's tone disturbed him. It felt as if the detective were reading from an itinerary, a detailed, step-by-step flowchart.

"Mike, you still with me?" Weissman asked.

"Yeah, I'm here."

"No, I mean, are we still on the same page about this afternoon? You're beginning to sound like you're wavering."

Carpo swallowed the last of his coffee. "I'm still with you."

"That's good, because we really need your cooperation," Weissman said. "Now, are you square on what'll happen this afternoon?"

"Yes."

"No interviews with the parents. No videotaping the chapel service and—"

"I know."

"—and all you can show is stuff that happens at the grave site."

"Detective Weissman, I said *I know.*"

"Wait, Mike, hear me out. The parents want to hold a little ceremony at the grave. They're going to leave some objects at the marker: a teddy bear and some other stuff. The bear was Cheryl's favorite stuffed animal when she was a kid. The parents say they don't mind if you use that video in your report."

"I'm sure the cameraman will roll on it."

"Make sure of it, Mike, it's about the only visuals you're going to have out there."

"Leave that to me," Carpo said. "I know how to do my job."

"Okay, okay," Weissman said. "I'm sure it'll work out fine. Stay dry and I'll see you at two."

Suddenly, Carpo remembered the strange postcards he had received over the past two days. "Hang on, Detective Weissman, I forgot to tell you something. I've been receiving some weird letters in the mail."

"What kind of letters?"

"Postcards. Two of them. I found the first one Tuesday and the second yesterday."

Carpo asked the detective to wait while he retrieved the postcards from his knapsack. When he got back on the phone, he read the cards to Weissman.

"I guess the view of a 'senseless fool' refers to what you saw out your window," Weissman said. "I'll bet they're from people who watched that interview you did on Channel 8 the night after the murder."

"I'm pretty sure they're from the same person. The handwriting is similar and neither card has a return address, a stamp, or a postmark."

"I wouldn't sweat it," Weissman said. "They probably came from someone in your building. You must have pissed them off by drawing attention to the street or the neighborhood."

"That's what I was thinking, until I heard something," Carpo said. "I ran into my mailman and asked him about them. He told me that last week Cheryl Street left a note for him complaining about getting hand-delivered postcards."

"Your mailman said this?"

"Yes, he said she left a note for him. He said he totally forgot about it until I mentioned my postcards."

"Why don't you bring them to the cemetery this afternoon and I'll take a look at them." Weissman moaned softly as if he were stretching. "And do me a favor," he said almost as an afterthought, "don't be telling anyone else about this brown-eye theory, okay? It could do a lot more than generate a few pieces of hate mail. It could jeopardize our entire investigation."

The Channel 8 News truck left for Queens beneath a pregnant charcoal sky. Carpo sat in the passenger seat as the cameraman, Roman Santiago, piloted the box-shaped van through bumper-to-bumper traffic on the L.I.E. The sweep of the windshield wipers transfixed Carpo as he stared out the window and anticipated the royal drenching he was about to receive. He had dressed that morning with a funeral in mind, not a monsoon. He was wearing a dark blue suit, a blue shirt, and a burgundy tie. His only concession to the weather were his waterproof hiking boots.

Roman had dressed more appropriately for the elements. He was wearing a large yellow rain slicker with elastic trim at his neck, wrists, waist, and ankles. Farther down, Roman's feet were encased in a pair of surplus firefighter boots; they looked as if they could withstand a tidal wave.

The traffic thinned once they passed the exit for LaGuardia Airport. As if foreshadowing their upcoming assignment, the expressway took them past several large cemeteries. In many, the graves were packed so tightly that it was hard to see any grass between the bone-white headstones. When they reached Elmhurst, they turned onto Woodhaven Boulevard, a route lined with dreary industrial complexes. A mile or so down the road they pulled into the parking lot of St. John's Cemetery.

There were six cars in the lot, all in a row; Roman steered to the end of the line and parked. He turned the key in the ignition so the van's radio and wipers would run off the battery, then he crawled over the seat and began preparing his gear. After a few minutes there was a knock on Carpo's window. He rolled it down to find Detective Spinks standing in the rain.

The detective was costumed in a knee-length police-issue slicker; the coat had an extra-long visor on the hood that completely shielded his face from the driving rain. "You're late," Spinks said as a way of a greeting. "I was just about to call your station and have them beep you."

"Sorry about that, we got held up in traffic." Carpo looked around the parking lot. "Is Detective Weissman here?"

"He got held up at the station house. I don't know if he's going to make it."

Carpo's hand tightened on the armrest. "What happened?"

"There was a minor development in the Street case. It couldn't be put off." Spinks broke into a grin. "Don't look so glum, Mikey, I ain't going to bite you."

"I didn't say you would," Carpo said.

The detective pulled a pack of gum from his pocket. He offered a piece to Carpo, which Carpo declined, then he slid it into his mouth. "Anyway, I'm glad you weren't any later," Spinks said. "The service is about to get under way."

"Where are the parents?"

Spinks pointed at the row of cars. "See the red car? The Mercury Sable? That's them."

Carpo could make out the outline of two heads through the car's rain-strewn rear window. "When did they get in?"

"Late last night. The drive from Roanoke took them seven hours." Spinks chuckled quietly. "They weren't so happy when I told them you guys were going to be here."

"We'll keep a low profile," Carpo said.

Spinks cracked his gum, filling the van with the smell of spearmint. "Now, you're square on the ground rules, right?"

"Yes, Detective Weissman already went over it."

Spinks continued speaking as if he hadn't heard Carpo. "When the service is over, the group will escort the casket to the grave site. After the casket is in the ground, Cheryl's mother will come forward and place a teddy bear on the tombstone. There's where you guys come in. It's the only stuff you're allowed to shoot."

"Detective Weissman already went over it," Carpo said again.

Spinks blinked a few times, his mind registering the statement. "What about your fellah?" Spinks nodded in the direction of Roman. "Is he square on it?"

"Everything is set," Carpo said. "We'll take over from here."

Spinks stopped snapping his gum. "Listen here, Mikey, don't be getting hot under the collar. I'm just making sure we're all on the same page."

"And we are."

"Okay, then," Spinks said, head moving in a tight nod, "I'll see you after the ceremony."

Spinks started back across the lot, his visor tilted against the rain. Carpo rolled the window up as Roman spat, "Who's that jerk?"

"His name's Detective Spinks. He's one of the lead detectives on the Sandman investigation. I guess he's also in charge here."

"Yeah? Well, he's about to get popped in the nose." Roman made a face as he mimicked, *Is your fellah square on it? Is your fellah square? What do I look like, a fucking trained seal?"

Carpo patted the cameraman on the back. "Don't let him get under your skin, Roman, he treats everybody that way. The cops are just paranoid about the way we shoot this story."

"If they're so worried, they should have hired their own crew," Roman grumbled. "The way this thing is being scripted, you'd think we were taping a Broadway production."

* * *

Roman kept the radio on while they waited for the chapel service to finish. The radio was tuned to an all-news station, WCBS-AM. Every ten minutes the weather forecaster came on and relayed the same information: *Rain, heavy at times, will continue throughout the afternoon and evening. Chance of late-afternoon thunderstorms. Clearing overnight.* The windshield wipers lent credence to the prediction, flicking aside the rain in a surflike spray.

After nearly an hour, the doors to the chapel opened and people began filing out. Carpo nudged Roman to wake him up. "Let's rock and roll, buddy."

Roman jumped out of the van and ran to the back. He strapped a large battery pack to his waist and slipped two half-hour Beta tapes inside his slicker. He hoisted the camera onto his shoulder and did a quick run-through to make sure everything was working properly. The camera was fitted with a clear plastic hood, leaving just the tip of the lens exposed to the elements. Carpo held up a sheet of white paper so Roman could white-balance the camera. When Roman was finished, he said, "Okey-dokey, your *fellah* is square."

Cheryl's parents filed out of the chapel, followed by Detective Spinks and a handful of people. Carpo spotted Irene among them, the upper half of her face covered by a black umbrella. The group waited by the door until the casket came out, carried by six men, three on each side. They walked down a narrow macadam path leading into the graveyard. Clouds of mist swirled along the path, concealing the casket and distorting the patter of the raindrops. Carpo and Roman followed a safe distance behind them.

The procession threaded in and out of the tombstones until it reached a freshly dug plot covered with a sheet of plastic. A man walked to the rectangular hole and threw aside the plastic. The men brought the casket to the hole and placed it on a stationary lift, then they lowered the casket into the hole.

"You getting all of this?" Carpo whispered to Roman.

The cameraman nodded, his eye pressed against the camera's rubber eye cup. "I'm rolling."

When the casket was in the ground, the priest stepped forward, shadowed by an altar boy clutching an umbrella over their heads. The priest read a short passage from the Bible, then he pulled a vial of holy water from his vestments. He whispered a few words as he sprinkled the water into the hole. When he finished, he turned and nodded at Cheryl's parents.

The father, Myron Street, came forward first. He was a tall, gray-haired man with a stiff, upright posture. He wore a black suit and a pair of L. L. Bean hiking moccasins. He pulled a rose from a bouquet of flowers at the gravestone, kissed the stem, and dropped it into the hole.

Cheryl's mother, Alice, approached next. Her eyes and most of her face were hidden behind a pair of sunglasses; a black dress showed from the bottom of her rain slicker. She pulled a small teddy bear from the coat, clutching it protectively to her bosom as she approached the grave. She kneeled before the hole, kissed the bear's nose, then propped it against the gravestone.

Altogether, the ceremony lasted five minutes. Roman shot it from a distance of twenty yards, covering all the aspects requested by the detectives. After it ended he spent several minutes rushing back and forth to tape cutaways. Each shot was taken from three perspectives: wide shot, medium shot, and close-up. He also took static shots of the grave marker, the open grave, and the teddy bear.

The crowd broke up and headed back to the parking lot, for the most part oblivious of Roman's work. Carpo waited for the cameraman under a water-logged willow tree. Even though it was raining harder, he didn't pressure Roman to hurry. Carpo knew the cutaways and static shots would be handy in the edit room; he would need several quick set-up shots of the burial plot before he could cut to the video of Mrs. Street placing the teddy bear on her daughter's grave.

Fifteen

The rain continued falling, as the weatherman had predicted, throughout the afternoon and evening, but it didn't create anything near the ripple caused by Channel 8's newscasts later that night.

The voice-over from Cheryl Street's funeral led the top of the six and ten o'clock shows. Both broadcasts began with a standard opening two-shot: studio lights coming up to reveal the anchors, Maria Gomez and Terry Chiltzom, seated at the desk. Between them, a graphic showed the file photo of Cheryl Street with the caption, "Laid to Rest." In the upper left a smaller graphic flashed: EXCLUSIVE.

"I'm Maria Gomez," Maria said once the opening music had faded.

"And I'm Terry Chiltzom. The Sandman's sixth victim, twenty-three-year-old Cheryl Street, was laid to rest in Queens tonight."

The angle switched from camera two to camera one, an isolated shot that framed a close-up of Maria's face with a smaller version of the "Laid to Rest" graphic over her left shoulder. At the same time, Maria started reading off the TelePrompTer.

"Just five days after she was found brutally murdered

*in her East Village apartment, friends and family of the
beautiful young flight attendant gathered to say a final
farewell."*

Maria's face dissolved into video from the funeral procession. The six men lumbered along the macadam path, hands
gripping the brass handles on the ebony casket. Cheryl's
parents came next, arms locked together for support, the
mother's face buried in her husband's shoulder.

*"The funeral took place just a few hours ago at St. John's
Cemetery in Middle Village, Queens. What you are seeing
is exclusive footage of the funeral, appearing only on Channel 8 News."*

The voice-over cut to separate, isolated images of the
burial: attendants lowering the casket into the ground; priest
reading from the Bible and sprinkling holy water into the
grave; Cheryl's father kissing the rose and tossing it into
the hole; and finally, a twenty-second chunk of video that
showed Cheryl's mother approaching the grave with the
teddy bear under her arm. The video zoomed to a close-up
as she knelt beside the grave, kissed the bear on the nose,
and placed it gently against her daughter's stone marker.

*"During an especially touching moment, a teddy bear
that once belonged to the victim was placed at the grave
site. Cheryl's parents, Myron and Alice Street of Roanoake,
Virginia, say the stuffed animal was their daughter's favorite toy when she was a young child."*

Carpo had written the script, he had also cut the video
and timed it to Maria's reading speed. As the anchor read
about Cheryl's mother leaving the teddy bear at the grave,
the video showed the woman stand and shakily retreat from
the camera shot.

"Today's funeral comes as police admit they are still no closer to catching the elusive serial killer, known as the Sandman. He is responsible for the death of at least six women in the past two years. Each of the crimes was committed in the East Village section of Manhattan."

When Maria had finished reading, the video stayed on the close-up of the teddy bear; alone, propped against the grave marker, its arms reaching into the air like a child seeking its mother.

Just above the bear's head, carved in the virgin white marble, was Cheryl's name, birth date, and date of death.

That image—teddy bear, grave marker, and CHERYL STREET: 1974–1997—appeared on the front pages of the *Daily News* and the *New York Post* a mere five hours after it first aired on Channel 8.

Carpo saw the pictures as he passed the newsstand in the lobby of the Chrysler Building on his way home from work. He bought all three local papers and read them during the short bus ride downtown.

The *Post* and the *News* had snapped their photographs right off a television set; the *Post's* shot even had squiggly lines running through it, evidently from bad reception. The headline on the *Post* read: FOND FAREWELL; The *Daily News*, REST IN PEACE.

While the page one billings impressed Carpo, it was the coverage in The *New York Times* that gave the truest sense of the funeral's impact. The so-called paper of record had put the file shot of Cheryl Street on its front page with a somber black headline across the top. Keeping with the paper's prosaic tone, the caption read: Funeral for Sixth Sandman Victim. Details Metro B1.

Inside the papers, coverage consisted of a brief recap of the funeral. Carpo noticed that more than just the photographs had been lifted straight from the television set; the recaps were almost word-for-word accounts of the script he had written for Channel 8. However, he also jealously noted the stories surrounding the main one: lengthy recaps of the murder, police statements on the status of their investigation, and an interview with the mayor about the Sandman's effect on his reelection bid. Carpo had tried to include similar information in his own voice-over, but the news editor had vetoed him.

"Time limitations," the editor had said as he deleted the passages from the script. "It's one of the prices you pay for working in show biz, Carpo."

Another price was the hours.

It was ten minutes before midnight when he finally reached his apartment. He dumped his knapsack on the couch and headed for the kitchen to make dinner. He opened a takeout bag from Little Poland and removed two warm potato knishes, a pile of greasy string beans, and a container of black coffee. He arranged the feast on a plate and carried it into the living room.

Just as he sat on the couch, the telephone rang. He snapped it up and, without thinking, gave his usual newsroom response: "Channel 8 News. Carpo here."

"Hello, Michael? It's me, Irene. Did I just dial your work number?"

"No, I'm at home." Carpo set the plate aside. "How are you, Irene?"

"Okay, I guess," she said in a small voice. "I hope I'm not calling too late. I saw your lights were on across the street, so I thought it'd be okay to try you."

"It's perfect timing, I just got home." Carpo waited a few seconds, then said, "Are you sure you're okay?"

"Really, I'm fine. A little sad, but nothing like before. You were right, I think it was good I went to the funeral."

"It's still going to take some time."

"I know. But I think it's . . . helping me come to terms with it."

"What did you think of the service?"

"It was nice. Small and, in a strange way, beautiful. The sermon was nice too. Did you hear it?"

"No, we weren't allowed in the chapel."

"That's too bad, because I think it was the best part. The priest talked for a long time about Cheryl. He even told a few stories about some of the crazy things she did growing up in Lancaster. I swear, it was almost like he knew her. He totally captured her spirit."

Carpo switched the phone to his other ear. "What did you think of the ceremony afterward?"

"It seemed a bit forced, especially that teddy bear business, but I guess it's what the parents wanted. By the way, did you see Steve Plotkin?"

"He was there?"

"Yes, for the whole thing. He was trying to look all incognito, standing in the background, wearing a ridiculous pair of sunglasses."

Carpo tried to recall a man fitting the description, but no one came to mind. "Did you talk to him?"

"No, there wasn't a chance during the service. I looked for him when it was over, but I guess he'd already left."

Suddenly, Carpo bolted upright on the couch. "What did you just say, Irene?"

"I said, he left before I could speak to him."

"No, no, before that," Carpo said. "When you were talking about the priest, you said he told stories about Cheryl in Lancaster."

"Yes, he told two of them."

"Don't you mean Roanoke?"

"No, I mean Lancaster."

"Lancaster, Pennsylvania?"

"Yes, that's where Cheryl was from."

"Are you sure?"

"I'm positive," Irene said. "Don't you remember what I told you the other day? About how Cheryl used to tell people she was from Dutch country?"

"That's right, I forgot about that." Carpo stood and began pacing the living room, the base of the phone in his hand, its elastic cord trailing between his legs like a limp tail. "It's so strange," he said. "Every time I think I'm getting a handle on this story, something new pops up."

"Like what, Michael?"

"Like just about everything. Cheryl's eye color, where she's from, her relationship with Steve. It seems like every person I talk to tells me a different story, one that totally contradicts the last story."

"I don't know where you're getting your information," Irene said, "but everything I'm telling you is the truth."

"I've been getting most of it from the police. Just this afternoon Detective Spinks told me the parents drove in from Roanoke. He said the drive had taken them seven hours."

"I don't know what Detective Spinks told you," Irene said, the strength flooding back into her words. "But Cheryl grew up in Lancaster, Pennsylvania."

With the phone still pressed to his ear, Carpo walked into the bedroom. He opened the blinds and stared across 12th Street. The lights were on in Irene's apartment, the only apartment above the third floor not in total darkness.

"Irene, what are you doing now?"

"Right this second? I'm standing in my kitchen, talking to you."

"No, I mean, do you have any plans tonight?"

"It's kind of late."

"I know," Carpo said, "but this is important. Can you meet me?"

"I suppose. What do you have in mind?"

Carpo stared at the pair of empty windows next to Irene's. They looked like the eyes of a shark: cold, black and forbidding. "I want you to help me get inside Cheryl's apartment."

"Michael, that's insane. We already went through this the other night. If we go into Cheryl's apartment, we're going to get caught."

"How?" Carpo said. "There's no burglar alarm in the place. How is anyone going to know we went in there?"

"What about the crime-scene tape?"

"We'll peel it off the door going in, then stick it back on when we're done. The cops won't even know someone went inside."

"People will hear us. The walls in this building are paper thin. They'll hear us walking around."

"Irene, I'm looking at your building right now. The only person we need to worry about is the guy who lives beneath 6W. There are no lights on in his apartment. He's either asleep or out of the building."

Irene sighed. "Fine, Michael. But don't forget to bring your sledgehammer. I already told you, I don't have a spare set of keys."

"That's okay," Carpo said, his eyes still locked on the set of windows. "I know who does."

Sixteen

"Are you fucking crazy?" George Bento said once Carpo finished explaining what he wanted the superintendent to do. "The cops told me to keep an eye on that apartment. I could get in a shitload of trouble if I let you in there."

Bento's T-shirt looked suspiciously similar to the one from Tuesday; sweat ringed his neck and armpits, the half-moons as yellow as nicotine stains.

"They won't find out," Carpo said. "I'll leave the apartment exactly the way I found it. No one will ever know I went inside."

"The door's taped up," Bento said. "They'd know in a second somebody'd been inside, and they'd know even faster that it was me who let them in."

"I'll replace the tape when I'm done. It'll look exactly the way it did before." As he spoke, Carpo pulled a plain white envelope from his pocket. Before going to the building, he had made a quick stop at the ATM machine down the street. Inside the envelope were one hundred dollars in twenties; he had folded the bills in half to increase the packet's bulge. "I know this is a lot to ask from you, so I'll make it worth your while."

Bento stared at the envelope without reaching for it,

then he looked at Carpo, eyes narrowing. "What business do you have in that girl's apartment?"

"I work for a TV station," Carpo said, hoping that alone would explain his motivation.

"It's more than that," Bento said. "You're looking for something."

Carpo pushed the envelope into the super's hand, pressing it against the palm to reinforce its width. "Do you really want to know, Mr. Bento? Seems to me, the less I tell you, the less you can get in trouble for."

The touch of money was apparently too much for Bento. He ran his long pinkie nail under the flap and peeked inside. What he saw made him swallow, once and very loud, as if he had gulped a mouthful of carbonated soda. He shoved the envelope into his blue jeans, then he produced a key ring from his belt loop. He chose one of the keys and peeled it off the coil. "You've got fifteen minutes," he said as he handed the key to Carpo. "Hear me? If you're not back by then, I'm calling the cops."

"What are you going to tell them?"

Bento shrugged. "That somebody's looting the dead girl's apartment."

The tape didn't come off the door nearly as easily as Carpo had been anticipating. He picked at the corners, hoping to start a larger piece, but succeeded only in ripping off thin strips. When he did get a piece started, it left behind most of its adhesive on the painted surface. Finally, Carpo finished the job with his key ring, a tiny silver coffee cup that he had purchased at Java The Hut. He used the sharp edge of the cup's handle to slice the tape along the door frame, then he unlocked the door and stepped inside.

He pulled a disposable flashlight from his pocket and turned it on. It created a diluted beam of light, no stronger than a match flame, but adequate for the job at hand. He shined the light across the room, bracing himself for signs of the evil deed—broken furniture, bloodstains, or worse—but everything appeared to be in order.

The apartment was the same size and shape as the other studios in the building, a small, box-shaped room with two windows overlooking 12th Street. A double bed squatted in the corner beneath a framed Matisse poster of four blue figures dancing in a circle. A night table and a small table with four metal folding chairs were the only other pieces of furniture. Since the floors had no rugs, Carpo peeled off his hiking boots for added silence.

After a quick inspection of the apartment, Carpo was struck by the lack of personal items. He had expected to find some clue to Cheryl's life—love letters, a diary, photographs—but such articles were noticeably absent. A cardboard box under the bed contained wool sweaters and the smell of mothballs. The drawer in the night table held tissues, a bottle of aspirin, and a paperback romance novel. The closet had nothing more than clothes, shoes, and a portable first aid kit. Everything was clean, neat, and predictable; too predictable, Carpo thought.

His final stop was the bathroom. A toiletries kit hung on the door, its plastic compartments holding travel-sized containers of toothpaste, deodorant, shampoo, and conditioner. Over the sink, two toothbrushes rested in a porcelain holder; under it, he found bath towels, spare toilet paper, and tampons. Carpo opened the medicine chest and flashed his penlight inside: birth control pills, a bottle of Motrin, Eyecare saline solution, and a plastic case for contact lenses. He picked up the case for a closer look; on the top was printed TRANSFORMATIONS. His interest piqued, he unscrewed one end of the case and looked inside.

Suddenly, a key slid into the door lock: Someone was entering the apartment.

Carpo turned off the flashlight and dropped to his knees. The door swung open and someone stepped into the apartment, making no attempt to conceal their presence. The person started to walk across the apartment. Carpo squeezed his body between the sink and the toilet, his heart slamming against his chest, almost drowning out the sound of the person's footsteps. He curled into a ball, eyes squeezed shut, and willed himself to disappear. The footsteps came closer and still closer, until they halted just outside the bathroom.

Who is it? Carpo wondered. The cops? George Bento? A nosy neighbor?

The Sandman?

The bathroom door swung open and the person entered the room, inches from where Carpo was hiding. He blinked his eyes in the inky blackness but couldn't see anyone. Just as fast it dawned on him: The footsteps were coming from the apartment below.

There was a clank as Tommy Abilene raised the lid on the toilet, then a muffled sigh as he began to tinkle into the bowl. Carpo turned on the flashlight. He put the contact lens case back in the medicine chest, closed the cabinet, and tiptoed across the apartment. He didn't bother putting on his hiking boots before he left. As quietly as possible, he closed the apartment door, locked it, and pasted the tape over the opening.

If someone looked closely, they would see in an instant that the apartment had been violated. But it should pass unnoticed for a while. Long enough for Carpo to find out what the hell was going on.

Irene opened the door to her apartment as soon as Carpo tapped on it. "What happened?" she whispered. "You look like you saw a ghost."

"Tommy Abilene came home," Carpo said. "Scared the shit out of me."

Irene stood aside to allow Carpo into the apartment, a studio roughly the size of Cheryl Street's place. A simple white couch stood between the kitchen and the bed. Carpo noted the three bookcases, each shelf filled with all types of books. Carpo noticed that most of the books were hardcover and carried formidable scholarly art history titles.

"Cheryl always complained about hearing Tommy," Irene said. "She used to say the walls were so thin, she could hear him snoring at night."

"Thin isn't the word. I thought he was in the apartment with me." Carpo sat on the floor and began lacing up his hiking boots.

"Did you find any of the stuff you were looking for?"

"Someone must have cleaned out the apartment after the murder. I didn't find anything. No papers, no personal letters, not even any photographs."

"Who would have done that?"

"I guess the cops or Cheryl's parents."

"So it was a complete waste of time going in there?"

"Not totally." Carpo stood and dusted off his pants. "I found out why there's a discrepancy in Cheryl's eye color. She wore contact lenses."

"Wow, I had no idea." Irene's face twisted into a frown. "Strange that she would lie to me about her eyesight. She told me she had perfect vision."

"She wasn't lying," Carpo said. "These aren't contacts for improving eyesight, they're colored contacts. I used to know a woman who owned a pair, which is why I recognized the lens case."

"What color did Cheryl have?"

"Blue."

"Blue," Irene said quietly. "So that explains why I remember her with blue eyes."

"Not only that, it lends credence to Detective Weissman's theory. Cheryl really had brown eyes." Carpo shook his head, grimacing. "I was starting to doubt it, but I guess it's true. The Sandman killed her."

Seventeen

As soon as Carpo woke up Friday morning, he went into the living room and called Detective Weissman at the 9th Precinct. Weissman sounded as if his mouth was full of something; Carpo figured he had caught the detective in the middle of breakfast.

"Nice job on the funeral last night, Michael," he said after a hearty swallow. "Channel 8's coverage was perfect, just what we were looking for."

"I'm glad you liked it," Carpo said. "It's actually part of the reason I'm calling."

"What's up?"

"I was talking to Detective Spinks at the funeral yesterday and he mentioned that Cheryl's parents came from Roanoke, Virginia. I think he said it took them seven hours to drive here."

"That's right."

"Well, last night I found out that Cheryl's parents aren't from Roanoke. They're from Lancaster, Pennsylvania."

The chewing noises started again. "That can't be," Weissman said. "I talked to the parents myself. They're from Roanoke."

"I'm pretty sure about this," Carpo said.

"I'm sure you are, but did it ever occur to you that the parents might have moved after she was grown up?"

"I suppose it's possible," Carpo said, "but I think it's worth checking out."

"Where'd you hear this anyway?"

"Irene Foster told me."

Weissman paused as he drank something. "Is this the same Irene who said Cheryl had blue eyes? So far she's batting a big goose egg with all of her theories."

"I can explain the blue eyes," Carpo said, needled by the detective's comment. "Cheryl Street owned a pair of colored contacts."

"A pair of what?"

"Colored contacts. They're cosmetic lenses that change the eye color on the person wearing them. Cheryl owned a pair of blue ones. Irene must have seen her in them."

"Why would she want to change her eye color?"

"I assume to give herself a different look, sort of like makeup. Anyway, it means your brown-eye theory is still intact." Carpo waited a few seconds, but the line remained silent. "Detective Weissman, did you hear me?"

"Mmm, yeah," Weissman mumbled, obviously lost in thought.

"Surely, I'm not telling you anything groundbreaking," Carpo said. "You must have seen her brown eyes at the morgue yesterday."

"What was that?"

"I said, you must have seen that she had brown eyes when you visited the morgue. Isn't that why you weren't at the funeral?"

"Yeah, Mike, that's the reason."

"Anyway, I hope you'll check on the parents," Carpo said. "I can't figure out why there's a discrepancy between their story and Irene's."

Weissman took another sip of something, then he said, "What made Irene think the parents aren't from Pennsylvania?"

"She said Cheryl used to joke about how she came from Dutch country—that's the nickname for the Lancaster area, Pennsylvania Dutch country. Cheryl used to like it when people thought she was from the Netherlands. Maybe the parents did move, but I think you should check it out."

"I'll do that," Weissman whispered as if his mind were still far from the conversation. "Anyway, Michael, I should get going. Talk to you soon."

Carpo hung up the phone, perplexed by Weissman's tone during the conversation. The detective had sounded as if he had been in a trance, his mind completely off the conversation. Carpo wondered if it was a sign of burnout or something worse. He also wondered if Weissman would go through with his promise to check where Cheryl Street's parents lived.

Carpo picked up the telephone again and dialed directory assistance. He asked the operator for the area codes for Lancaster and Roanoke, then he called information in both cities. An operator in Roanoke informed him that there were five Streets listed in the local environs, none with the first name Myron or Alice. Checking under initials, Carpo learned there was one *M* Street and two *A*'s. In Lancaster an operator found listings for three Streets. No Alice or Myron among them, but one had the first initial *A*.

Carpo sat with the telephone in his lap as he reviewed

the list. He could try calling each of the six families, but what if the Streets hadn't returned home yet? There was also the possibility that the Streets didn't live in either city, but out in the suburbs or a neighboring town. Suddenly, Weissman's reluctance didn't seem so odd; finding out where the Streets came from was almost an impossible task.

"Almost," Carpo mumbled as he got off the couch.

Almost, because he knew one surefire way to find the answer.

After a quick breakfast and shower, Carpo walked to the 8th Street subway station and boarded an N train headed downtown. It was ten in the morning, well after the morning rush, and for most the trip he had the entire car to himself. He was thankful for the privacy, since he was dressed in the same clothes he had worn to the funeral. The cuffs on his trousers felt damp and the sleeves on his jacket had shrunk so much, his wrists showed.

Carpo got off at the Cortland Street station, in the basement of the World Trade Center. He rode an escalator to the lobby and followed signs to the World Financial Center, crossing the cavernous lobbies of the Twin Towers, then the pedestrian bridge spanning the West Side Highway. In the farthest tower of the complex, he located the world headquarters of Merrill Lynch.

The entrance to the tower was gained through a series of narrow, waist-high chutes similar to subway turnstiles. Employees threaded single file down the slots, placing their picture IDs on a special scanner that unlocked the metal bar. Carpo watched the entrance for a few minutes, then he found a pay phone in the visitors' center and dialed upstairs. The secretary who had taken his previous calls answered.

"Good morning," Carpo said, "may I please speak with Steve Plotkin?"

"Whom may I say is calling?"

"Just say it's Michael."

The woman placed Carpo on hold. After a minute or so, the line clicked over. "This is starting to get old," Plotkin said hotly, "and I'm starting to get tired of it. If you don't knock it off, I'm going to slap a harassment complaint on you."

Plotkin's tone took Carpo by surprise. He had figured he was bugging the man; he hadn't realized just how much. "All I need is five minutes of your time. I need to ask three quick questions. When they're answered, I promise I'll never call again."

"I already told you, I'm not talking to you."

"Steve, at this moment I'm standing in the lobby of your building, and I don't plan on leaving until you meet me. If I have to, I'll wait here until you come down for lunch or try to leave the building." Carpo paused to let his intentions sink in. "Why don't you make it easy on both of us? Come down and meet me."

When Plotkin spoke again, his voice had lost some of its punch. "You're bluffing."

"Maybe I am, maybe I'm not. You'll find out when you see me."

"You don't even know what I look like."

"I saw you at Cheryl's funeral yesterday," Carpo said, straining to remember how Irene had described him. "Maybe you thought those sunglasses would hide your face, but they sure looked out of place in a rainstorm."

Plotkin was silent for a while. "If I wanted to, I could make one phone call and have security remove you from the building."

"Yes, but then you'd have to explain who I am and why I'm bothering you. Do you really want a scene like that?"

"There're three different entrances to this tower. I can get in and out of any of them."

"That might work a couple of times," Carpo said, "but I'll run into you sooner or later. This is the only story I'm working on, and it doesn't matter how I fill my days. If I don't see you today, I'll come back tomorrow, and the day after that. I'll keep coming back until you meet me."

"So let me get this straight: I either meet you or you'll ambush me? That's some noble profession you're in, Carpo. How the hell do you look yourself in the mirror in the morning?"

Carpo ignored the jab. "The ball's in your court," he said. "Meet me and I'll be out of your life forever."

Plotkin swore under his breath. "My entire morning's booked. I don't have time to dick around with you."

"Go to your meetings, do what you have to. Like I said, I've got nowhere else to go."

"Fine. I'll be down when I get a chance, you goddamned son—"

Carpo set down the phone before Plotkin could finish the pleasantries. He sat in the booth for a few seconds and forced himself to stare, eye to eye, at his reflection in the phone's metal frame, just to prove that he could.

He walked to a small newsstand down the hall and bought

a *New York Times*, then he returned to the visitors' center and chose a conspicuous seat facing the turnstiles. He breezed through the paper, then he flipped to the crossword puzzle. He was halfway through it, trying to come up with a six-letter word for "prevaricator," when a pair of shiny tasseled loafers appeared at his feet. He looked up from the paper as a man said, "You Carpo?"

The two hours had drained most of the anger from Steve Plotkin. The man's hands were shoved deep in his pockets, fingers jingling together coins and keys. Carpo set the paper aside and extended his hand. "Nice to meet you, Steve."

The man glanced at Carpo's hand and waved it off. "I thought you said you knew what I looked like."

Carpo shrugged. "I lied."

Steve Plotkin looked much older than Carpo had expected, mid-thirties, perhaps even forties. Gray had taken a firm root in his thinning brown hair, and gravity was doing its own magic with his face, dragging down the skin beneath his eyes and chin. He was dressed in an immaculate gray suit, designer quality, and his shirt looked as if it had been pressed under a steamroller. "Where do you want to do this?" Plotkin asked.

"Is there a coffee shop nearby?" Carpo asked. "It'd probably be better than talking here."

"There's a couple of places in the Winter Garden." Plotkin pointed toward the entrance to the World Financial Center, where Carpo had passed a large glass atrium. "It's a little more private than here."

They didn't talk as they walked to the atrium. To Carpo's dismay, Plotkin skipped an appealing coffee shop by the name of Pasqua's in favor of a Starbuck's franchise. They each bought coffee and carried them to the end of the atrium, where four steep flights of stairs created a natural seating arena. Workers and tourists alike sat on the steps, eating lunch, drinking coffee, and watching people. In the middle of the second flight a bride and groom in full wedding regalia were posing for a photographer. A handful of people in the wedding party, betrayed by their tuxedos and matching long dresses, looked on. Carpo and Plotkin moved one level above the group.

"Let's get this over," Plotkin said as soon as he had taken a seat. "What do you want to know?"

Without asking for permission, Carpo pulled out his note-book and balanced it on his knees. "As I've told you, I'm working on a profile of Cheryl for Channel 8. I'm trying to present Cheryl as a real woman, a complete person, not just another victim of the Sandman."

"How noble," Plotkin mumbled.

Carpo ignored the comment. "I can pretty much narrow this interview to three questions. First, I'm having trouble finding out where Cheryl was from."

"What do you mean? Where she was born?"

"That, and where her parents live now."

"Why is it important?"

"I don't know if it is. It's just a discrepancy that's come up during my interviews."

"What have other people said?"

Carpo shook his head. "I'd rather not say in case it influences your answer."

Plotkin pulled the tab off the container's lid and sipped his coffee. "Cheryl was born in Pennsylvania, I can't remember where exactly."

"Was it Lancaster?"

Plotkin's eyes moved to Carpo. "Yes, I think so."

"What about her parents?"

"I'm not sure. I think they're still in Lancaster."

"Is there any chance they moved to Roanoke, Virginia."

"I don't know. I suppose it's possible, but I don't remember Cheryl mentioning it."

Carpo opened his own cup and sampled some of the bitter Starbuck's brew. "How long did you and Cheryl date, Steve?"

"Two years."

"That's a long time."

"I guess." As Plotkin spoke, he stared down at the newlyweds. The photographer had arranged them for a new pose: the bride kneeling on a step, wedding dress fanning the floor; the groom crouching a step higher, top hat perched under his arm. "It sure didn't feel that long," he muttered.

"Steve, I've got to tell you, I find it strange that you're so unwilling to talk about Cheryl. From what everyone tells me, she was an incredible woman. Don't you want people to know that?"

Plotkin's head remained facing the couple, but Carpo noticed he wasn't looking at them. He was looking over their heads, somewhere past the glass wall, at New York harbor or farther off at Brooklyn Heights. He whispered, "She was."

"She was what?"

"Incredible." Plotkin rubbed his eyes, as if he were trying to clear a mirage. "She was the most amazing woman I've ever met. Ever will meet."

"But you still don't want to talk about her?"

"I wish I could. God, I wish I could." Plotkin pushed his

hair back roughly, then dragged his fingers down his face. "Jesus, you have no idea what this has been like."

"It must be very difficult."

"Sometimes I feel like I'm about to go insane. Bottling up feelings, pretending I don't miss her, acting like this isn't ripping me to pieces inside. I swear to Christ, I can't take it anymore."

"Then let it go. If not to me, then to someone you trust, a family member or a friend. You shouldn't keep it inside."

"A family member," Plotkin said before he broke into a hearty chuckle. "Christ almighty, you just don't get it, do you, Carpo? You don't have a fucking clue."

"About what?"

"I'm married. I've got a wife and a fifteen-month-old baby girl. Who the hell am I going to talk to? You think anyone wants to hear about my problems?"

Without thinking, Carpo checked Plotkin's hand: the left one, four fingers over. He wasn't wearing a wedding band.

Plotkin noticed the glance. He draped his right hand over his left, but it was too late to hide the empty finger. "You think I'm a sleaze, don't you?" he asked Carpo. "You think I don't wear a ring so I can pick up women."

Carpo didn't say anything.

Plotkin stared at his hands, as if he were wondering where the ring had gone to. "I am a sleaze. I've been one ever since I laid eyes on Cheryl."

Carpo took a breath and asked, "How did you meet?"

"I was on a business trip, San Francisco, I think. I saw Cheryl as soon as I stepped on the plane. She was at the door, in this cute little uniform, and she smiled at me and said something liked Welcome to our world, or whatever the hell they say when you get on a plane. All I remember thinking was, Oh, God, I am in big, big trouble. I knew right there I was going to fall for her."

"What happened?"

"Nothing on the plane, if that's what you mean. I was up in business class, she was working back in coach. We ran into each other at the baggage claim. We started talking while we were waiting for the bags to come out. I had a limo waiting, so I offered to give her a ride to the city." Plotkin smiled ruefully. "I didn't think she'd go for it. Honestly. That was part of the reason I asked her, it seemed so . . . improbable."

"But she did?"

"Yes, she did," Plotkin said. "When we got to her building, I asked if she'd like to get together sometime. Drinks or dinner. It nearly plowed me over when she said sure."

"Did she know you were married?"

"Funny thing is, she knew it immediately. I've never worn a wedding band, but I guess I'm the type who flashes the No Vacancy sign." Plotkin stared at his finger again. "I want to make one thing clear, Carpo, I don't wear a ring because I'm hoping to pick up a woman. I've got eczema, it's a skin rash, and the ring aggravates it." He rolled up his sleeve and showed his bare wrist. "Look, I can't even wear a watch because of it."

"You don't have to make excuses, Steve. You were two consenting adults. I'm not about to judge either of you." Carpo turned to a fresh page in his notebook. "I've got to ask you a few more questions, Steve, and they're not pleasant."

"Were the earlier ones? I hadn't realized."

"Several people have said that you and Cheryl had bad arguments, violent ones. Is it true?"

"We argued a lot, but they weren't violent."

"Nothing physical at all?"

"No way."

"Did you have a good relationship?"

"Under the circumstances, yes."

"What does that mean?"

"She had to put up with a lot of crap," Plotkin said, "me being married and all. At times things got . . . rocky."

"Was it rocky recently?"

"For about a year or so, ever since my little girl was born. I was planning to leave my wife, but the stakes changed after she was born."

"Cheryl know that?"

"She never asked, but she must have sensed it."

Carpo pretended to write something in his notebook, stalling before the next question. "Steve, this is a hard thing to bring up now, but in a few of my interviews people have said that Cheryl was dating other men. Do you know if she was?"

"I have no idea."

"None at all?"

Plotkin stared down at the newlyweds again. "Maybe she was, I don't know. Cheryl was a beautiful girl and we had an open relationship." He gave a tired shake of his head. "For chrissakes, I'm married. What was I supposed to do, demand that she be faithful?"

A smattering of applause broke out as the bride and groom finished their photographs. The groom, top hat cocked at a crazy angle, picked up the woman and carried her down the stairs. When they reached the bottom they kissed, bringing another eruption of applause.

"I've got to go," Plotkin said. "My office is going to send out a search party if I'm not back soon."

"One more question. Why did Cheryl wear colored contacts?"

Plotkin's jaw dropped. "Gosh, Carpo, you really did your homework. How'd you find that out?"

"It came up in a conversation."

"Why's it important?"

"It's just another discrepancy."

"Yeah, she wore them. A pair of blue ones."

"Do you know why?"

"She told me once her fantasy growing up was to have blue eyes. I guess she hated her natural eye color." Plotkin drained the last of his coffee and crumpled the cup. "She didn't wear them all the time. In fact, the first time we met she wasn't wearing them."

"Was it purely a cosmetic change?"

"I think so."

"Why did she hate having brown eyes?"

Plotkin frowned. "What are you talking about?"

"You said she hated her eye color growing up. Why did she hate having brown eyes?"

Plotkin didn't say anything, but the frown on his forehead showed something was bothering him.

"What's the matter?" Carpo asked.

"What do you mean by brown eyes?" Plotkin asked. "Cheryl didn't have brown eyes. They were green."

Eighteen

"That's the second time this week someone has dropped a complete bombshell on me," Carpo said.

"What do you mean?" Irene asked.

"Learning from Steve Plotkin that Cheryl didn't have brown or blue eyes after all. They were green."

"I know about that bombshell," Irene said. "I don't recall the first one."

"Try your little revelation last night, that Cheryl's parents were from Lancaster, Pennsylvania, instead of Virginia. That one also did a complete number on me."

It was late Friday night, about ten hours after Carpo had met Steve Plotkin at the World Financial Center. He and Irene were seated at a table in the back of Taste of Siam, a small Thai restaurant on Second Avenue, just around the corner from 12th Street. The restaurant was very crowded and filled with a dinnertime buzz—plates clattering, snippets of random conversation, and an occasional sizzling food platter. Smells of garlic, peanut oil, and fried meats perfumed the air.

"That reminds me," Irene said, "just so you don't think I'm utterly cuckoo, I found a photograph of Cheryl. It's not the best, but you can make out her blue eyes in it."

She pulled a framed photograph from her purse and handed it to Carpo. The frame was circular and the photograph had been cropped accordingly. In it, Cheryl had on a pair of Ray-Ban sunglasses, worn low on her nose. She stared into the camera with a seductive pose: head tilted back, a pout on her lips. Even though the photo was slightly out of focus, Carpo could see the aqua-blue color of her eyes.

"When was this taken?" he asked.

"Last summer."

"By you?"

Irene nodded. "It was during that awful heat wave in August. We went out to Jones Beach for the day. They have this special deal on the train where you can use your ticket stub for a free ride on the shuttle bus to the beach. Have you ever done it?"

"No."

"We should do it sometime. It's a lot of fun."

"What did you and Cheryl do there?"

"We ended up spending the whole day and most of the night there. There's a big stadium nearby where they put on shows, and we scalped some tickets to a Blues Traveler concert. I'm not crazy about them, but Cheryl was absolutely wild for the lead singer, the chubby guy who plays the harmonica. She kept threatening to go backstage and ask if he'd join us for a drink."

"Did she?"

"No, thank God."

Carpo held up the photo. "Mind if I hang on to this?"

"Sure, go ahead." Irene sipped her beer without taking her eyes off Carpo. "So have you told the cops yet about Cheryl's real eye color?"

"Not yet. I tried calling this afternoon, they were both out of the precinct. I left a message, but never heard back from them."

Irene scraped a fingernail across the label of the bottle. "What did they say when you told them where Cheryl was born?"

"Detective Weissman didn't seem too shocked. He raised the point that Cheryl's parents may have moved within the past few years. Anyway, he promised to check it out."

"I remember Detective Weissman," Irene said. "He seemed like a decent man, like he cared about Cheryl. I wouldn't say the same for his partner."

"You mean Detective Spinks?" Carpo chuckled. "The guy really is a total jerk."

"Would you believe he called me after they questioned me and asked me out on a date?"

"Spinks did? That's so unprofessional. What did you say?"

"No, of course."

"No, I mean, how did you get rid of him?"

"I told him I was dating someone."

Carpo managed a weak smile. "That's a good deterrent." He watched her face for some hint of whether it was true or not.

Irene picked up her napkin and scrubbed her chin. "What's the matter? Is there food on my face?"

"No."

"The way you're staring at me, something must be wrong."

"No, nothing's wrong." Carpo looked down at his plate. "Except . . ."

"What?"

"Do you?"

"Do I what?"

"You know what I'm talking about, Irene."

"If you're asking if I have a boyfriend, the answer is no." The smile stayed on her face. "Why do you ask?"

Carpo could tell she was enjoying making him squirm. "I wanted to call the guy and extend my condolences."

"Very funny."

A waiter came by to clear their plates and announce the dessert specials. They decided to forgo dessert and coffee in favor of another round of drinks. After the waiter had left, Irene said, "So what about you?"

"What about me?"

"Do you have a girlfriend?"

"Would I be sitting here if I did?"

"Don't act so surprised, Michael. It wouldn't be the first time a guy told me they didn't when they really did."

"I assure you, I don't."

"What about that woman at Little Poland?"

"Who, Candi?" Carpo said. "No way. I love her and all, but she's like my sister."

"Then what was going on between you two the other night? The way you were winking and making comments, I thought I'd stepped right in the middle of a lovers' quarrel."

"What you stumbled upon was Candi's lame attempt to set us up. She spotted you as you entered the diner and started pestering me to ask you to sit. I refused, so she basically asked for me."

"Is that what she does, help you pick up women?"

"Not at all. If anything, it's just the opposite. She gets on my case because I don't date."

"As mattter of choice?"

"It's not like I don't want to. I just haven't found the right opportunity."

"What's gone wrong?"

"Irene, what is this? A background check?"

"No, it's a before-ground check. I'm checking you out before I get to know you." Irene drummed her fingers on the table with mock impatience. "Let's go, spill the beans, mister. Who did you date?"

"Some woman I knew in college. That's all."

"Does this *some woman* have a name?"

"It's Karen."

"And what did Karen do to you?"

Carpo spotted the waiter approaching with their beers. He waited, hoping the interruption would cause a change in topic, but as soon as the waiter had set them down, Irene said, "So what did she do to you, Michael?"

"Do we have to go into this?"

"Did she dump you? Is that what happened?"

"Do we?" Carpo said louder.

"I guess it's still too hard to speak about her," Irene said, picking up her beer. "Don't worry, I understand. You still love her."

"Irene, please, I don't still love her."

"Obviously you do if you can't even say why you guys broke up."

Carpo closed his eyes. He wished he were like a genie: one blink and he'd disappear. *The evening was going so perfectly*, he thought. *Why'd I have to ask if she had a boyfriend?*

With his eyes still closed, he said, "First we dated in college, for about three years. We broke up before graduation."

"What happened?"

"I messed up."

"What did you do?"

"Irene, please."

"What did you do, Michael?"

Carpo squeezed his eyes tighter; small flares began to explode on the inside of his eyelids. "I got caught . . . being unfaithful."

"That's very thoughtful."

"Irene—"

"Shut up and tell me what happened next."

"I ran into her again in the city, about two years ago. She was involved in a story I was covering for Channel 8."

"Do you often meet women connected to the stories you're covering?"

Carpo's eyes flew open; he felt a charge of anger. "What are you talking about? I don't use my job to meet women!"

"Pipe down, Michael, I'm just joshing," Irene said without a trace of a smile. "So, let's see, you haven't dated anyone in . . ." She looked up at the ceiling, making like she was counting out the years in her head. "Lord, two whole years. That's a long time. No wonder Candi's been trying so hard to set you up."

"Thanks for your thoughtfulness too."

"Are you over her yet?"

"Yes."

"I mean, *over* her, Michael. Completely."

"Yes!"

Irene brought the beer bottle to her eye and squinted through the glass. "I take it this Karen chick had some sort of job in the art world?"

Carpo's face registered shock. "How did you guess?"

"The time we first met, when you came to my building, you made this awful face when I said I was studying art history. I asked what was wrong and you mumbled something about having dated a person who studied art history."

"Now I remember," Carpo said. "You snapped at me after I said it, something like, Well, it's a good thing we're not dating!"

"I said that?"

"You sure did."

Irene set the beer bottle down. She reached across the table and slid her hand into Carpo's. "I've been known to tell a fib or two in my time," she said quietly. "And don't you look like the Cheshire cat. Wipe that silly grin off your face, Mr. Carpo, or I'll ask for more details on Karen what's-her-name."

After dinner, as they headed up the avenue to 12th Street, the silence pressed in on Carpo. Conversation that had flowed so effortlessly at the table now eluded him altogether. Making matters worse, Irene was nestled against his body, her hand slipped through the crook of his arm, fingertips lightly brushing his wrist. The sensation felt wonderful: her nails tracing slow circles that raised goose bumps on his skin. The lightness of her touch, the proximity of her body, the sweet smell of her perfume—these were the only things on which Carpo could concentrate.

And so, he remained silent.

"Hey there," Irene said, nudging him with her elbow, "gotten kind of quiet, haven't you?"

He shook his head as if to clear it. "I'm just thinking about what we were saying over dinner."

Her whole hand moved, like the brush of a feather, fingers sliding into his palm. "Are you having second thoughts about Karen?"

"No, no, no," he said quickly, "that's not at all what I was thinking."

Her fingers tightened then released, a quick reassurance. "I'm only teasing. In a way, I'm happy that you told me about her. It means you trust me."

Her grip relaxed and they continued walking. After a minute she said, "You know, I still don't know what to call you. I hear people refer to you as both Michael and Carpo."

"Either one's fine."

"Which do you prefer?"

"My friends call me Carpo. My parents, and anyone else who doesn't know me, call me Michael."

"I guess that settles it. Carpo it is."

They waited at the corner of 12th Street for the light to change, then they crossed Second Avenue. The movie marquee was turned off. It was quiet on the street. Quiet enough to hear the buzz of the streetlamps.

What will happen when we reach her building? Carpo wondered. *Will she invite me upstairs?*

He looked up the street, gauging the distance that remained to her building. Less than half a block. He could see the black railing on the stairway, the yellow light over the entrance. On the sidewalk, a man was rummaging through the garbage pails.

"What are you doing tomorrow?" Irene asked.

"I'm working on the profile."

"On a Saturday?" She took a step back so she could see his face better. "Why don't you take a day off? You've been working nonstop on this thing, I think you deserve one. Besides, how much can you accomplish on the weekend?"

"I was thinking of taking a trip to LaGuardia, see if I can find anyone at TWA who knew Cheryl. I may also take this photo around the neighborhood, try to dig something up that way."

"When do you begin the on-camera interviews?"

"Early next week, Monday or Tuesday. I've got to have the piece shot, written, and edited by Friday."

Irene sighed. "Well, that's a bummer. I was hoping we could spend the day together. Have a late breakfast, maybe catch a movie or even head out to Jones Beach. I guess I'll have to wait until the series is finished, huh?"

"I'm afraid so."

At the sound of their footsteps, the man at the garbage pails straightened up and looked at them, the lapels of his coat falling open. He bunched the coat around his body and went back to prospecting in the trash.

Ten yards from the building, Carpo felt his pulse quicken. *Should I invite myself upstairs, or would that seem too forward?*

Irene must have sensed the finale too, because she squeezed his arm. "If you're busy this weekend and all next week, when am I going to see you again? I don't think I want to wait until next week."

"I didn't say I was busy tomorrow night."

"I'm not sure I want to wait until then either." A shy smile spread over her face. "For heaven's sake, Carpo, do I have to hit you over the head with a club?"

"What do you mean?"

"I mean, would you like to come upstairs with me?"

The man at the garbage pails stood up again, his arm holding the coat in place. The coat was a trench coat, black, and reaching down to his knees. Without a sound Carpo clamped down on Irene's arm and pulled her away from the building.

"Carpo, what're you—"

"Shut up," he hissed. "Please, Irene, don't say anything."

The man in front of the building was the same man he had seen last Saturday, the one in the long black trench coat that he had spotted from his window.

It was the Sandman.

Nineteen

With her arm pinned to his side, Carpo guided Irene down the sidewalk. Not once did she cry out, even as she struggled to free herself, yanking her fist against his elbow. Carpo placed his right hand on top of his left and pressed harder; their bodies collided awkwardly with each step. The man in the trench coat did not look up at them, though Carpo got the impression he was listening.

When they reached Third Avenue, Carpo relaxed his hold. Irene stumbled back, massaging her wrist as if it hurt. Her face was pained too, a mixture of shock and anger.

"Goddammit, what's wrong with you? What the hell was that about?"

"Shh, Irene," he pleaded, "keep your voice down."

"I will not! Not until you tell me what the hell is going on!"

Carpo circled her until his back was toward 12th Street. "Look over my shoulder," he said. "See, the man back there? The one outside your building? I think it's the Sandman."

The color instantly drained from Irene's face. She looked down the street, then back at Carpo, eyes blinking with disbelief. "That's not the Sandman," she said, "it's just some homeless guy collecting cans."

"I'm telling you, it's him. It's the same guy I saw from my window Saturday night. The one who ran away when you started screaming."

She squinted at the shadowy figure. "Are you sure?"

"I'm positive, Irene. He looks exactly the way I remember him. Black trench coat, dark hair, same build. I'd bet my life it's him."

Her hand was trembling as she ran it through her hair. "We've got to do something, Michael. We've got to call the police."

"No, we should call Detective Weissman," Carpo said. "He might want to handle this a certain way."

"It's too late to reach him. There's no way he'd still be at work."

"I've got a pager number for him." Carpo located the detective's business card in his wallet. "He said I could reach him twenty-four hours a day."

Irene checked all four street corners. "I don't see a pay phone."

"There's one down on 9th Street, outside St. Mark's Books."

"Okay, let's go."

"Wait a sec, Irene, we both can't go. What if this guy wanders off?" He handed her the business card. "Here, you call Weissman. I'll wait for you."

"But what happens if he does wander off? What'll I tell Weissman? Hi, Carpo just spotted the Sandman, but I don't know where they went?"

Carpo checked over his shoulder. The man had finished picking through the garbage outside number 228 and was moving on to the next building, the one in their direction.

Carpo noticed he was dragging a plastic bag crammed full of soda cans.

"We need a contingency plan," Irene said.

"How about this: You call Weissman and tell him what's happening. Have him wait by the precinct phone for us to call back, then you come here. If I'm not around, you'll know that the guy left and I followed him. Then you call Weissman and tell him that I'll phone as soon as the guy stops."

"But what if I come back and you're still here? We'll be in the same boat. I'll have to go back and call Weissman, which means the guy could still leave."

Carpo rolled his eyes. "Weissman would be here by now."

"Don't get smart with me," Irene snapped. "I'm not calling Weissman until I know our plan."

"Do what I said: Call and tell him what's happening. That's the most important thing. Tell him I'll call once this guy takes root."

"You're forgetting something." She waved the business card in the air. "I have Weissman's number. Unless you have it memorized, how are you going to call him?"

The man moved to a new set of garbage cans, a mere twenty yards away. One more set and Carpo feared he'd be able to hear their conversation. "Read me the number," Carpo said, his impatience growing. "I'll memorize it."

Instead of answering, Irene rustled through her purse for a pen and a piece of gum. She opened the gum wrapper and wrote the detective's number on it. She started to hand it over, then stopped and added a second number to the list.

"What are you doing?" Carpo asked.

"Adding my number too."

"Irene, you're wasting time."

"Be quiet." She finished writing and gave him the wrapper. "Here, take it with you."

Carpo slipped the wrapper into his shirt pocket. "Okay, now go call Weissman."

Irene stood her ground. "Carpo, you be careful."

"Irene, if you'd gone and called him the first time, Weissman would have the handcuffs on him by now."

"I don't care," she said in a tone that sounded almost angry. "You watch out, hear me? I want you back in one piece. And alive."

The man in the trench coat did move on. About two minutes after Irene had disappeared, the man shouldered his enormous bag of cans and walked to Third Avenue. Carpo melted into the small crowd of people waiting at the bus stop. After rustling through the wire rubbish bin on the corner, the man headed uptown.

Carpo kept a distance of a block between himself and the man. It was easy to keep him in sight; the man seemed in no particular hurry and his blue plastic bag was conspicuous. On 18th Street, the man crossed to the west side of the avenue and entered a Gristede's supermarket. Carpo crossed too and waited on the sidewalk. He peeked between a cluster of "Best Buy" signs taped to the window; the man was feeding his cans into a recycling machine. When the bag was empty, the man punched a button on the machine that spat out a receipt. He brought it to the checkout counter and collected his money.

The man emerged from the supermarket and headed west along 18th Street, with Carpo following a safe margin behind. They passed a row of people eating at the tables outside Pete's Tavern, then walked up Irving Place to Gramercy Park. Old-fashioned gas lamps lit the center of the private park, its private status guaranteed by the eight-foot-high fence circling the perimeter. The man stepped into the shadows and urinated through an opening.

The man walked halfway around the park to Lexington Avenue and continued north. On 23rd Street he ducked into a liquor store and emerged a moment later with a fifth of something hidden in a brown paper bag. He unscrewed the cap and took a thirsty, twenty-second pull on the bottle. He walked with the bottle near his mouth, pausing every block or so for another swig.

A few blocks north they entered the area of Manhattan known as Little India, the avenue and side streets crammed full of restaurants, convenience stores, and spice shops. Most of the businesses had closed for the night, but the smell of curry and incense lingered in the humid air. Lexington Avenue was dark and deserted, so Carpo lagged back a block and a half. The man stayed in the middle of the sidewalk, maintaining his slow, deliberate pace. Not once did he make an unpredictable move or check over his shoulder.

The buildings grew taller and more modern as they reached the 30s. Traffic grew heavier in the streets, the sidewalks congested. Carpo quickened his pace until he had closed within a half block. He noticed the man starting to weave in his path, his steps shorter and uncertain. The time between swigs off the bottle shortened as well, until it seemed as if the man was wetting his lips every ten steps or so.

At the corner of 40th Street the man stopped, tilted the bottle upside down, and drained it. He wiped his mouth on the back of his hand, then tossed the bottle at a garbage can. It missed badly, smashing into hundreds of sparkling fragments. The man seemed oblivious of the miss. He burrowed his hands into his pockets and turned west, the soles of his shoes scratching like sandpaper as he trod over the glass shards.

As they crossed the belly of Manhattan, in the direction of Times Square, the street pounded with a pulse and energy found nowhere else in New York City. People loitered outside delis, newspaper stands, and pizza parlors. Traffic clogged the intersections, bubbling with a cacophony of car horns, boom boxes, and thousands of human voices. Garbage piled along the curb; grates in the pavement secreted clouds of steam that smelled of the subway.

Fearful of losing the man in this quagmire of humanity, Carpo shortened the distance between them to a mere twenty feet. He could see the man's stringy black hair skidding over the collar of his trench coat. The coat itself was mottled with grease smudges; along the bottom the fabric was frayed. They passed Times Square, where the sky filled with bursts of neon brighter than a fireworks display. The sounds of traffic and people grew louder and louder, until the noise was a dull, steady roar that seemed to hover directly above Carpo's head.

The man continued farther west, moving into the porno district that had once occupied Times Square. All that remained from that era were a pair of Triple-X movie rental stores, their front windows painted black. The man entered the store to the right with the vapid name: Girls, Girls, Girls.

Carpo waited on the street a few minutes to see if the man would reappear. When he didn't, Carpo jogged to a cluster of pay phones on the corner. The first one was empty. He pinned the receiver between his ear and shoulder as he patted down his pockets for a quarter. He dropped one into the slot and pulled out the gum wrapper. Just as he started to dial Weissman's number, he felt a heavy tap on his shoulder.

"Whatcha think yer doin', jack?"

The voice belonged to a white kid, maybe twenty years old, with a buzz haircut and a pair of mirrored sunglasses. The kid wore a tank top stretched to transparency by a set of massive pectorals, each one as wide as Carpo's head. By the look of his physique and acne-scarred face, Carpo figured the kid had spent a little time in the weight room to compliment his steroid program.

"I says, whatcha doin', jackrabbit," the kid said, his jaw muscle tensing like a fist.

"I'm making a phone call," Carpo said evenly, unsure if the kid was bluffing.

The kid lunged forward, bumping Carpo with his chest. "No you ain't, jackass. Dese phones is outtah ordah."

"No problem," Carpo said, resisting the urge to wipe the kid's sweat off his cheek. He set the phone back into its cradle. "I'll call somewhere else."

The quarter fell into the return slot with a metallic ding. Carpo reached for it, but the kid's hand beat him there. "Now yah ketchin' on, jackshit," the kid cackled as Carpo backed away. "You go an' find anudder tell-a-phone."

A block north, Carpo came across another telephone, a single unit mounted on the wall outside Casey's Coffee Hut. Carpo rifled through his pockets but couldn't find another quarter; he walked inside the diner to make change. At the register, a waitress holding a carafe of coffee approached him. "Table for one, hon'?"

"No, I just need some change for the telephone."

"Sure, let me drop this off."

She walked behind the counter and put the carafe on a hot plate. Steam lifted from the brown stuff like bubbling hot lava.

That's what I want, Carpo thought, *a cup of mud that'll set my hair on end. Tall, black, and scalding hot.* He checked out the window at the entrance of the rental store; still no sign of the man in the trench coat.

"You have the dollar, sir?"

Carpo turned to find the waitress before him, her open palm displaying four shiny quarters. He glanced back, just in time to see a swatch of long black fabric exiting the peep show.

"Son of a bitch," he said as he slapped the dollar bill on the counter and scooped up the quarters.

"I beg your pardon?" the waitress said, planting her hands on her hips. "What did you call me?"

Carpo didn't answer her, he was already out the door.

The noise and bright lights of Times Square faded as the man resumed his westerly course, his arms swinging purposefully, causing the lapels of his trench coat to flare out behind him. Carpo dropped back a block, fearful that the man might see him if he looked over his shoulder. By 10th Avenue, Carpo was checking over his own shoulder too. A gang of young punks loitered on the steps of a burned-out tenement. They eyed Carpo as he passed, one of them cracking an inaudible joke that brought peals of laughter from the group. The man in the trench coat walked halfway to 11th Avenue and stopped in front of the tallest building on the block. He cast a quick glance over his shoulder, the only time that evening he had looked back, before he entered the Hotel Bellmarc.

At one time, back in the twenties or thirties, the Bellmarc must have been a grand hotel. It had sleek art nouveau lines, curlicues that framed the front entrance and windows and reclining nudes along the ledge of the first floor. Now the Bellmarc was an SRO hotel, sandwiched between the gutted shell of a brownstone and a U-Lock-It self-storage center. The hotel sign was missing a few letters; the light-bulbs looked as if they hadn't been replaced in a long while—perhaps since the twenties or thirties.

Carpo waited on the street for ten minutes before he entered the building. An obese white man with a sweat-ringed forehead was sitting inside a caged reception area. The man had his feet on the desk, on either side of a twelve-inch black and white TV that was playing the late movie. The cage wreaked of Chinese takeout and cigar smoke.

"Excuse me," Carpo said. "Do you work here?"

The man glanced at Carpo with a pair of bulging yellow eyes. "I ain't here for my health."

"I was wondering if you could tell me the name of the guy who just walked through here."

The man snorted like a bull. "I ain't here for my wealth neither."

Carpo took a five spot out of his wallet and slid it under the grille. "Okay, who is he?"

Without looking at the bill, the man said, "Cost you better than that."

Carpo pulled out another five and slapped it down.

"Keep going," the man said.

Carpo started to reach for another bill, then stopped. "No," he said. "It's not worth more than ten."

The man's hand shot forward, surprisingly fast for its girth and swallowed the money. "Name's Al," he said, tucking the bills in his pocket, "Al Dicenzo. Least, that's what he goes by around here. Could be Peter Pan for all I know."

The man went back to his TV program. Carpo looked around the lobby. "Excuse me," he said again, "where's the pay phone?"

The man looked at Carpo again, his big head swiveling within a bulge of flesh, as if it weren't really attached to his body, just spinning on his shoulders. "You can use the house phone."

"Where is it?"

The man motioned at the black telephone on his desk.

Carpo grimaced. "How much?"

"Ten more."

Carpo swore under his breath. "You sure there's no public phone?"

"Nuh-uh, owner had it removed. Kept complaining he was getting ripped off by the phone company."

"Imagine that," Carpo muttered as he slapped a ten on the counter. "All right, pass it over."

The man's hand devoured the bill, then he moved the phone across the desk and passed the receiver through the grille. "I gotta dial for you," he said. "What's the number?"

Carpo recited Detective Weissman's number off the gum wrapper. As the call started to go through, he turned his back on the man in the cage.

On the first ring, the detective answered. "It's Weissman."

"Detective Weissman, it's Michael Carpo."

"Michael, I've been waiting for you to—"

Carpo tried to keep his voice a whisper, but his excitement was getting the better of him. "He's here, the Sandman is here. It's the guy I saw Saturday night, the guy on 12th Street."

"It's funny you should say that, Michael. Are you sure?"

"One hundred percent positive. He looks the same, he's wearing that same black trench coat. You've got to hurry over here. I'm at the Hotel Bell—" Carpo broke off in mid-sentence, mouth agape. "What do you mean, it's funny I should say that?"

"We took a suspect into custody about three hours ago. A white male, crying like a baby on Cheryl Street's grave at St. John's Cemetery."

"But that can't be," Carpo said, his grip tightening the phone. "I'm absolutely sure this is the guy."

"Maybe he is, Mike, but he's not the Sandman. The guy we caught tonight is a perfect fit. He was hugging that teddy bear like it was Cheryl herself, sobbing for her to forgive him. We got it all on tape, the crying, the confession, everything." Weissman chuckled giddily. "The sick fucker was sobbing, *Please forgive me.* Can you believe that, Mike? He was saying, *please fuckin' forgive me.*"

Twenty

Carpo stared across the lobby of the Bellmarc, his face paralyzed by an expression of utter shock. *Is Weissman joking? Did they really arrest the Sandman?*

"Michael, are you there?" Weissman asked.

Carpo blinked a few times and shook his head. "Yeah, I'm here."

"You got so quiet, I thought maybe you'd hung up on me." Weissman chuckled again. "This is great news, isn't it? I mean, who would have thought we could nail this guy just by staking out the victim's grave. I don't think it's ever been done before. Hey, Mike, you there?"

"Yeah, yeah, I'm here."

"What's wrong with you? I figured you'd be jumping for joy over this."

"I am, I am," Carpo said, even though inside he wasn't feeling quite right. "I'm just a little shocked by it. I wasn't expecting it to happen so soon."

"Neither were we, I can assure you. Funny thing is, you're the reason for most of it. Without your coverage of the funeral last night, the guy would never have gone to the grave site. In that respect, we totally lucked out."

"Thanks," Carpo said modestly. "So tell me, who is he?"

"His name's Ronald Bailey. He's a forty-three-year-old truck driver from Bensonhurst. And get this, irony of all ironies, the guy lives ten blocks from Detective Spinks."

"Has he confessed yet?"

"Just what we got at the grave site. This guy's a smart one, clammed right up as soon as we put the cuffs on him. Either way, we've got the tape of him, which should be enough." Weissman paused for a moment. "I've got a good feeling on this, Mike. He looks like a perfect fit."

"Congratulations," Carpo said, "you guys did a great job. I'll do my best to see you get credit for your work. Which reminds me of our little bargain. I hope you and Detective Spinks are going to honor those interviews you promised me."

"We're not allowed to say much from here on in, but I'm sure we can work something out after the arraignment." Weissman yawned heavily on the line. "Listen, Mike, I got to go. I'll be back in touch with you in the next couple of days."

After they had disconnected, Carpo stayed with the phone pressed to his ear. He stared across the lobby, lost in his thoughts. It was amazing news, practically a miracle. *And I played a part in it*, he thought. *As small as it was, I helped them catch the Sandman.*

The Bellmarc manager rapped on the cage. "You done yet?"

"I need to make another call," Carpo said. "Would you dial 555-2211?"

"Sure thing, just as soon as you pay for it."

"I just gave you ten bucks."

The man shrugged. "I ain't running Ma Bell here. You wanna make another call, you gotta pay up."

"This is ridiculous," Carpo grumbled as he slapped down a five dollar bill. "Dial 555-2211."

The man glanced at the money but didn't budge. "You gave me ten the last time."

"I'm not paying ten more dollars for a phone call. I'll go on the street and find myself a public phone."

The man started reeling in the cord, as if he would yank the phone out of Carpo's hands.

"Son of a bitch," Carpo said, picking up the five and replacing it with a ten.

"Watch your language, son," the man said as he stuffed the bill into his pocket. "Now, what was that number again?"

Carpo repeated it, then presented his back to the manager as the call went through. The phone on the other end rang twice before a man picked up. "Channel 8 News."

"It's Carpo. Who's this?"

"Hi, Carp. It's David."

"David? What are you doing there so late? Didn't your shift end hours ago?"

"Not tonight. I've still got three crews on the street covering the arrest. You've heard about it, haven't you? The cops nailed the Sandman."

"I just found out. Any chance Sisco's still around?"

"He punched out an hour ago. If it's real important, I could probably beep him."

"It can wait," Carpo said. "I presume he'll be in tomorrow, even though it's Saturday."

"More than likely."

"Just leave a message that I called. Tell him to call me first thing."

"Will do, Carp."

After they said good-bye, Carpo remained on the line, staring at the same spot across the lobby. A smile was on his face, frozen there. Inside, he wasn't sure how he felt.

He was happy about the arrest, of course, and the fact that everything had turned out okay. But a sense of disappointment lingered over him. Big stories came along just once every few years, and the arrest of the Sandman was easily the biggest he had ever covered. Somehow he felt cheated by not being there to witness its conclusion.

Then he remembered the reason, a very good reason, why he had not been there to see the conclusion. One that made him turn to the Bellmarc manager and say, "Let me guess, another ten bucks for a call, right?"

The man nodded, the flab under his chin wobbling like a tray of Jell-O.

Carpo pushed a twenty under the partition. "Here, give me back a ten, then dial this number." He recited Irene's phone number, which she had scratched on the bottom of the gum wrapper. After four rings, she answered the phone.

"Carpo, it's you," she said, drawing out his name in a yawn. "I'm sorry, I just dozed off in front of the TV. Have you heard about the Sandman yet?"

"I just got off the phone with Detective Weissman."

"It's wonderful news, isn't it?"

"Sure is."

She yawned again. "Are you home yet?"

"No, I'm all the way on the west side, 40th and Tenth.

You were right about the guy I followed. I don't think he's anything more than a can collector."

"Don't sound so disappointed."

"I'm not. I just wish I weren't the last person to find out about the arrest."

"I'm sorry, Carpo," she said sincerely. "I know you've been working hard on the story. I hope you're not too upset."

Carpo grinned without making any sound. "Aw, well, I guess the entire night wasn't a washout."

"Oh?"

"At least I got a decent meal at Taste of Siam."

She gasped in mock horror. "If I were near you, Michael Carpo, I'd slug you."

"Mmm, sounds good to me. The *near* part, that is."

"Don't get any ideas, it's late." There was a pause on the line, then Irene said, "My God, it's after two in the morning. No wonder I fell asleep."

"Since tonight's out, maybe we can see each other tomorrow night. Actually, I guess now I should say tonight."

"Carpo, are you asking me out on another date?"

"I guess I am."

"Before I accept," she said testily, "I want you to promise one thing."

"Your wish is my command."

"At the end of the night, when we're walking down the street and I invite you up to my apartment, do me a favor and warn me before yanking my arm out of its socket."

Twenty-One

At eight-thirty the next morning the telephone began jingling. Six rings, then the answering machine picked up. Carpo's voice came on, recited his home phone number, and asked the caller to please leave a message after the beep. The machine beeped and started to record, but the caller, whoever it was, hung up without leaving a message.

Carpo rolled over in bed and went back to sleep.

Fifteen minutes later the phone rang again. Same drill, only this time the machine picked up after three rings. Carpo's voice repeated the same instructions. Beep. Nothing.

Carpo buried his head under the pillow, determined that the calls would not disturb his sleep.

Only twenty seconds later—about the length of time someone would need to hang up the phone, reestablish a dial tone, and call again—the phone rang. This time, after the beep, the caller began to speak.

"Hello, Michael? This is Mitch McLaughlin calling from the *Post*. Are you there, Carpo? I know it's early, but could you please pick up?"

Mitch McLaughlin was a *New York Post* columnist, one of the most prominent and most controversial reporters in the city. His local coverage and hard-hitting columns had won him a Pulitzer a few years back; his abrasive style and wild ambition had won him the disdain of the entire local news corps. Carpo knew that McLaughlin was someone to be handled very carefully.

Carpo yanked a sheet off the bed, wrapped it like a toga around his naked body, and ran for the living room. He snapped up the telephone before the columnist could finish his message. "I'm here, Mitch. What do you want?"

"I'm so glad you picked up," McLaughlin said. "I wanted to talk to you about the arrest last night in St. John's Cemetery."

He wants to interview me about the Sandman. Carpo relaxed enough to take a seat on the couch. "What do you want to know?"

"Has anyone else talked to you yet?"

"About the arrest? No, not yet. I didn't learn about it until late last night, a couple of hours after it was announced."

"So you missed the press conference?"

"I guess so," Carpo said. "I didn't even know there was one."

Carpo could hear papers rustling on the other end. "Let's see," McLaughlin said, "I understand a . . . Detective Weissman and a . . . Detective Spinks from the 9th Precinct, the arresting officers, I understand they mentioned you as playing a role in their investigation."

"I told you, Mitch, I didn't see the press conference."

"Either way, could you tell me a little about this role you played?"

Carpo took a seat on the couch. "I don't know if I'd call

it a role. I was involved mostly because I spotted a possible suspect in Cheryl Street's murder."

"Right, right," McLaughlin murmured. "You saw the man on the street, the one in the black trench coat." More papers rustled. "But is it true that these detectives asked you to provide special coverage of Cheryl Street's funeral the other day?"

Carpo frowned at the question. "Yes, they did. Did they mention that at the press conference?"

"Mm-hmm."

"They asked if I'd get Channel 8 to cover the funeral for a pool feed."

"Did you have to do anything in return?"

Carpo's frown deepened. "What do you mean, Mitch?"

"I mean, did you have to promise to cover the funeral in a certain way? A way that they told you to?"

"I'm not sure I understand."

"Did they ask you to shoot certain things during it? Or maybe I should say *not* shoot certain things?"

"Yes, they asked me not to interview the parents."

"Do you regret that?"

"No."

"You don't?"

Carpo sat upright on the couch. *What the hell is going on?* "No," he said, "I don't regret it at all."

"Why not?"

"Look, why don't you get to the point, Mitch? What are you trying to find out?"

"I'll explain in a sec, just answer the question."

"The answer is no, I don't see anything wrong with not interviewing them. The parents asked the cops to shield them from the media. It was their daughter's funeral and I felt I should respect their wishes."

"I'm not talking about that part," McLaughlin said. "I'm wondering whether the cops asked you to cover any specific parts of the funeral."

Carpo thought about the question for a moment. The only thing Weissman and Spinks had asked him to include was the final shot of the teddy bear. It had seemed a bit strange at the time, but nothing to cause major concern.

"They asked me to include one shot," Carpo admitted, "the last shot in the piece, of Cheryl's teddy bear on the grave. To tell you the truth, I probably would have used it anyway, it was so dramatic."

"Did the detectives ask you to stay away from the parents?"

"I just told you they did."

"But did they specifically say no interviews?"

"What the hell is—"

"Just answer the question, Carpo."

"Yes, they said no interviews."

"Okay," McLaughlin said, his tone a little too jolly. "Let me fill you in on a few things, Carpo, then I want to get your reaction."

"Yes, Mitch, why don't you get to the point."

"The man and the woman who appeared in the funeral the other night, Mr. and Mrs. Street"—more papers rustled over the line—"their real names are Douglas Driscoll and Allison Oshinsky. Doug is a detective at the 9th Precinct. Allie is a captain, same precinct."

Carpo's head began to swim. *Is McLaughlin telling the truth?*

"Detective Driscoll and Captain Oshinsky were posing as the parents of Cheryl Street," McLaughlin continued. "They were part of an overall police sting designed to capture the Sandman."

"Are you joking?"

"Check with Public Information if you don't believe me. They've got the names and ranks of every cop on the force. Driscoll's been a dick eight years. Oshinsky? Shit, she's been saddling the night desk seventeen years."

Carpo got off the couch and began pacing the room. "Mitch, I've got to admit, they pulled the wool over my eyes. I had no idea those weren't Cheryl's parents."

"How does it make you feel?"

Carpo shrugged, which described the way he felt better than words could. "I don't know. I guess it makes me—"

"Angry? Does it make you angry?"

Is it anger? A little bit, Carpo thought. Mostly hurt though. If only because he had done Weissman and Spinks a favor and they had allowed it to get back to him. It showed a certain lack of respect.

"I guess I'm a little angry," Carpo said. "I had no idea what they were up to."

"Really?"

"Yes, really."

"Not even an inkling?"

"No, Mitch," Carpo said hotly. "And before you blow this thing all out of proportion in your column tomorrow, let me say this: The most important thing is that they caught the Sandman. Whether or not I was manipulated by the police, that's the thing we should all be happy about."

"Yeah, yeah, I hear you. Actually, I could use your reaction to that too."

"Reaction to what? The arrest?"

"Not the arrest, Carpo. The *false* arrest."

"What the hell are you talking about?"

McLaughlin laughed, a deep, drawn-out chuckle that showed just how much he was enjoying himself. "Jesus, I really am the first person you've talked to. The man they arrested in the cemetery last night? The one allegedly sobbing for forgiveness on Cheryl Street's grave? It turns out, he's not the Sandman. The cops nailed the wrong guy."

Carpo didn't wait for McLaughlin's chuckle, which he knew was on the way. Nor did he wait for an explanation. Instead, he slammed down the telephone.

Hide, that was his first impulse. Pull the blinds, fasten the chain over the door, then get in bed and bury his head under the pillow. And no matter what, never, never, never answer the telephone again.

Before Carpo could enact the plan, the telephone rang.

"Damn, damn, damn," Carpo said. He nervously paced the living room, waiting for the answering machine to pick up.

No matter who was calling, he vowed that he wouldn't answer the telephone. He might make an exception for McLaughlin, just to tell him to fuck off. Same went for Detective Weissman and Detective Spinks. Anyone else, he was not home.

"Carpo, it's me. Pick up the phone. Come on, Carp, I know you're there. Answer the damn phone."

Carpo picked up the phone. "Hi, Sisco."

"Good morning, Carpo."

"How are you?"

"Cut the crap," Sisco shouted, "I'm terrible, just terrible, and you're even worse. Have you heard this news about the Sandman yet?"

"I just got off the phone with Mitch McLaughlin. He was trying to get my reaction to it."

"What did you tell him?"

"I didn't say anything. I hung up on him."

"Way to deal with adversity, Carp, bury your head in the sand."

Carpo winced at the image; what he had really wanted to do was bury his head under a pillow. *Why did I answer the phone?*

"So you know the story?" Sisco asked.

"Only what McLaughlin told me."

"And what was that?"

Carpo took a deep breath. "He said two cops were posing as Cheryl's parents at the funeral. He also said that they arrested the wrong man at the grave site."

"Did he tell you that Cheryl Street's casket was empty? That the teddy bear never belonged to her? That the entire funeral was a sham?"

Carpo rubbed his eyes, wishing he was back in bed, having a bad dream. Meekly, he asked, "The entire thing was fake?"

"Yes, whole damn thing. Why do you think they offered us exclusive coverage? The less media hanging around, the less of a chance someone would start asking questions."

"What about the guy they arrested?"

"His name's Ronald Bailey." Sisco said the words like

he was spitting fire. "Three months ago he was involved in a hit-and-run that killed a young girl. I remember when we did the story at Channel 8. Apparently, this guy went to the girl's grave last night to ask for forgiveness, only the fool ended up on the wrong grave. Before he knew it, he was handcuffed and being read his Miranda rights. Bailey figured he was under arrest for the hit-and-run, so he didn't tell them anything. It wasn't until this morning when he met his lawyer that he realized the cops were accusing him of being the Sandman."

"Wow," Carpo said, "that's bad luck."

"Damn straight it's bad luck. It's bad luck for him, and it's real bad luck for you. Did you have any idea this funeral was a hoax?"

"None whatsoever."

"How about that the cops were using it to set a trap for the Sandman?"

"No."

"Is it true they asked you to include that shot of the teddy bear at the end?"

Carpo rubbed his temples. "Kind of."

"What the hell does that mean?"

"They asked me at the funeral to use it. I didn't know why at the time, but it didn't seem like a big deal."

"Did you know Cheryl's parents were cops?"

"No."

"Carpo . . ." Sisco said, voice filled with doubt.

"No way," Carpo said firmly. "The police told me they were Cheryl's parents. Why would I have questioned them?"

Carpo had believed the answer would mollify Sisco; instead, it had quite the opposite effect. Sisco bellowed so loud that Carpo had to hold the phone away from his ear. "Because you're a journalist! You're supposed to ask questions and dig for answers. You're also supposed to check facts. Got that, Carpo? Check facts!"

"But the cops told—"

"I know, I know, the cops told you the facts, so why bother? You bother because sometimes the cops are wrong, sometimes they lie, and sometimes they try to manipulate. That's why."

Carpo slumped onto the couch. "Sisco, I'm sorry. Flatout, no excuses, I totally screwed up. It never occurred to me that the cops might be lying. I promise you, it will never happen again."

"You're right, it won't, but not because of your own doing. Effective immediately, you are off the Street story. Hear me? No more field-producing, no more interviews, no more Sweeps series." Sisco paused a moment, letting the edict register with Carpo. "Do you understand the magnitude of what you've done?"

"Loud and clear."

"So help me God, if I find out you're still working on the story, in any capacity at all, I will come down on you so hard, you won't know what hit you!"

"Okay, okay, I understand," Carpo said, hoping to calm the executive producer.

But it was too late. Major Sisco had hung up on him.

Twenty-Two

For the rest of the morning and early afternoon, Carpo stayed on the couch and watched television. He started with an episode of *American Gladiators*, in which muscle-bound men and women with names like Thor and Blaze competed in various bizarre athletic events. Then he sat through an hour-long infomercial featuring a hyperactive man with a ponytail who was trying to sell an abdominal exercise machine. Finally, he watched an episode of *This Old House*. The program taught him everything he needed to know about lawn irrigation systems—not exactly pertinent information for a city dweller, but it did an adequate job of calming his nerves.

Sometime around three, craving food and information, he got dressed and ran to the newsstand on Second Avenue. He bought a bagel at the deli counter, along with the three newspapers. He didn't look at them until he was out on the sidewalk.

The local rags all headlined the Sandman story, but he quickly discovered that the stories inside were staler than his rock-hard bagel. "NABBED!" was splashed across the front of the *New York Post* in massive black letters.

Beneath it there was a photo of the press conference where the police had announced the arrest of the Sandman. Crowded together on the dais at One Police Plaza were the mayor, police commissioner, and Manhattan D.A. A bevy of lesser officials jostled behind the platform to get their faces attached to the biggest story of the year. The focus of all their attention: Weissman and Spinks. The detectives stood behind a cluster of microphones, apparently fielding questions from the media. The caption beneath the photograph explained their cocksure swagger: *Hero Cops Capture Sandman.*

The *Daily News* targeted sentimental readers with its coverage of the arrest. The front page carried the headline "SANDMAN SNAGGED!" with a snapshot of Cheryl Street's grave, the soggy teddy bear propped against the stone marker. The photo caption, in smaller lettering, read: *Serial Killer Arrested at Grave of Victim.*

The *New York Times* also carried the story on its front page, appearing in a box outlined in the lower left corner. No photograph, and just a story sedately headlined: *Alleged Serial Killer Taken into Custody.*

Carpo noted that the *Times* was the only paper to insert "alleged" in the headline, as was proper when referring to an unindicted suspect. The paper had also gotten it right when referring to the status of the case. At the time the papers went to press, the police had not charged Ronald Bailey with a crime; they had only taken him into custody.

None of the papers made any mention of false arrests, police stings, or fake parents. Nor were there details on a Channel 8 employee who had conspired with the authorities to capture the Sandman. Despite the absence of these revelations, Carpo felt little solace. He knew his luck was bound to change once the local news shows aired at six o'clock.

He tucked the newspapers under his arm and trudged to 12th Street. As he crossed the street, a familiar-looking late-model sedan zipped toward him. The car ground to a halt and Detective Weissman poked his head out the window. "Michael, we were just coming to talk to you."

Carpo didn't break his stride. "Really? I don't think we have much to say to each other."

Spinks was behind the steering wheel. He kept the wheels of the car rolling, matching Carpo's pace down the sidewalk. Weissman held his arms out the window, as if he meant to physically stop Carpo. "Wait, Michael, we really need your help."

Carpo smirked at the detective's statement. "I'm sure you do."

"Seriously, Michael, we need to discuss the guy you followed last night. His name's Al Dicenzo. We ran a check on him this morning. The guy's got a rap sheet longer than *War and Peace*. He looks promising."

"More promising than Ron Bailey?"

"I'm sorry about that, Michael. It was a little miscalculation. Sometimes these things don't turn out the way they're supposed to."

Carpo stopped walking. "Is that what you guys are calling this, a little miscalculation? Seems to me it's a big fuck-up."

"Cut the shit, Carpo," Spinks shouted across the front seat. "Quit acting like a damn baby and get in the car."

The word "baby" hit Carpo like a slap in the face. His eyes started to water and chin quivered. Without thinking, he curled his hands into fists and charged the car.

"You're an asshole, Spinks, you hear me? You're nothing but a damn Keystone Kop! Now, get the hell out of my sight before I kick your—"

Spinks wrenched the wheel of the car toward Carpo, as if he meant to run him over. Before he did, he slammed on the brakes and rammed the car into park. A shudder traveled up the length of the sedan.

"Kick my what?" Spinks yelled back. "You goddamned baby, come over here and say it. I'll give you something real to cry about."

"Knock it off!" Weissman shouted at his partner. He turned to Carpo. "You're right, Michael, we totally messed up. I thought we had him, I swear I did, or I never would have gone public with the story."

Carpo whirled on the detective. He pointed his finger at Weissman's face "What happened to you Thursday? Why didn't you meet us at the cemetery like we had planned?"

Weissman eyes widened, but he didn't answer.

"You went to the morgue to check Cheryl's body," Carpo accused. "We had spoken just that morning and I told you that your brown-eye theory didn't hold up. Whatever came of that?"

Weissman opened his mouth as if to speak, but nothing came out.

"Damn you, Weissman, level with me! Cheryl's eyes weren't brown, were they?"

"No," Weissman admitted, "they weren't."

"Why didn't you tell me the truth?"

Weissman looked to his partner for help, but Spinks was busy scraping dirt from his thumbnail.

"I'm through with it," Carpo announced as he backed away from the car. "You guys have known since the get-go that the Sandman didn't kill Cheryl Street. You've been playing me this entire time."

"Mike, I'm telling you," Weissman said, "Dicenzo's our man. I got a real feeling on this one. Just give us five minutes, that's all we're asking, five minutes of your time."

"This is the only five I'm giving you," Carpo said. He held up his hand and waved good-bye at the detectives. "Now get out of my life."

Back in his apartment, Carpo settled back on the couch. He forced down the bagel, then he watched most of the Yankee game. It was a blowout, and even under the circumstances he stuck with it longer than he should have. When a eighth-inning homer put the Yanks up by eleven runs, Carpo grabbed the remote control. He channel-surfed through the cable box, settling on a wild animal documentary on the Discovery Channel. At six o'clock he said a silent prayer, then switched to the local news.

As he had anticipated, WCBS and WNBC both led with the stunning developments in the Sandman case. Channel 2 started with the announcement by a police official that forty-three-year-old Ronald Bailey of Bensonhurst, Brooklyn, was under arrest for vehicular homicide. Almost as an afterthought, the official mentioned that police were now ninety-nine percent certain that Bailey was not the Sandman. Channel 4 ran the same police statement, followed by a background story on Ronald Bailey. The reporter had managed to land an interview with Bailey's girlfriend, who expressed shock that Bailey had been arrested for the hit-and-run death of a fourteen-year-old girl.

Both news reports consumed roughly five minutes of the first section. Carpo flipped back and forth between them, bracing for any mention of his name or his involvement in the case. It never happened. The reports ended, the newscasts moved on to other stories, then the stations broke for commercial.

He sighed heavily and headed to the kitchen for a soda. As he passed the telephone, it started to ring. He could see by the blinking red light that messages had been piling up all day. The phone rang just three times before the machine picked up and his voice came on. The machine beeped several times as the tape fast-forwarded, then a higher-pitched beep sounded, signaling that it was recording. Irene's voice filled the apartment.

"Carpo? Are you home? I just heard the most incredible thing on Channel 4. If you're there, would you please pick up?"

Carpo fidgeted by the telephone, wondering if he should answer it. Finally, he snapped up the phone and quickly said, "I'm here, Irene, I'm here," before she could hang up.

"Carpo, where have you been? I must have left five messages for you today."

"I'm sorry. I've been . . . busy."

"Did you hear what they just said on Channel 4? The reporter said they arrested the wrong man at Cheryl's grave last night. Is it true?"

"Yes," he said hoarsely, "I'm afraid it is."

Irene was quiet for a moment. "I don't understand. Detective Weissman sounded so confident on the phone last night. What could have gone wrong?"

Briefly, Carpo recapped the story of Ronald Bailey and his false arrest, leaving out the portions concerning the police sting at the graveyard and his use of the teddy bear video.

"So you've known about this all day?" Irene asked. "Why didn't you tell me?"

Carpo sucked in his breath and held it. He felt the pressure rise in his temples. *How much should I tell her? Should I say that I'm in trouble? That my name's probably going to be in the paper tomorrow. That I might even get shit-canned from Channel 8.*

"What's going on, Carpo? Are you in trouble? Is that why you didn't call?

Should I tell her?

"Damn you, Carpo, answer me! Are you in trouble?"

He released the air with a tense whoosh. "Yes, yes, I'm in trouble," he said, "I'm absolutely screwed. Weissman and Spinks set me up. Cheryl's funeral was a fake. It was a complete setup so the police could capture the Sandman."

Irene's voice sounded hollow as she said, "The funeral was fake?"

"Remember how Spinks told me Cheryl's parents were from Roanoke, Virginia, instead of Pennsylvania? It's because those weren't her parents. They were two cops from the 9th Precinct playing the part. The whole thing was a sham. Even the coffin was empty."

Carpo waited for a response, but the line remained silent.

Tell it all, he thought. *If you want any chance of a relation-ship, you can't keep secrets from her.*

"I'm in big trouble, Irene. The cops were using the funeral to lure the Sandman to the graveyard and I was their bait. They asked me to include a shot of Cheryl's teddy bear at the end of my report Thursday night. I went along with it, not realizing what they had in mind."

"You had no idea it was a trap?"

"None at all, I swear. I thought it was strange, but I didn't question it."

He waited for her to speak; all he could hear was the sound of her breathing. "Irene, say something."

"I'm sorry, Carpo, I don't know if there's anything to say. I don't feel . . . I guess I'm not . . . comfortable with the way this is turning out."

Carpo collapsed on the couch. He closed his eyes and buried his face in his hands. *She's blowing me off. She's telling me she doesn't want to see me again.*

And then she said it. "I think I need some time, Carpo. Time to think. Time to decide what I should do. Just be patient with me, okay? I'll . . . call you later."

Carpo shook his head, stunned by her words. *Time? Space? Patience?* How could she ask such things of him? Wasn't he the one in trouble?

She said good-bye and, without waiting for his response, disconnected. Carpo stayed on the couch, receiver pressed to his ear, until a recorded voice came on the line and told him to hang up. As he did, he actually wondered if he would ever see Irene again.

*   *   *

At six-thirty the three independents aired their versions of the Sandman story. Carpo kept his set tuned to Channel 8, figuring that they would be under the most pressure to report his involvement in the case.

Like the networks, the broadcast started with the biggest development: the false arrest of the Sandman suspect. When the opening credits finished, the studio lights came up to reveal Maria and Terry at the anchor desk. Between them, a graphic of Cheryl Street's grave with the caption *Setup!*

"Good evening, I'm Maria Gomez," Maria said once the opening music had faded.

"And I'm Terry Chiltzom. It's back to square one in the Sandman investigation."

The shot switched to camera one, a close-up of Maria's face with the same graphic over her shoulder. She began to read off the TelePrompTer.

"Just hours after announcing the stunning arrest of the Sandman, police now say it was all a mistake. They arrested the wrong man. We get more on this shocking development from Mary Snow, who's live at St. John's Cemetery in Queens. Mary?"

The picture dissolved to a fuzzy remote shot in the parking lot of the cemetery. The reporter, Mary Snow, briefly and breathlessly recapped the major events of the day: Ronald Bailey was under arrest for vehicular homicide; he was no longer a suspect in the Sandman murders; police had no new leads in the case.

As the reporter wrapped up her report, Carpo squirmed

to the edge of the couch. He knew his turn was next. His entire body was tensed like a metal spring; one false move and he'd likely catapult across the room.

The remote feed cut to the studio: camera two, showing Maria at the anchor desk. " *Thanks, Mary,*" Maria said, then she looked at her co-anchor. *"Terry?"*

The shot cut from camera two to camera three, an isolated shot of Terry, who began reading.

"The latest news in the Sandman case has tarnished the police department's work up to this point. It has also raised some troubling questions about the media's involvement in the investigation. For that story, we turn to Jerry Russo, who's live outside the 9th Precinct. Jerry?"

The camera cut to a remote shot of Jerry Russo standing on the front steps of the precinct house. The shot was framed to include the front door of the precinct. A chyron along the bottom of the screen identified the location as "5th Street, the East Village." In the upper left corner, a smaller chyron reminded viewers that the report was "live."

"Terry, for the past eighteen months the 9th precinct has been the headquarters for the Sandman task force. Last night this place was abuzz with excitement after officials announced they had finally captured the elusive Sandman. Well, what a difference a day makes. Tonight tempers are flaring and fingers are pointing after a big arrest turns out to be . . . a big mistake."

The reporter dissolved behind video from Friday night's press conference. There was a short pop of natural sound, then Jerry's voice came on tape.

"Several details have come to light in the aftermath of

last night's blockbuster police announcement. Perhaps the most startling: Police now admit Thursday afternoon's funeral for the Sandman's sixth victim, Cheryl Street, was a fake, nothing more than an intricate sting operation designed to capture the Sandman."

The video dissolved to the footage Carpo had shot at the cemetery on Thursday. It started with the processional moving down the path toward Cheryl Street's grave. The video ground to super slow speed as the fake Mr. and Mrs. Street walked into the shot.

"Not only was the victim's casket empty, police now admit that Cheryl Street's parents were actually two New York City police officers in disguise. The reason for the deception? Police were hoping this video would lure the Sandman to the grave site."

The video dissolved again; Carpo winced when he saw his face appear. It was the video from the interview he had given almost a week earlier, when he had described the man he had seen from his window.

"The controversy has done more than tarnish the reputation of the NYPD," Jerry said in a solemn tone. *"It has damaged the reputation of the local media as well as the reputation of this station, Channel 8 News. One of our employees—news writer Michael Carpo—was apparently working with the police to get coverage for the fake funeral. As a result of his involvement in the sting, Channel 8 has suspended Michael Carpo from his job, effective immediately. They have also released the following statement."*

The screen cut to a graphic printing the Channel 8 statement, which Jerry narrated as well.

"We apologize to our viewers for the scandal surrounding

*the funeral of Cheryl Street. We hope it will in no way
diminish our viewers' confidence in the integrity of Channel
8 News."*

Carpo grabbed the remote control and turned off the
TV. He didn't need to see the reporter come back onscreen
and wrap up the live shot. Nor did he need to hear any more
details about the Sandman investigation and the conse-
quences it might have for him. All he needed to know he
had just learned.

Channel 8 had suspended him from work.

For the first time ever, Carpo called down to Little
Poland to have his dinner delivered. He couldn't bear the
thought of going to the diner, not after the entire city had
seen his picture in connection with the false arrest. He actually wondered if he would ever feel comfortable going out
in public again.

The delivery man arrived with his parcel of food. As
Carpo paid him, he watched the man's face for any sign of
recognition, but the man seemed more interested in the five-
dollar tip Carpo slipped him.

Carpo unloaded the food and ate it on the couch. When
he was done, he stacked the dishes in the sink, on top of the
pile of dirty coffee mugs. As he was drying his hands on the
dish towel, the telephone rang. When the answering machine
started recording, Irene's voice came on.

*"Hi, Carpo, it's me. I know you're there and I under-
stand if you don't want to talk to me. I just wanted to tell
you that I'm sorry. I didn't mean to freak out like that
before, I just didn't understand what was happening. I*

want you to know that I'm sorry, really, really sorry, for everything—"

Carpo snapped up the phone. "Hi, I'm on."

"I'm so glad you picked up," Irene said. "I was starting to worry that you'd never talk to me again."

He smiled, despite the circumstances, and muttered, "That's not possible."

"Did you hear what I said on the machine? I'm sorry, Carpo, really sorry, for deserting you this afternoon. I don't know what came over me, I just freaked out when you started telling me about the funeral."

"That's okay, I was pretty freaked out myself."

"I can't imagine what this day has been like for you. Is there anything I can do to help?"

"Can you get me my job back?"

"If there was any humanly way possible, I would. I feel terrible about this. Just before I called, I was staring across the street at your windows, thinking, how can I make this up to him? How can I make him trust me again?"

"Irene, I never stopped trusting you."

As he spoke, he wandered into the bedroom; the phone cord trailed behind him, reaching all the way to the window. He pulled open the blind and stared across the street. In one of Irene's windows he spotted a shadowy figure, backlit by the lights in her apartment. He waved at the figure and said, "Hi there."

He heard her gasp of surprise, then the figure waved back. "Hi, Carpo."

A mere twenty yards separated them, so little that he could almost make out her face, but the psychological distance made her feel miles away. Suddenly, Carpo ached with the desire to be with her. On the same side of the street. In the same room.

"I owe you an apology too," he said. "I should have called you this morning, as soon as I found out I was in trouble. It wasn't right to let you learn it from a news report."

"I understand. You were upset and needed to be alone." She moved the telephone to her other ear, the movement producing a crackle of feedback in Carpo's ear. "But I hope you won't always be like that," she said. "Someday I hope you let me crack that hard shell you wear around you all the time. I want a chance to see what you're carrying around inside there."

Her words brought a reluctant smile to his face. He stared hard at the fuzzy, faceless figure—visible, audible, yet totally intangible.

"I . . . miss you," he said.

"What?"

He blushed. "I said, I miss you."

Irene didn't answer, which caused him to blush even deeper. He turned away from the window, just in case she had a clear view of his face.

"Where are you going?"

"Nowhere. "

"Did you just say you miss me?"

"Two times."

"I'm sorry I didn't answer, but I was trying to think if a guy's ever said that to me before."

"That they miss you?"

"Yes."

He waited for a second, then asked, "Has anyone?"

"No." Irene paused, then said, "Carpo, do you realize we've never even kissed?"

"It's not by choice.

"True, but I kind of wish it would happen. I thought it was going to happen last night, and then we ran into the guy on the street. That seems to be the story for us, huh? We never catch a break."

"No, we sure don't."

Suddenly, Irene exclaimed, "Oooh, I'm so jealous!"

"What about?"

"There's a man and a woman walking arm in arm down the street, just like we were last night. Gosh, I'm envious."

"Why?"

"Silly! Because I wish it were you and me."

Carpo looked down at the street but couldn't see the couple. "Where are they?"

"They're on your side of the street. I'll bet they just ate a nice dinner at the Taste of Siam. Say, I could go for some Thai. How about you?"

"Unfortunately, I just ate." He put his face in the opening between the window and the sill and looked down at the street. "Where are they?"

"Who, the couple? They're on your side of the street."

"I know, but which direction?" He craned his neck forward until his hair brushed against the screen. "I can't see them."

"They're on the right. No, wait, actually that's your left. A man and a woman. Carpo, let's go out tonight. I know you ate dinner, but we could just hang out somewhere, get a drink or something. It would take your mind off all this Sandman business."

"I don't know if I feel comfortable enough. They plastered my face all over Channel 8 tonight. I'd feel like everyone was staring at me."

As he spoke, Carpo continued to look at 12th Street. On his side of the street he could see the cars parked along the curb, the trees and the tops of the streetlamps. He still could not see the man and the woman. "Are they on my left?"

"No, now they're underneath you. Forget about them. I've got an idea. Why don't I run out and buy a bottle of vino and come over to your place? We can just hang out. That way, there won't be any other people. What do you say, Carpo? Carpo, are you listening to me?"

"Uh—yeah," he muttered as he checked straight below, then to the left, then to the right.

"Don't sound so excited."

"No, no, it's not that. It's just … damn it … I still can't …" A jolt passed through Carpo's body. His hands locked onto the windowsill as if he were being pushed into the street. "My God, Irene, I still can't see them! Do you hear me? I still can't see the couple!"

"Carpo, why are you yelling? It's no big deal. They're already down the street."

"But before, when I was trying to—" He stood up too fast and cracked the back of his head on the window. "Ouch!"

"Carpo, what's wrong with you? I can hear you all the way across the street."

"Ouch, ouch, ouch," he sang as he hopped around the bedroom in pain.

"What are you doing?"

He didn't answer. He kept his eyes squeezed shut as he rubbed the egg-sized bump that was already popping out of his scalp.

Despite the pain shooting through his head, all Carpo could think was: *I know who murdered Cheryl Street.*

Twenty-Three

There was no light showing from beneath Edith Garbanzo's door when Carpo walked down to the fifth floor of his building. He knocked on the door, waited twenty or thirty seconds, then knocked again.

The lights came on, under the door and through the peephole, then footsteps gingerly approached the hallway. The old woman demanded, "Who's there?" her voice husky with fear.

"It's me, Mrs. Garbanzo, Michael Carpo. Can I talk to you for a moment?"

The floor creaked, then the door shifted. Carpo imagined her leaning against it as she studied him through the peephole.

"Who are you?"

"It's Michael Carpo. The guy who lives above you, in apartment 6E. I'm the one who always carries your trash down to the street."

"What do you want?"

Carpo stared at the peephole, hoping to make eye contact with her. "I know this sounds strange, but I need to look out your window."

"What for?"

"I need to see a man and a woman who are walking down the street. I think I know them. It'll only take me a second, Mrs. Garbanzo, I promise. All I need to do is peek out the window."

The door shifted again. "How do I know you're really Michael?"

He centered himself before the peephole and took a step back so as to cast himself in the hallway light. "Look at me, Mrs. Garbanzo. You know what I look like."

"Yes, I can see you there. But I don't let strangers into my apartment."

"I'm not a stranger, Mrs. Garbanzo, I live right above you. We talk practically every day."

"No matter, young man, I'm not letting you in. I don't open my door for anyone unless I've invited them." The pressure released on the door and the floor creaked again, this time signaling Mrs. Garbanzo's retreat.

Carpo swore silently. He had to get into the apartment. Somehow, some way, he had to look out Mrs. Garbanzo's window and see the street.

He knocked again.

"Go away!" the old woman shouted. "Leave me alone or I'll call the police."

Carpo reminded himself to stay calm. Mrs. Garbanzo was only doing the right thing. The thing Cheryl Street and five other women had failed to do.

"Mrs. Garbanzo, please hear me out. This is very important. I absolutely must look out your window tonight.

If it'll make you feel any better, you can stand in the hallway while I look. That way, you can run or scream for help if I do something that makes you feel uncomfortable."

"How do I know you don't have a knife or a gun? I've seen it done on TV. As soon as I open my door, you push your way in."

Carpo held his hands up in clear view. "But look at me, Mrs. Garbanzo. My hands are empty. I don't have any weapons."

She stepped close again and studied him through the peephole. After several seconds she said, "How long is this going to take?"

"One minute. Not even, thirty seconds. I just need to peek out the window, then I'll leave."

"Why can't you look out your own window?"

"Because I live too high up. I can't see anything."

"Oh, all right," Mrs. Garbanzo said, "if you really must. But if you do anything to frighten me, anything at all, I'll scream. I'll scream so loud, the entire block will hear me."

"I promise, I won't scare you."

A lock clicked, then a second one. The door opened three inches, the chain still fastened. Carpo kept his hands in the air as Mrs. Garbanzo's face, wrinkled and wary, appeared in the space. She looked him up and down, appraising him in the light, her milky eyes glaring with suspicion.

If everyone had been this cautious, Carpo thought, *there wouldn't even be a Sandman. He wouldn't have gotten into anyone's apartment.*

Mrs. Garbanzo slid the chain off the door. She opened it an inch at a time, then stepped quickly into the hallway.

She was wearing a white robe and furry slippers; her blue hair was secured beneath a thin mesh net. In one of her hands she held a bag of trash. "You can carry this down when you're through," she said, dropping the bag near the stairs.

"I'll take it right down, no problem." Carpo stepped around her and entered the apartment. "I really appreciate that you're letting me do this."

Mrs. Garbanzo shrugged and gave a little shake of her head, making it clear that she thought he was crazy. "For the life of me, Michael, I can't figure out what's wrong with the view in your own apartment."

As it turned out, there was nothing wrong with the view from his apartment: It was almost identical. The only difference was the sight line, captured by Mrs. Garbanzo's windows ten or twelve feet lower. Instead of looking down at the tree, Carpo was now able to see it from the side. The branches looked gnarled and filthy, coated with years of black soot. On the sidewalk, the base of the streetlight was visible, the gray paint peeling off in giant flakes. The fire hydrant squatted next to it like a small red figure holding out its arms, about two feet from the curb.

But Carpo couldn't see anyone or anything else on his side of the street. Not the pedestrians that he knew had to be down there, strolling along the sidewalk, on their way to dinner or a movie. Nor any of the trash cans, which he had seen stacked by the wrought-iron fence outside his building. Most important of all, he couldn't see the steps leading to the entrance of his building.

* * *

"Did you find what you were looking for?" Mrs. Garbanzo asked a moment later when he emerged from her apartment.

"Yes, thanks, I did," Carpo said, even though quite the opposite was true.

He hadn't found what he was looking for. He had found what he was expecting.

Back in his apartment, Carpo made a few phone calls before he went into the kitchen and ladled a half-dozen scoops of coffee into the filter of the Rancilio. As he waited for the coffee to brew, it occurred to him that he had forgotten to pay his weekly visit to Java The Hut. He couldn't recall the last time that had happened.

More incredible, a full week had passed since he had heard Irene's cries for help. Seven full days, almost to the hour, since her screams had erupted on 12th Street, shattering the calm of the night and destroying the comfortable routine of his life. The time had passed like a blip on a radar screen; he had to struggle to remember all the crazy twists and turns that had filled it.

When enough brown liquid had piddled into the carafe, he carried a mug into the bedroom and dragged a chair to the window. Twenty yards away, the windows of Cheryl Street's apartment stared back at him, wide and blank, like a pair of dead eyes. Earlier that week, the sight had disturbed him; it had served as a reminder of the unspeakable atrocities that had occurred within spitting distance of his bedroom. Tonight, however, this view served to strengthen him. It reminded him of his purpose, of all that was still at stake.

In a short time, he thought, *I'll put the story of Cheryl's murder to rest forever.*

Over the next two hours, as the sun dipped below the buildings, Carpo sipped coffee and maintained a silent vigil over the face of Cheryl Street's building.

Though not readily apparent, there was plenty of life beneath the skin of dirty red bricks and rain-spotted windows. Shadows that whisked past windows; lights that turned on and off; the sounds of a piano, television sets, and the occasional ring of a telephone.

Carpo saw Irene leave the building and return a short time later with two brown paper bags filled with groceries. Ludwig Monroe came down and sat on the front steps. He smoked two cigarettes and chatted with Violetta Ignacio when she emerged with Suki. The tiny dog exploded with a frenzy of barks when George Bento stepped outside. The super made a motion as if he would kick the dog, which served to silence the animal. Bento walked to the sidewalk and dragged the building's trash cans to the curb for the morning pickup.

Sometime before eight, the streetlamps flickered on with a phosphorescent buzz. In their pale white glow, a young man walked down 12th Street from the direction of Third Avenue. He was alone, and dressed in a flannel shirt, faded jeans, and a pair of Timberland work boots. The boots made a dull, scratchy noise as he trudged up the steps and entered the building.

Carpo stomped his own feet a few times to get the blood flowing to them. He kept his eyes riveted on the set of windows beneath Cheryl's apartment. After a minute or so—about the time one would need to gather the mail, climb four flights of stairs, and unlock the door—the lights came on in the apartment. Carpo stood and slowly backed away from the window.

Tommy Abilene was home.

Twenty-Four

An hour later, when Tommy Abilene answered his door, he was still wearing his blue jeans and bulky construction boots, but he had removed the flannel shirt. He stood bare-chested in the doorway, his neck and biceps ringed by a taut tan line. The contrast in flesh color was so sharp, it appeared as though he were wearing a skin-colored T-shirt.

"What's up, Carpo?" Tommy asked as he cast a sideways glance at the Channel 8 cameraman, Roman Santiago. "What brings you here?"

"Sorry to bother you so late," Carpo said, "but I got the go-ahead from my boss to begin shooting interviews for my special project."

"The series on Cheryl," Tommy said. "Sure, I remember from the last time we talked."

"If it's not too much trouble, I was hoping we could do a quick interview," Carpo said. "Shouldn't take more than ten or fifteen minutes."

Tommy's eyes dragged across the pile of equipment next to his door: two duffel bags, a folded tripod, and a Betacam video camera. "I don't know how much help I'll be, I hardly even knew her."

"As I found out, not many people did. I thought we could

go over the stuff we talked about last time, just to get it on tape."

Tommy nodded but didn't move out of the doorway. "I can repeat what I said the last time, but if you're looking for some sort of insight on her life, I won't have much to say."

"Just answer the best you can," Carpo said. "If there's something you don't know, we'll skip it and move on to another question."

"Okay, I guess." Tommy stepped aside. As Carpo and Roman began lugging equipment into the apartment, he asked, "How did you get into the building? Did someone buzz you in?"

"We interviewed a few other people," Carpo said. "When we passed your apartment, I saw the light was on, so I decided to give it a shot."

"Who did you speak to?"

"Let's see, we talked to Irene Foster, Ludwig Monroe, Victor Mendez, and your super, George. I forget his last name."

"It's Bento." Tommy scratched a patch of blond fuzz in the center of his chest. "I can see you interviewing Irene and Ludwig. Maybe even Georgie. But why waste your time with Victor? The guy's an Uncle Pervie."

Carpo set down one of the duffels. "He's a what?"

"An Uncle Pervie. You know, a pervert. The guy thinks every girl on the planet wants to jump his stump. Cheryl used to say he made her uncomfortable."

"It's not going to make a difference," Carpo said. "He didn't say anything we could use."

When the equipment was inside the apartment, Carpo

stood in the center of the room and appraised the space. The apartment looked as it had the last time: dirty dishes stacked in the sink; mail scattered on the breakfast table; clothes scattered over the furniture and across the floor. He turned to Roman and said, "Let's shoot this by the window. We'll move the chair aside and go handheld. Ten minutes of Q-and-A, then we'll wrap."

Roman nodded and began carting the equipment to the window.

"How long's it going to take to set up?" Tommy asked.

"Five minutes or so," Carpo answered.

"Maybe I'll go put on a shirt and comb my hair," Tommy said. "I don't want to come across as a total grub." He went to the closet and selected some clothes, then he walked into the bathroom and shut the door.

Carpo helped Roman with the lighting. They pulled two aluminum stands from a duffel and erected them on either side of the window, about five yards apart. On top of each one Roman fastened a metal light box. He made Carpo stand by the window as a target while he adjusted the height and direction of the bulbs. Afterward, he used wooden clothes-pins to clip a variety of colored gels over the light boxes. He adjusted the plastic gels, experimenting with their thickness and color, until the wall behind Carpo was bathed in a warm blue swath of light.

Next, Roman went to work on setting up the camera. He unfolded the tripod and locked down its rubber treads, then fiddled with the built-in leveler until the unit was perfectly aligned. He clipped the camera into place and turned it on, then slid a thirty-minute field tape into its body. Finally,

Carpo held a piece of white paper in front of the lens so Roman could white-balance the camera.

Tommy emerged from the bathroom as they were setting up the microphone. His hair was combed immaculately off his face, held in place by water or styling gel. He had changed into a blue-striped button-down shirt, a pair of khakis, and shiny penny loafers. The transformation was startling; the rugged, construction worker edge was supplanted by a clean-cut, preppie appearance. Suddenly it didn't seem so strange to Carpo that Cheryl might have fallen in love with him.

Roman slipped a Channel 8 flag over the microphone, handed it to Carpo, and said, "Gimme some sound."

"Test, one-two-three," Carpo said into the microphone. "This is Michael Carpo, test, three-two-one."

Roman adjusted the audio levels, then he half crouched behind the camera and peered through the viewfinder. He adjusted the height on the tripod again, then he winked at Carpo. "Your fellah is ready."

"Tommy, how about you?" Carpo asked. "Ready for the interview?"

"Yeah, sure. Where should I stand?"

"Over here, by the window." Carpo steered Tommy in front of the camera so they were facing each other, the window in between them. "Turn a bit toward the camera," Carpo told Tommy. "A little more. That's it, so Roman can get your face."

Tommy stood stiff as a lead toy soldier, arms pinned to his sides, eyes staring directly into the camera. "How come it's not pointing at you?"

"Because I'm not supposed to be on camera."

"How come?"

"I'm only field-producing the piece," Carpo explained. "If I stay off camera, I can drop pieces of the interview anywhere in the story. That way it looks like the reporter was here doing the interview." Carpo waved his hand in the air until he caught Tommy's attention. "Tommy, I said stop staring at the camera. I want you to look at me during the interview."

Tommy nodded, then turned back to the camera and resumed his wide-eyed stare. "What are you going to ask me?"

"Just some general questions about Cheryl."

"Like what?"

"I'd rather not say, so it comes out fresh during the interview." Carpo shot a glance at Roman and asked, "Are we rolling?"

"You've got speed," Roman said, keeping his eye pressed to the viewfinder.

Carpo pushed the microphone under Tommy's chin, two inches from the man's quivering Adam's apple. "Okay, Tommy, last time we talked was Wednesday. It was three days after Cheryl Street was murdered in her apartment. Is there anything new you can tell me about her?"

Tommy swallowed nervously. "I don't think so."

"Okay, why don't we discuss some of the stuff we went over the last time? We'll start with an easy question. Give me your impression of Cheryl."

"Well, like I said the last time, Cheryl seemed like a nice girl. Friendly, real pretty, and she seemed to have her head screwed on straight. I used to pass her sometimes on the stairs or down by the mailboxes. She used to tell me about the places she'd been to, the cities she'd seen. She was lucky 'cause her job took her to a lot of different cities. Sometimes she'd—" Tommy broke off when he noticed that Carpo was shaking his head. "Something wrong, Carpo?"

Without answering, Carpo pulled out his notebook and began flipping through the pages.

"What's the matter?" Tommy asked.

"Nothing, Tommy, it's just"—Carpo tapped a page in the notebook—"here it is. Last time we talked you said you didn't know what Cheryl did for a living. From what you just described, I take it you knew she was a flight attendant."

"Did I say that? Maybe I read it in the newspapers or something. They've been all over this thing."

"But you said that Cheryl talked about the places she visited. Surely that was before it got into the newspapers."

Tommy chuckled and pretended to slap his face. "You're right, Carpo. Gosh, I gotta wake up. I guess I didn't remember that she had said that until now."

"That's okay, Tommy, it happens all the time. Why don't we start over again? In fact, we'll go back to the very first question. Tell me anything new you remember about Cheryl?"

"Like I said, not much. I only ran into her once every couple of days. Usually we just said hi, how are you, what's new. Stuff like that. Sometimes, if I saw her with a suitcase, I'd ask where she'd been to."

"It sounds like she trusted you," Carpo said.

Tommy squinted one of his eyes. "What do you mean?"

"Just what I said, she must have trusted you."

"I don't know, I guess so. Why are you asking?"

"A few minutes ago you said that Cheryl told you that

Victor Mendez made her feel uncomfortable. If she told you that, she must have trusted you."

Tommy stepped back from the microphone. "Can we stop taping a second?" He looked back and forth between Carpo and Roman. "Listen, guys, maybe this interview isn't such a great idea. I'm telling you, I barely knew Cheryl at all."

"Don't worry," Carpo said, "you're doing fine."

"I don't feel like I am. I keep messing up my story."

"You're thinking too much. Just answer the questions truthfully and you'll do fine." Carpo waited for Tommy to step back into place, then he returned the microphone to the spot under his chin. "Let's move on to a new question. Last time we talked, you mentioned that you ran into Cheryl's boyfriend a few times. Tell me about him."

"I didn't ever meet him."

"But you told me that you used to hear them arguing. You said they had violent arguments."

"I said that?"

"Yes, I wrote it down here."

"I don't remember."

"Do you know his name?"

"No."

"Can you describe him, at least?"

"Yeah, sure," Tommy said, wiping his forehead. "He seemed like the typical Wall Street type. Short hair. Suit. Briefcase. I suppose he was good-looking, if you're attracted to those guys. Frankly, I was—" Tommy broke off when he saw Carpo flipping through the notebook again. "What's the matter?" he asked. "Did I say something wrong again?"

"This is an interview, Tommy, not a test. You can't give a wrong answer." Carpo pointed at one of the pages. "Last time we talked, you said you didn't know where the boy-friend worked. How did you learn about Wall Street?"

"Did I read it in the papers?" Tommy asked hopefully.

"I doubt it. To my knowledge, it's never been in the papers. Nobody knows what Cheryl's boyfriend does for a living except me. And that includes the cops and the media."

Tommy blinked with surprise, then he pushed the micro-phone away from his face. "Sorry, Carpo, but this isn't going to work. I don't know what I'm supposed to be saying to all these questions."

"But I'm going over stuff we've already covered."

"I know, but I can't remember what I told you the last time."

"It doesn't matter what you told me, Tommy, just tell me the truth."

A spark flickered in Tommy's eyes. Through clenched teeth he said, "I am telling the truth, man."

"Then why are you so worried about getting the questions right?"

"Because I feel like I'm on trial. You've got that damn notebook you keep flipping through, checking every little thing I'm saying. How do you expect me to feel?"

"Is this what's making you edgy? The notebook?" Carpo snapped the notebook shut and tossed it on the floor. "Does that make you feel better? You shouldn't be so threatened by a bunch of innocent questions. I'm trying to learn about Cheryl Street, not Tommy Abilene."

Tommy released the microphone, splotches of pink rising on his cheeks. "I'm sorry, Carpo, I don't know what gets into me sometimes. It must be nerves. I've never been in front of a TV camera before."

"Try not to think about the camera. Look at me and pretend we're standing here alone, having a friendly conversation."

Tommy nodded solemnly. "I'll do my best."

"Okay, let's try those questions again. How did you learn that Cheryl Street was a flight attendant, and that her boyfriend worked on Wall Street?"

"Beats me. I must have heard them talking in the hallway or something."

"Did you know Cheryl, Tommy?"

"I already told you, I didn't—"

"Tell me the truth."

"What?"

"I said, tell me the truth."

"Carpo, I—"

"Come on, Tommy, quit wasting my time. Tell me the truth for once."

"What the hell is your problem?" Tommy stepped toward Carpo, pinning the microphone between their chests. "I'm getting sick of hearing that, man. I *am* telling the truth."

"Then why are you avoiding my question? Did you know Cheryl?"

"But I'm telling the truth!"

"Then tell it again." Carpo freed the microphone and shoved it under the man's chin. "I'm going to keep asking the same question until you spill it."

"Dammit, there's nothing to spill. I must have read about it in—"

"Don't say the newspapers," Carpo said, emphatically shaking his head. "The things you know about Cheryl were *not* in any newspapers. Level with me, Tommy, did you know her or not? Give me a simple yes or no."

"I ... I ... fine, yes. Are you happy? Yes, yes, yes. I knew Cheryl Street. Is everyone happy? Huh? Now, get the hell off my back before I end the interview."

Carpo heeded Tommy's warning; he stepped back and lowered the microphone. He couldn't push Tommy so hard that he lost the interview. Not yet, at least.

When Tommy seemed to have relaxed, Carpo raised the microphone. "Can we get started again?"

"I don't know, Carpo," Tommy said, staring at the floor. "This interview is starting to get to me."

"Just a few more questions and we'll be done." Without waiting for Tommy's assent, Carpo said, "Tell me how well you knew Cheryl."

"I was friendly with her, that's all. We used to talk in the hallway and down at the mailboxes."

"You already told me that, Tommy. I think you knew her better than that."

"We were casual friends."

"What sorts of things did you talk about when you ran into her?"

Tommy pondered the question, the knot jiggling in his throat. Suddenly, his face brightened. "She used to tell me about the trips she'd gone on. That must have been the way I knew she was a stewardess. And I think she told me about Steve." Tommy smiled, relieved to have found a way to explain everything that he knew. "That must be why I said he worked on Wall Street. See, Carpo, that's how I know that stuff. All along I've been telling you the truth."

"I thought you didn't know the boyfriend's name."

The smile froze on Tommy's face. "What do you mean?"

"A little while ago you said you didn't know his name. You just called him Steve. You did the same thing the last time we spoke. How did you know that?"

"I . . . I don't know. I must have heard Cheryl use it and just remembered it."

Carpo tightened his grip on the microphone; time for another stab. "You and Cheryl were dating, weren't you?"

"What're you talking about?"

"You two were lovers, right?"

"Me and Cheryl? Hell, no. No way."

"Come on, Tommy, you can tell me. Cheryl was your girl, wasn't she?"

"No. I swear, no." Tommy turned to Roman and asked, "What's he doing to me?" as if he hoped the cameraman would intercede.

"I'm just trying to discover the truth, Tommy," Carpo said.

"Okay, that's it, now you've gone too far."

"But it's a simple question."

"Doesn't matter, I've had enough. This isn't even an interview. It's a . . . it's a . . . ."

"A what, Tommy? Tell me what it is."

"It's an inquisition. You're making me feel like I did something wrong."

"No, I'm just trying to find—"

"I know!" Tommy screamed. "You're trying to find the truth."

"Actually, that's not what I was going to say." Carpo smiled at the man, surprised at how calm he felt. Calm and mean. He actually wondered if he was enjoying himself.

"What I was going to say is, I'm trying to find out about you and Cheryl."

"I don't want to talk anymore." Tommy looked at Roman again. "Please, dude, stop taping."

"I'll tell you what," Carpo said, "I'm not going to ask you anything else about Cheryl. Okay? We'll move on to something else. An entirely new subject."

"No, I don't want to talk anymore."

"Come on, Tommy, one more topic. Nothing at all to do with Cheryl. Tell me about the guy you saw on the street Saturday night. The guy we rode around looking for in the squad car."

"Shit, Carpo, you know what I saw."

"I want to hear you describe him."

"But it's the same thing you saw."

"I know, but what am I supposed to do, interview myself? I need your version."

"He was a guy in a long black trench coat. That's all."

"Where was he standing?"

"He was on the front steps of my building. He ran away when that woman started screaming."

"Which step was he on?"

"Huh?"

"I said, which step was he on? The top one, the bottom, in the middle? There's four steps down there, which one did you see him on?"

"I don't know, somewhere near the middle."

Carpo smiled again, in spite of himself. He liked watching Tommy squirm. "Which step was it?"

"I said, the middle."

"The middle one?"

"That's what I heard myself say."

"Then I guess you and I didn't see the same thing after all."

Tommy swallowed a few times, very fast, as he tried to comprehend what was happening. "What do you mean?"

"The guy I saw wasn't on the steps. He was down on the sidewalk, by the garbage pails. When are you going to start telling me the truth, Tommy?"

"I told you twice already, you'd better quit saying that."

Tommy edged closer to Carpo, his chin two inches from Carpo's nose, the microphone squished between them. Carpo held his ground, even though he suddenly had the feeling he was going to get punched. "Take it easy, Tommy, I'm just trying to figure out how we saw two different things."

"Maybe he moved," Tommy spat out, his hot breath hitting Carpo's face. "Maybe you're the one who's wrong. Just because you've got that goddamn microphone in your hand doesn't mean you know everything."

"I'm not saying it does. I'm just trying to find—"

"Say it," Tommy snarled. "I dare you to. So help me God, I'll punch you right in the face."

"You never saw him, Tommy. I know you never saw him—"

"—I dare you, Carpo, say it—"

"—look out your window right now, Tommy. You can't see anything, not even the sidewalk—"

"Get out of here! Damn it, Carpo, get out! Both of you, out!"

"Look down at the street." Carpo pointed at the window. "Go on, take a look. You never saw the guy from this window.

It's impossible. You could have seen him only if he was on the opposite side of the street."

Try as he might, Tommy couldn't resist looking. He turned to the window and peered down, then he stepped closer to see the sidewalk. One more step and his head bumped the glass.

Then he spun and went for Carpo.

"That's it, interview's over!" Tommy bear-pawed the microphone from Carpo's hand and flung it to the ground. He clamped his other hand over the lens of the camera.

"Turn it off, dude!" Tommy shouted at Roman. "Right now, turn the camera off or I'll break it."

Carpo picked up the microphone and held it toward Tommy. "What are you so upset about? What are you hiding?"

"I . . . I . . . nothing. I'm not hiding anything."

"Then why are you so upset? What are you afraid of?"

Tommy and Roman tussled for control of the camera. Roman had the heavy end and appeared to be winning the battle.

"Knock it off, dude!" Roman shouted. "If I put down this camera, you'll be one sorry muthafuckah."

"You're the one who's afraid!" Tommy shouted at Carpo. "You hide behind your microphones and your cameras and your goddamn questions. You're the one who's a coward."

"But I'm not the one who's lying," Carpo said. "I didn't lie and say I didn't know Cheryl. I didn't lie about not being her lover. I never said I saw someone on the street when I clearly didn't. Tell the truth, Tommy. What did you do to her?"

"That's it," Tommy whispered on a deep intake of breath.

He let go of the camera and went for Carpo, his right hand balled into a fist.

"Yo, yo, yo," Roman shouted. "Carpo, watch out!"

When Tommy released his fist, it looked as if it were coming from a million miles away. Carpo saw it clearly, a sweeping roundhouse, traveling through the air in super slow motion. The next thing he knew, he was on the ground, his face totally numb, blood roaring in his ears.

Somehow he found the presence of mind to look at Roman and see if the camera was still rolling. Roman had to capture the rest. Tommy still hadn't said it.

"Tell me what you did!" Carpo shouted, tasting blood on his tongue. "Tell the truth."

Tommy swung at him again, but his movements had gone out of sync and he missed badly. "Don't say it. Don't you dare."

"What could she have done for you to kill her? What could she have done to make you pluck out her eyes like that?"

Tommy made another lunge, but it was too much. The weight of it, the awful weight, came crashing down on his narrow shoulders. "Please," he sobbed, "please, stop."

"Come on, Tommy," Carpo said, bringing his voice back under control, "put an end to it. Only you can make the madness stop. Tell me what you did."

"Oh God, oh God, oh God," Tommy wailed. "You are sick, Carpo. Sick, sick, sick!"

"End it, Tommy. Why did you kill Cheryl? Did you hate her? Is that why?"

"No, no, no." Tommy's sobs turned into ragged coughs, his lungs starting to hyperventilate. "How can you . . . say

I hated . . . her? I . . . loved her. Nobody loved her . . . more than me. I swear, I'd . . . die for her. I'd die . . . today to have her back."

The anger drained from Carpo's body, leaving him exhausted and strangely full of pity. It was frightening to see Tommy's face: eyes cracked with red; cheeks glistening with tears; spit flying from his mouth with each sob.

"Why did you kill her?" Carpo whispered. "What did she do?"

"She . . . she was—" Tommy clamped both hands over his mouth and screamed. He gasped and said, "I can't say it. I can't do it."

"Tell me, Tommy. End it forever."

"She . . . was still seeing him. She was still seeing Steve. She told me it was over between them. She told me she loved me. Carpo, she lied to me."

"And you killed her?"

"I didn't mean to, I swear I didn't. She wasn't supposed to get back until Sunday. But I heard . . . her footsteps Saturday. I ran up there, thinking she'd come back to see me. She was all dressed up, makeup, jewelry. As soon as I saw her I knew it was for him."

Tommy scrubbed the tears off his face with his palm. "I asked her where she was going, and she got this terrible look on her face. Like she felt sorry for me. Like I was someone to be pitied. I got so angry. Angrier than I've ever been. I swear to God, I wanted to . . ."

Tommy sank slowly to the floor, arms hugging his knees to his chest. He didn't bother covering his face anymore.

He sobbed from deep within his body, one of the loneliest sounds Carpo had ever heard. "Why, why, why?" he cried. "Why didn't she love me?"

Carpo got Roman's attention and made a slicing motion across his throat, signaling for Roman to turn off the camera. Then he walked to Tommy and knelt beside him. "It's over now, Tommy. It's all over. I'm going to get you some help, okay? You don't have to carry this around inside anymore."

Roman ejected the tape from the camera and whispered, "I'll be right back."

After he had left, Carpo got to his feet. His ears were ringing and his face felt funny, numb and drenched with sweat. He put his hand to his nose and discovered that the sweat was blood. Gently, he felt along the bridge of his nose. It hurt when he pressed it, but the cartilage felt intact.

"Carpo, what's going on?"

Carpo turned to find Irene in the doorway, peering around the corner as if unsure whether it was safe to enter the apartment. He walked over to her, his knees wobbling.

Irene made a face and said, "Your nose, it looks terrible. What happened to you?"

"I got punched."

"Is it broken?"

"I don't think so. It's just bleeding."

Irene looked at Tommy, who was still sobbing in the corner. "What happened?"

"He confessed. We got it all on tape."

Irene studied his face. "Should I go call Detective Weissman?"

Carpo started to say yes, then shook his head. "Weissman

and Spinks don't deserve this one. Just dial 911 and tell them to send a squad car over."

Irene checked Tommy again. "Is it okay to leave you alone with him?"

"Yes, he's done." At the words, Carpo felt relief surge through his body. "It's all done. Finally, this thing is over."

Twenty-Five

Tommy Abilene's arrest didn't create anything near the stir created one day earlier when the police announced that they had captured the Sandman. Carpo chalked up the relative lack of media interest to the lack of several key elements in the story: a hastily called news conference; an arrest at the victim's grave site; the capture of an elusive serial killer. All the same, the arrest generated ample airtime and column inches in the local press. For Carpo, that meant ample time spent at Channel 8.

On both Sunday and Monday he worked fourteen-hour days in the newsroom, cranking out story after story on the arrest. New angles developed quickly, each one pounced upon by a reporter, covered in exhaustive detail, then discarded for the next fresh lead. Sunday night Channel 8 covered Tommy's perp walk at the 9th Precinct. The station also aired interviews with Tommy's parents in Bayside, Queens, and with his former high school sweetheart, now living in Bridgeport, Connecticut. Monday night the station devoted its coverage to his arraignment at the Criminal Courts Building, followed by interviews with the foreman of Costanza Construction, a waitress at Dan Lynch's bar, and Tommy's academic adviser from junior high school.

Unfortunately for Channel 8, the most sought-after interview surrounding the case was unavailable for broadcast. As soon as the Manhattan district attorney learned of Tommy's on-camera confession, the tape was subpoenaed and confiscated as evidence. Channel 8 wasn't even allowed to air silent portions of the footage for fear it would taint the city's potential jury pool.

On Tuesday the focus in the newsroom shifted from Tommy Abilene to Cheryl Street, as Major Sisco gave the go-ahead for Carpo's special profile. Carpo returned to 12th Street with Roman Santiago and conducted interviews with the residents of number 228. Of all the people he had met the previous week, he decided to interview Irene, Violetta Ignacio, and Ludwig Monroe. He spent the entire day Tuesday screening field tapes and archive tapes, then most of the night writing a script. Wednesday, he cloistered himself in an edit bay with an editor and cut the profile. After consulting with Major Sisco, the series was narrowed to two parts: Cheryl Street's life in the city and her untimely death at the hands of a former acquaintance. The pieces aired Thursday and Friday night, the first two days of the vital May Sweeps period.

Friday afternoon, his work finally complete, Carpo headed straight home. He napped until seven, then he showered, dressed, and picked up Irene for dinner. They settled on Jule's, a loud, crowded French bistro on 8th Street, just down the street from St. Mark's Place. A waitress seated them by the window, at a small table with a three-pronged candelabrum that dripped red wax on the white tablecloth. Carpo ordered a bottle of wine, which they started on as they read over the menu.

After a waiter took their order, Irene settled back in her chair, wine in hand, and asked, "What was going through your mind Saturday night when you went over to Tommy's place? I can't imagine what you were thinking, knowing you were about to confront Cheryl's killer."

"Truthfully?" Carpo asked. "I wasn't that nervous. I knew that once I got Tommy talking about Cheryl, he'd mess up somewhere."

"But weren't you scared? Just a little? I mean, the guy had murdered someone. What was to prevent him from going after you?"

Carpo sipped some of his wine. "I had my cameraman with me, so it was two against one. I suppose if Tommy had pulled a knife or a gun, I wouldn't sound so cocky, but at the time all I was worried about was getting in trouble with my boss."

"Why would he have gotten angry?"

"Saturday morning he took me off the series on Cheryl, and later that afternoon I found out I'd been suspended from Channel 8. There's no way they would have let me check out that crew. The whole time, I had my fingers crossed that I wouldn't get caught."

Irene swirled the wine around her glass. "What did he end up saying?"

"So far he hasn't made a peep. I'm lucky it turned out the way it did, otherwise I'd probably be standing in the unemployment line."

Irene ripped a chunk of bread off a baguette in a basket. "Was it the view alone that made you suspect Tommy?"

"That's what triggered it. When we were talking on the phone and I couldn't see that couple on my sidewalk, I realized there was something wrong with his story." Carpo reached for a piece of bread too. "After that, everything fell into place. I got to thinking about what he had told me the first time I interviewed him. He knew things only a person well acquainted with Cheryl could know."

"Like?"

"First off, he knew Steve Plotkin's name. He also knew Cheryl was a flight attendant. Nobody else in the building mentioned either of those things except for you."

"So you put two and two together?"

Carpo brushed aside the bread crumbs on the table. "When I learned that Cheryl's eyes were green instead of brown, I had proof that the Sandman hadn't killed her. After that, everything sort of clicked."

Irene took another sip of wine, a frown settling on her face. Carpo noticed her expression. "What's the matter?"

"It still doesn't explain why he did it."

"He said he lost his temper when he discovered that Cheryl was still dating Steve."

"But why did he step forward and tell the police he saw the man in the trench coat? It seems like a stupid thing to do, especially since there was a good chance he'd screw up his story."

"There's probably no logical explanation for it," Carpo said, "besides the fact that he was curious. That night, he told the police that he had come home, taken a shower, and then heard your screams. I'll bet what really happened is that he killed Cheryl and took a shower to clean off any physical evidence."

Irene shuddered. "That's a horrible thought."

"I can't think of any other reason for him to take a shower so late in the day."

"What could he have hoped to gain by getting involved?"

"I can think of two things right off the bat. First, who would ever suspect an eyewitness to be the actual murderer?"

"Certainly not Weissman and Spinks."

"Certainly not," Carpo said, "which explains the other part of my theory. I think Tommy was trying to find out what the cops knew about the case. If I remember correctly, when we were driving in the squad car together, he asked the officer if the Sandman had committed the crime. I think from the very beginning he was trying to plant the idea that the Sandman was responsible."

"Still, it was a brazen thing to do."

"Irene, this guy had already strangled a woman, a woman he supposedly loved, and then poked her eyes out so it looked like a serial killer had murdered her. After doing that, I don't think it would be very difficult to lie to the police."

"It makes me sick just to think about it."

"You should have seen what Tommy looked like after he confessed. Curled up on the floor, bawling like a two-year-old. I'll never forget the sound of him crying as long as I live. He had this awful expression on his face, one of complete and utter horror, like he couldn't believe what he'd done."

Irene set her wineglass down. "You make it sound like you feel sorry for him."

"Maybe I'm a total sucker, but I get the feeling Tommy Abilene is going to be tortured by this for the rest of his life."

"I hope so," Irene said, her voice gaining strength. "That

son of a bitch still has his life. What's Cheryl got? I hope he's so tortured he ties his bedsheets together and hangs himself in prison. That's the only way I'll ever believe that Tommy Abilene felt remorse."

After dinner Carpo and Irene lingered at the bar for another drink. Eventually the conversation moved from Tommy Abilene to other topics. As they talked, perched on two barstools, Carpo staring into Irene's bottomless brown eyes, he couldn't help thinking about how much his life had changed over the past week and a half. At one point he even wondered: *Is it happening again? Am I falling in love?*

"What are you smiling at?" Irene asked.

Carpo looked down at his hands. "Nothing."

"Is something funny?"

"Not at all."

"Then what is it?"

"I'm just happy," he said, shrugging, "that's all."

Irene took his hand out of his lap and brought it to her mouth. Softly, she laid her lips on the back of it. "So, are you over her?"

"Over who?"

"You know who, Carpo."

In a deadpan voice, he said, "I haven't slightest idea."

"Karen what's-her-name."

"Never heard of her."

Irene stared up at the ceiling, pretending to strain for her name. "Let's see, what was her name. Was it Blackhead? No, that's not right. Blackheart?"

Carpo reversed the position of their hands so his was on

top. He kissed it, his head filling with the scent of her. "For the life of me," he whispered, "I can't remember."

Outside, the breeze carried a strong hint of the East River, mud and algae, like a pond in midsummer. Carpo began walking toward home, when he noticed that Irene was not at his side. She was back by the restaurant, standing at the curb, her arm raised high in the air.

"What are you doing?" he called back.

"Hailing a cab."

"But it's such a beautiful night, let's walk."

She stayed in the same position, like Lady Liberty herself, unflinching and mute.

"Irene, did you hear me? We're a ten-minute walk from here."

Just then a taxi with a vacancy light turned onto the block. The driver caught sight of Irene and sped toward her, pulling to a stop with a creak of its weary brakes.

"Come on, Carpo," she said as she opened the door and climbed inside.

Carpo followed her into the backseat and closed the door. "What's the rush?"

"I don't want anything to go wrong."

"But what could go wrong?"

She gave him a stare, as if to say he should know better. "I don't care if you're in the mood to walk. I don't care if you're dying for fresh air. I don't even care if the Sandman himself is sitting on my doorstep, waiting to pounce on us."

He looked into her face and tried desperately to contain the smile that was pushing through his lips. "You know, with brown eyes like yours, I wouldn't be surprised if he *is* waiting for us."

"I said I don't care." She put her hand behind his head and pulled him close. She kissed his forehead, his cheek, then the bottom of his ear. "Tonight you're mine," she whispered, her moist words raising the hair on his neck. "All mine."

Twenty-Six

The next morning Irene's apartment looked as if a twister had blown through. Clothes were scattered on the far side of the studio near a small white couch, a springy old thing that had creaked and groaned with each of their movements. Two untouched glasses of wine sat on a table nearby; Irene had poured them as soon as they reached the apartment, and almost as quickly they had been forgotten. A jasmine-scented candle still flickered on the table, its wick burned deep within the cylinder of yellow wax.

Carpo awoke with Irene's back facing him. He wiggled close to her and spooned his body against the entire length of hers. Languorously, he kissed her exposed cheek and earlobe until she stirred from sleep. She rolled over, eyes still closed, and purred, " 'Morning, Mr. Buzz Saw."

"Mr. Buzz Saw? What does that mean?"

She smiled and kissed the tip of his nose. "You're quite the little snorer, Carpo."

Carpo pulled back from her in mock disgrace. "Sorry 'bout that."

"Not to worry." She wrapped her hands around his waist and tugged him close. "It's something I'll just have to get used to."

Carpo nuzzled her neck, nibbling the parts his mouth could reach. "So it occurs to me," he said between kisses, "since I don't have to go to work today, what do you say we scrounge up some breakfast and do something fun?"

"What do you have in mind?"

"I don't know," he said. "A museum, a movie, the flea markets? You choose."

She moaned softly and rolled her head back, allowing him to nibble farther up her ear. "Where are these flea markets?"

"They're over on Sixth Avenue, in the flower district. A bunch of dealers lay out their stuff in a big parking lot every Saturday and Sunday, except when it rains."

"I've been looking for a new couch."

"Yes, you could use one. But I've got to warn you that nothing's new there, just a bunch of hand-me-downs. Occasionally one does find a hidden gem."

"Either way, it sounds like fun. It's such a beautiful day, it'd be a shame to stay indoors." Irene nudged Carpo with her elbow. "Come on, my lover, let's go."

"Okay."

Neither of them moved.

Irene nudged him again. "You first, Carpo."

"I'm not going first."

Irene curled the covers around her body like a cigarette wrapper. "Yes, you are. You're the man. You have to go first."

"But I'm the guest." Carpo grabbed the covers before she could steal them all. "The guest gets to do whatever they want."

"Please, Carpo."

"No way."

Just then the intercom buzzed.

Irene sat up in bed. "Who could that be?"

"Who cares," Carpo said. "Don't answer it."

"But I've got to. What if it's something important?"

Carpo checked the clock on the nightstand. "At eleven o'clock on a Saturday morning? What could be important?"

The buzzer sounded again.

"Damn, damn, damn," Irene said as she wiggled to the edge of the bed. Before leaving the sanctuary of sheets, she turned to Carpo. "What do you think you're looking at?"

"I'm checking you out."

"Turn around and face the wall." She glared at him until he flipped on his side. Just as he relaxed, she ripped the covers off the bed.

"Hey!" Carpo shouted. "Give those back."

She scrambled away from the bed, squealing excitedly as she wrapped the sheets around her body. Carpo grabbed a pillow and covered himself.

Irene walked to the door and pressed the talk button on the intercom. "Who is it?"

"Mailman," the intercom responded. *"I've got a package for a Ms. Irene Foster."*

"I thought your intercom was busted," Carpo said.

"Only downstairs." Irene pressed the button again. "Leave it inside the door, please. I'll pick it up later."

The intercom stayed silent for a moment, then it buzzed again. *"Package for Irene Foster,"* the mailman said, slowly enunciating each word.

"Leave it downstairs, please," Irene said again.

"Sorry, can't make out what you're saying," the mailman

responded. *"I need a signature on this package, or I'll have to return it."*

"Damn it all," Irene whispered as she pressed another button that unlocked the door. "Come on, Carpo, get up. Go hide in the bathroom."

"What for?"

"The mailman's coming up."

"What difference does it make?" Carpo asked, doing his best to hide behind the pillow. "The mailman doesn't care."

"I know," Irene said, "I care. I don't want him to see you. Go hide in the bathroom."

Carpo scooted off the bed, the pillow pressed over his front. As he passed, she reached out as if to yank the pillow off him, shouting, "Woo, woo, woo." Carpo sidestepped her, scooped his clothes off the floor, and ran into the bathroom.

As he dressed, he could hear footsteps coming up the stairs, then a tap on the door. "Mailman," a voice shouted from the hallway.

"One moment," Irene called.

Carpo heard her rifle through the closet for a robe. He opened the bathroom door an inch to watch, whispering, "Woo, woo, woo."

She stuck her tongue out at him, then walked to the front door and opened it. "Hi," she said to the mailman, "sorry I took so long."

"That's okay, ma'am."

Carpo pushed the door open a few more inches. He recognized the man immediately. It was Darryl Foote, the same mailman who worked his side of the street.

The mailman was holding a package wrapped in brown paper and a clipboard. He stepped into the apartment and handed the clipboard to Irene. He pointed at a spot on the page. "The John Hancock goes right there, please."

As Irene scribbled her name, she said, "I didn't know you worked Saturdays."

"I usually don't," the mailman said, "but the regular guy is out. Or that's what he claimed. He's probably sacked out on some beach in the Hamptons, enjoying the weather."

"It is a beautiful day," Irene said as she handed back the clipboard.

The mailman gave her the package. "It's not very heavy."

"Thanks."

The mailman started toward the door, then stopped. He studied Irene's face, his forehead crinkling as if something weren't making sense to him.

"What's the matter?" Irene asked.

When the mailman spoke, his voice had changed; deeper and harsh, as if he were growling. "I forgot to ask for something."

Irene took a step back. "What?"

The mailman reached into his pocket and pulled out an object. Through the three inches of door space, Carpo could make out only its general shape; thin and about eight inches long, with a shiny finish that glinted wickedly in the sunlight. "I forgot to ask for your eyes."

Irene screamed as she fell back, but the mailman was already upon her, pouncing like a leopard. He grabbed Irene by the hair, punched her once, then yanked her onto the floor.

Carpo burst from the bathroom, not understanding what was happening until he was in the room. The mailman had an ice pick in his hand, raised in the air.

"Get off her!" Carpo screamed. "Get the hell away from her!"

The mailman looked at Carpo, ice pick over his head, a surprised expression on his face. And then Carpo understood everything: why he had received the strange postcards in his mailbox, just like Cheryl Street, and why so many women had opened their doors to the Sandman.

The Sandman's face contorted with a crazy rage as he howled, "Carpo, I warned you!"

Carpo tackled the man at his waist, ramming him into the door. He swung his fists desperately, punching the cap off the Sandman's head and clawing at his face. His head was down so he couldn't see what was happening. He felt a sting in his shoulder, then another in his arm. Each time the ice pick penetrated him, he felt searing heat and numbing cold, as if he were being jabbed with an icicle.

"Carpo, watch out!" Irene screamed. "He's stabbing you."

Carpo shoved the man away just as the ice pick penetrated his back, right between the shoulder blades. His arms went dead, heavy and limp. He shoved the man again, creating a few inches of space between them. When the Sandman raised the ice pick for another stab, Carpo slapped it out of his hands.

The Sandman punched Carpo in the face and squirmed free. He started for the ice pick, then changed his mind and bolted from the apartment.

There was a moment of silence in the apartment that seemed to last forever, the quiet disrupted by the sound of the man's retreating footsteps. Then Irene was at Carpo's side, her face drained of color.

"Carpo, are you all right? Where did he stab you? Please, Carpo, tell me you're okay."

Carpo's stomach was churning, the shock and pain triggering a swirl of nausea. Something was wrong in his chest too. Each breath felt as though the ice pick were still lodged in his back, pinning his lungs to his rib cage. He nearly screamed from the pain, but he remained silent, knowing to scream would only worsen the pain.

"Speak to me, Carpo. Tell me where you hurt."

He wiped his face, which was soaked with cold sweat. The room seemed blurry, shimmering like a mirage, and his ears were ringing. "Lock the door," he whispered, "and call for help."

"Carpo, tell me where you're hurt?"

"No, Irene, please," he gasped. "Call me an ambulance. I think I'm dying."

Epilogue

What felt like death to Carpo turned out to be pneumotho-rax: the medical term for a punctured lung. The Sandman's ice pick had nicked the lining of his right lung, causing a small pool of blood to gather in the organ. While the injury was not life-threatening, it was serious enough to require a three-day hospital stay at Cabrini Medical Center.

After facing the Sandman, and what he had believed to be certain death, three days of bed rest felt like a month's vacation to Carpo.

Of more concern to the city, the police were unable to capture Darryl Foote after the attack at Irene's apartment. Foote eluded a stakeout at his Upper West Side apartment by climbing up the fire escape. He made off with a small bag of clothes and an unknown amount of cash, then he hopped a Peter Pan bus at Port Authority headed to Hart-ford, Connecticut. He transferred to another bus headed to Chicago and vanished.

When the police finally entered his apartment, they found a shoe box under the bed containing newspaper clippings on each of the murders. They also discovered a rack of videotapes chronicling his exploits in the local media, including Carpo's interview on Channel 8 News.

The most gruesome discovery was revealed in Foote's freezer, where a plastic bag held a collection of his victims' brown eyes.

Carpo was released from the hospital on Wednesday afternoon; later that night he was treated to a celebratory dinner at Little Poland. Candi had decorated one of the booths with balloons and streamers, and Irene chipped in with a pound of Black Magic from Java The Hut. The three of them stayed in the booth until one in the morning, drinking coffee, smoking Candi's cigarettes, and talking about whether or not the police would ever capture the Sandman.

After dinner Irene led Carpo by the arm to her apartment. She uncorked a half bottle of champagne to toast their reunion. No sooner had Carpo sipped from his glass of bubbly than Irene led him to the bed.

They broke up in August, just before Irene started classes again at New York University. As the summer had worn on, Carpo noticed a strain developing in the relationship. Much of it was due to a new series Major Sisco had placed him on at Channel 8, a special report on the Sandman investigation, which consumed most of Carpo's time.

The final straw came on a Wednesday night, when Carpo arrived an hour late for a dinner date at the Taste of Siam. Irene didn't mention the tardiness during the meal. But when they arrived at her building afterward, instead of inviting him up, she stopped at the front steps.

"Carpo, there's something on my mind," she began, "and I might as well get it off my chest."

Carpo noticed that she avoided looking into his eyes, and he immediately sensed trouble. "I'm sorry about tonight, you have every right to be angry. I should have called as soon as I found out I was going to be late."

"That's not the problem anymore, I'm used to it." She took a step back and finally looked at him. "The problem is me, I don't feel the same about you."

"But I won't be late again. Cross my heart, I'll never let it happen again."

She cracked a paper-thin smile, one that almost made Carpo's eyes sting with tears. "God, I wish I could believe that, but it'll happen again. You're so wrapped up in what you do, you would work twenty-four hours a day if you didn't have to sleep. I can't deal with it anymore. Next week I start school and it's going to be a hard semester. I'm not going to have time to wait for you every night."

Carpo swallowed hard, the panic building. "Please, Irene, give me a second chance. I'll change, I swear I will."

"A second chance? Carpo, I've given you twenty chances. It's time for me to get wrapped up in my own life. There's things that I want to do, things I need to accomplish. I'm not ready to give up my own life just so you can fulfill yours."

"Are you"—Carpo swallowed, almost unable to speak— "breaking up with me?"

"I haven't decided what I'm doing. What I need right now is a break from you. Just for a while, to see what my schedule is like and how much work I have."

"How long is a while?"

"I'm thinking a few weeks."

Now it was Carpo who couldn't make eye contact. He shook his head dejectedly. "You're breaking up with me."

"I said, I don't know." She backed away, walking up the steps, and then unlocked the door.

"Irene," he called out, hearing the anguish in his voice, "please don't do this to me."

She grimaced, a look of pity that made Carpo's heart plummet. "I have to," she said. "I'm sorry, I just do."

As the door slammed shut, Carpo found himself screaming for her. "Irene, wait. Please, Irene."

She opened the door, the awful expression on her face more apparent now. "What do you want, Carpo?"

"Please, I ... could I ..."

"Could you what?"

The lump in his throat was so big, he almost couldn't breathe. "Could I hold you?"

"You want to hold me?"

"Yes, please," he whispered. "Just for a second. I promise, I won't make a scene or anything. I just want to hold you."

She shook her head, eyes filling with tears. "I'm sorry, Carpo, I can't. I can't do this anymore."

One week later, the FBI mailed Darryl Foote's photograph to every post office, police station, and social services department in the United States. One day later Foote was apprehended at a post office in West Palm Beach, Florida.

Incredibly, Foote had been employed at the post office as a mail carrier for the entire month of August.

*   *   *

On a blustery day in September, the wind buffeting the leafless trees, Carpo noticed that the lights were on in Cheryl Street's apartment.

Dusk was falling on 12th Street, so he could easily watch a man and a woman in the small studio as they unpacked several large boxes. The man went to work installing a pair of curtains over the window; the woman walked back and forth, putting things in their new places. After a while a delivery of Chinese food arrived. The couple camped out on the bare wood floor, a candle between them, and pushed the meal into their mouths with chopsticks.

The lights were on in Irene's apartment too, but the shades were drawn, as they almost always seemed to be now. He prayed that it wasn't because of him. He thought often of Irene; he looked for her every time he walked along 12th Street. But long ago he had given up any real hope of getting back together with her.

Some nights, for no particular reason, her phone number popped into his head. He toyed with the idea of calling her, just for the hell of it, just to see how she was doing. One night he even dialed the first six digits of her number before he lost his nerve and hung up the phone.

What would I say to her anyway? he wondered. *Hi, it's Carpo. There something I want to tell you. If you'd give me the chance, one more chance, I could make you so happy.*